BONES OF THE RAIN

A BLUE-EYED INDIAN MYSTERY

BONES OF THE RAIN

RUSS HALL

FIVE STAR
A part of Gale, Cengage Learning

GALE
CENGAGE Learning

Detroit • New York • San Francisco • New Haven, Conn • Waterville, Maine • London

Copyright © 2010 by Russ Hall.

Smith & Wesson® is a trademark of Smith & Wesson Corporation in the United States and its use herein shall not be deemed to imply Smith & Wesson's endorsement or sponsorship of this work.

Five Star Publishing, a part of Gale, Cengage Learning.

LIBRARY OF CONGRESS CATALOGING-IN-PUBLICATION DATA

Hall, Russ, 1949–
    Bones of the rain : a blue-eyed Indian mystery / Russ Hall. —
1st ed.
        p. cm.
    ISBN-13: 978-1-59414-809-5 (alk. paper)
    ISBN-10: 1-59414-809-0 (alk. paper)
    1. Murder—Investigation—Fiction. 2. Texas—Fiction. I. Title.
PS3558.A373395B66 2010
813'.54—dc22   2010007277

First Edition. First Printing: June 2010.
Published in 2010 in conjunction with Tekno Books and Ed Gorman.

Printed in the United States of America
1 2 3 4 5 6 7 14 13 12 11 10

Down these mean streets a man must go who is not himself mean, who is neither tarnished nor afraid. The detective must be a complete man and a common man and yet an unusual man.

—Raymond Chandler, *The Simple Art of Murder*

CHAPTER ONE

People like to say your friends are your silver and gold, but when they call you out into a night where the rain beats down angry hard on the canvas sides of the tent where you sit hunched on the floor with the cold and damp seeping up into the pants of your suit, and lightning is flashing in bursts like white upside-down trees accompanied by thunder that sounds like timpani drums rolling sideways down a hill, you begin to think they haven't done you any real favors, that instead they've lured you all the way out to the other side of nowhere.

I did the best I could to try to regain some positive spin about being in Texas Hill Country on a night when the elements tugged and hammered in what seemed an effort to tear the tent in half. Rain cycles, I reminded myself, were vital to the Indian tribes of the west. They had good things to say about rain, even danced to get it. The Cheyenne, who were no strangers to sleet and hard rains, called something like this "the bones of the rain." The Comanche used the Shoshone word *emar* for rain and called a rainbow "sunlight on ripened rain." For the Kiowa, the word for rain, I'd been told, was the same as bow. Maybe it seemed to them that rain was being shot from one. That felt like the case tonight. Another hard sheet of it hit the tent and swayed and buckled the sides. The damp cold had at last soaked all the way through to my crotch and I suppressed a shiver. I wasn't doing such a great job of getting to the half full glass on this one.

"Well, it sure enough is a dark and stormy night out there." Johnny Gringo let the tent flap drop back into place with a wet smack and headed back to where he had been sitting.

"Will you knock that off and sit back down a spell," Jimmy Bravuro said. He turned back to me. "Trish Mirandez, the absolute prettiest little songbird in the entire Austin live music scene, put down her guitar, the stage lights dimmed, and she slipped off toward her trailer. The next thing we see and hear is the stage manager flipping on the full lights and rushing out onto center stage to yell as loud as he could, 'Someone's killed Trish.' Now, that was *just* what a Kasperville Folk Festival crowd needed to hear right then."

The stark worried lines of Jimmy's face, three feet from me in the light of a swaying Coleman lantern, looked like something you might see crawling out of a grave on a rainy Halloween night. His long hair had gone stringy inside the damp tent. The tanned tint of his face, like mine, showed an indication of a Native American heritage that traced itself back to when Oklahoma was an Indian territory.

No one would mistake him for the rugged outdoorsy type, or me either, for that matter, given the suit and tie I wore, albeit an outfit that by this point wouldn't get me into a dress-code-restricted restaurant. A steady drip plunked down onto my left shoulder. Beneath my suit jacket, my long-sleeved white shirt had begun to cling to me. I felt another slow damp shudder shiver through me.

The breathy notes of a saxophone began to lift and fall in a far back corner of my head.

"You drag me all the way out here to an event I'm as likely to attend as a Grateful Dead concert, in the teeth of a storm, with a case for me that's not really all that pressing. Then I get here and find a murder just happened?" I said.

"That's about the sum of it, Trav." Jimmy's eyes would have

twinkled if a corpse hadn't been found. The trademark of his singing is his intensity—the kind that makes you wonder if at any moment he might climb right out of his own skin. When he's not on stage he usually assumes a folksier, more laid-back, even jovial persona, something that was heightened by circumstances more than usual at the moment.

"All I'm saying is it wasn't in the plan. I was having a quiet night at home."

On the way out, through black skies and rain that slashed across the twisting road in horizontal lines the color of steel piano wires snapping, I'd negotiated hills and S-curves to the constant roll of thunder and lightning the like of which I hadn't seen in many a moon. It had been sinister enough to make me reach for the heater control in my relic of a car before remembering it didn't work.

"Quiet night at home. Do you hear that? This coming from the one private detective who never gets the girl. I mean *never*. That while hanging 'round the music biz too." Jimmy turned to Johnny Gringo, who now sat like some thirty-year-old skinny Buddha with a can of beer in his hand, careful not to touch the wet tent walls or get near the one or two small puddles forming in the corners of the tent.

"Was my need to come out here urgent or not?" I said.

He ignored me and turned to Gringo to speak in the slow measured way of imparting wisdom. "You know, we often think of someone who craves being alone as a failure. There are those who think the hermit merely enjoys a different kind of marriage, off to commune with himself, nature, to stay home. What we see as a retreat, he sees as an advance. What we'd view as poverty, he views as luxury. That hermit, recluse, solo flyer in the world of human relationships, whatever you want to call him, may be simply one who discerns the difference between loneliness and solitude."

I crumpled the empty beer can in my hand in my fist. If there'd have been a table I'd have pounded on it. "What you don't take into consideration is the attitude of rural law enforcement officers when a murder—something that happens about as often as the Borzoi ballet performing out here—occurs in their backyard, and minutes later a private investigator appears."

"Don't like it, do they?"

"No, they don't."

"I only asked Hal to call for you to get you some social life."

"I don't need a social life."

Johnny Gringo's eyes followed us back and forth like he was watching a Ping-Pong match, a not particularly riveting one.

Jimmy shook his head in mock sadness. "You look at him, this detective of ours—go ahead, look at him, I said—and you see someone who looks like the world not only stepped on him, but gave the foot a little twist, like putting out a cigarette butt. I mean, the suit's rumpled, the hair's black and likely to stick out in more than one direction with the least insubordination from the wind, and the sparkle of blue eyes above high cheekbones hardly compensates for a heritage that has more Indian in it than is even fashionable these days, excepting, of course, for myself."

People grieve or deal with death in different ways. I'd been too close too many times not to have picked up a mental scrapbook of every variation. I knew Jimmy did not mean to make light of a tragic moment. The much younger Johnny Gringo didn't seem so sure of that. This was a folk festival, after all, and one that had been brought to a screeching halt.

There should have been music outside right now—lively, peppy, foot-tapping music—with the sound of fireside chatter, and the convivial clinking of bottles. Instead, there was the steady sound of rain, the rustling of cans being yanked from paper bags, and the kind of subdued grumping you get when a body has turned up like a turd in the punch bowl.

The festival's an annual event, makes you think of Woodstock with cowboy hats—folk music shows all day long, campfire sing-alongs at night, tents, campers—you get the picture.

There wasn't supposed to be a body there, and I should have been dry back in my musty old office looking, in the dim light from street lamps that filtered through the heavy rain, at the shadowed parts of the Indian relics hanging on the opposing wall. They were the most valuable things in the office, except I couldn't sell them. I'd earned them as fees for all the tribes I'd helped during the years before settling in Austin. But, no, I was here instead, in a tent, a wet tent, and I was pretty sure my butt was getting chapped even as I sat there. The tent was some undetermined sort of green canvas army surplus job, not one of those nice, expensive waterproof Gortex types. Its canvas floor showed the darker damp of puddles forming in a couple of spots. The pulsing, swinging white light from the camping lantern's twin mantles lit half of everything in the tent, leaving the other half in black shadows.

There were just the three of us in the leaky tent at the moment—Jimmy, me, and the younger new kid from Oklahoma by way of Nashville, John Murray Greenberg, who had, in the tradition of country singers out this way, already been given a new handle, Johnny Gringo.

"Don't you do most of your detecting in cities?" he spoke for the first time in a while. "What do you know about cops out here?"

"What I do know is that cops everywhere don't like PIs in general, and usually me in particular. No local cop is going to feel good about some PI being in the area right now. A county this size, some ninety miles from Austin, is bound to have so few murders they'll take them as personal. They're not going to believe that a professional snoop like me being out here has nothing to do with a murder they're investigating."

"You still don't believe Trish is the one who's been murdered, do you?" Johnny Gringo said. He had the hubris it takes to be a performer, which is a necessary thing. It's a bumpy career path he'd chosen. Even though I respected what it took to be a singer and a songwriter, I was getting tired of the youthful thinly veiled sarcasm in his face at a time of death and probable inconvenience for me.

"He's the cautious type, your gringoness," Jimmy Bravuro said. "He won't believe Trish is dead until he stands looking at the corpse. He's been burned before believing things on hearsay without proof, haven't you, Trav?"

I could feel my forehead tighten into one real bowline hitch of a tension knot. "Tell me what it was that made you think I ought to come all the way out here in the rain from Austin."

"He was called," Johnny Gringo said, "couldn't go. Went anyway. Weren't wanted." Johnny's no more an original talking Texan than I am, but that made him try extra hard, in a way that scratched fingernails across my chalkboard.

I struggled to my soggy feet, got all the way upright and had turned toward the tent flap door when Jimmy waved at me to sit back down. "Oh, take a chill pill. We'll go into the case we have for you later. This Trish thing is bigger just now."

I eased back down. The spot where I sat hadn't gotten any drier in my absence.

He had to stretch from where he sat cross-legged on his sleeping bag to reach for the can of beer on the ground beside him. The downpour outside hammered on the tent's surface like Marine Corps drummers for a parade having a serious practice. The tent flap pushed inward and open. Dutch Hitchcock shoved himself inside and stood dripping like some wet-and-wear lumberjack. He tugged a blue handkerchief loose from the back pocket of his jeans and wiped across the deep lines of his weathered face. Water oozed in at the bottom of the front flap onto the already soggy tent floor.

"It still raining out there?" Jimmy asked, in that same casual tone I'd come to recognize as his not entirely successful tension-cutting comedy in the face of death. We all moved back in the small tent so that Dutch wouldn't drip all over us.

Dutch's head snapped to Jimmy.

"One plain, plumb frog-walloper. That's what she is," Johnny Gringo said, pushing that heavy-handed Texas accent that was still fresh to him.

Dutch swung his head to look at John. His face looked like a few miles of hard road. Meeting him for the first time, you might take him for a construction worker, or wrestler of alligators. His roots were out in Lubbock, what they call a flatlander in Texas. No one was going to hand him any unsolicited beauty contest prizes either. The general cut of musicians out this way ran to the rustic model. Dutch had presence, though, the kind that made the inside of the tent seem much smaller with him being in it.

"Raining hard enough to fill a wire basket," Jimmy said, playing along with Johnny Gringo.

"Like a cow pissing on a flat rock," Dutch finally snapped back.

"You wouldn't drink so much of our dwindling supply of beer, you wouldn't have to go out there so often," Jimmy said.

"Next time I won't." Dutch glanced around at the corners of the tent in a bathroom-searching way that worried me. I had nothing to add. I felt as cooped up as they did. As some of Texas' top musicians, they had more experience with outdoor versions of road trips like this than me.

Dutch said, "And who was it inspired you to buy this crappy beer, the worst tourist-swilling diarrhea beer south of Yankee land?"

"It's all they had. You're the one was going to fix us up in a motel, remember?"

"Full. All of them. You know that." Dutch tugged off his jacket. In the process he managed to hit both Jimmy and myself with a spray of water.

Jimmy said, "Well, hell, Dutch, no one ever said the music business is all tits and champagne."

"Hey, guys . . . ," I said.

"Come on, Trav, lighten up. There's nothing any of us can do right now," Jimmy said.

"Let the private detective talk, Jimmy. You drag him all the way out here, probably tearing him away from a case where someone's robbed a Cheyenne reservation casino or some other bleeding-heart damned thing." Dutch sloshed over to rustle around in the paper bag that held the last of the beer. "Though none of those jolly moments are going to weigh much with the local law I met."

"I already took my beating in there answering their questions," Jimmy said.

"What d'you mean by that? They didn't really hit you, did they?" Gringo's voice nearly cracked. There was no Texas twang this time.

"Why'd they bust your chops? You didn't have anything to do with Trish's death, did you?" I asked.

Jimmy just shook his head.

Dutch said, "That's one deputy in serious need of a laxative. You'll see what he means. You've got more've an Indian look than Jimmy does. Man's not fond of anyone who's not a white-bread born-in-Texas white man like himself is the way I read it."

"People aren't really still like that anymore, are they?" Gringo asked.

I heard steps outside splashing toward us through the rain.

They had the official sound of deputy-sheriff boots. "Maybe I'll find out soon enough," I said. "I'd guess my chance to talk with the local law is approaching."

A hand pulled aside the tent flap. The Smoky the Bear hat came in first, then the dark wet uniform. The soaked front of her uniform was pressed out in a significant way that was hard to miss. I looked up, caught the long blonde hair tucked up into her hat, the smooth attractive face. She pointed a finger at me and beckoned.

"Well," Jimmy said to Dutch, "at least it's not all champagne."

We slogged our way through the puddles and mud toward the music hall. The deputy, in her taut, wet uniform, might have been worth watching closer, but my head stayed down, mostly, watching each step. A lot of people were still at the folk festival, huddled in their tents, as miserable as I was, no doubt. Spreading out from the entertainment center, through the relentless rain, I could see quite a few more tents, campers, and RVs. It was quiet as a stone here in the center of things. Only one or two people were stirring on the muddy creeks the streets had become. I saw Ponty Bone load his accordion case into the back of a van and then drip his way back toward the hall. It made me realize how different tonight was. There'd be none of Ponty's zydeco tunes to pep or cheer us up.

Usually, at the Kasperville Folk Festival, the key part is singers and songwriters out by campfires trying out new tunes on their devout fans. The event has happened every year since 1972, and has featured the likes of Willie Nelson, Peter, Paul & Mary, Gary P. Nunn, Nanci Griffith, and Kinky Friedman. It's usually more peppy, weird, and fun. Even on the rainiest of days, you can hear guitars strumming and songs carrying out from the lit tents. Tonight was as silent as death, and I heard only an occasional cough, low mumbling, or the whoop of someone tying on a semi-toot as my tent roomies were, while I trudged through ankle-deep puddles with sheets of rain hammering down onto my uncovered head.

I got thinking about how the Cheyenne wouldn't drink water that's been left standing overnight. The women would always go down to the stream to get water each morning, because the Cheyenne believe it's live water, while water left standing overnight is considered to be dead. There seemed to be more live water going on out here tonight than live music. Some of it was soaking all the way through my suit as I walked.

Then I saw Hal Jansen himself, the guy who'd called me on behalf of Jimmy and dragged me into this predicament. Now wasn't the time to give him a piece of my mind. He and his camera were being escorted out of the main theater building by a deputy at the same time I was being escorted in. Hal didn't look my way, and I whooshed along myself to keep up with the deputy; but I promised myself I'd chew on his ear later about this mess.

The Armadillo Theater, where they hold the sundown concerts, was as quiet as I'd ever seen it, even with the handful of uniformed people gathered around at the center of the empty stage. Someone had set up a command post, comprised of a table for a desk and three straight-backed chairs. The bulky guy seated behind the table probably had a cushy chair behind his desk back at his office, which he visibly seemed to be missing. His face twitched in a scowl and he twisted to get more comfortable in his chair as I sat down across from him after squishing across the empty dance floor and hiking around up the stairs onto the stage.

"You Travis?" he said. "The one the newspapers call the Blue-Eyed Indian?" His angry eyes flicked to the other deputies.

Before I could comment that the handle was only used by Austin's version of a *Daily Planet* and a few other newspapers, not me, he added, "And don't you *look* like you just crawled off a buffalo nickel, too. Whooee."

My face, with its high cheekbones and dark reddish tint, does send a certain strong signal. Most folks these days don't make as much of it as this deputy. I mulled over which side of that antique nickel he meant, hoped he didn't mean the buffalo butt side.

I don't want you to get the impression that all Texans are prejudiced against Indians. Though you *can* come across individuals here and there, like the deputy before me apparently, whose sentiments still ran along the lines of the late General Sheridan's comment that the only good Indian's a dead one.

Without waiting for a response from me, he glanced down at a sheet of paper on a clipboard in front of him and said, "Never met a real live private detective before." He said it the way I might have commented about never having stepped in a cow pie. I glanced around at the other deputies. Something was lousy here. The one who'd escorted me here, with Winnick on her uniform nameplate, stood back and looked off at nothing. Another deputy stared at us, his weasel face leering at me like I was a dartboard and all he needed was a triple eighteen to go out.

My head panned back to the beefy guy across from me. He said, "My name's Alvin Turnbull. I'm the acting sheriff here." He said it the way Alexander Haig said he was in charge that time. I caught an eye roll from the weasel deputy. The word dysfunctional zipped across the wasteland of my skull. "Sheriff Harmon Cuthers is away, camping with his grandkids down to Big Bend."

I gave Alvin the benefit of a careful look. His hair was trimmed as close as you can get without resorting to a razor. The wide square face, chiseled on top of a thick neck, did little to diminish the look of pit bull menace which he seemed to crave and cultivate. He either lifted weights or had been recruited from the San Antonio Zoo. He had the beefy rounded look you'd expect to see of a fellow climbing out of a pickup truck in the gravel lot beside a late-night honky-tonk with an ax handle in his hand. Oh, I was getting good vibes from this one. His Texas drawl was as heavy as that Johnny Gringo had been trying for, but his was genuine. He was *from* here.

He squinted at me. "Later I might could take time to actually be impressed at meeting a real-to-life private dick like yourself . . . and an Injun besides. But for now, what I want to know is what brings your suit-and-tie ass out here to the Laughing Burro Ranch. You sure as shit don't look like the other moonie-eyed dropouts from life who think this is the sixties all over again."

This time I caught the eye roll from Deputy Winnick. Her eyes clicked on mine and skittered away again. I began to wonder how Alvin came to be in charge, how he even came to be in his line of work. His colleagues seemed to wonder the same thing. Something had gotten under his skin, and it was more than just his having a long and stressful day.

I felt irritated myself—at Jimmy Bravuro for not telling me what case he had for me, and at Hal for calling me in the first place. I couldn't tell this gorilla of a deputy anything, even if I wanted to. It bugged me too that the deputy, in advance of me talking to him, was aware I was a PI, and one with Indian blood, something that didn't endear me to him.

A hubbub came from behind the stage, back where small trailers were lined up to act as dressing rooms. A fellow came out of the wing of the stage and came across toward us. His heels clicked on the wooden stage. He wore a black rain slicker that said "Medical Examiner" in white letters. He looked like one of the crew instead of the ME himself. Alvin turned to glare at him, but the guy plopped a clipboard onto the table and ignored me. "Better sign here," he said, "and we can haul her away."

Alvin picked up a pen, looked up at the man, back down at the paper, then signed. He tossed the pen to one side, ignored the fellow and called over to the weasel deputy, "The boyfriend still around?"

Deputy Winnick started to say something. Alvin held up a hand to stop her. "The men are talking, honey," he said. Her mouth shut with a click I could hear without straining.

"Yeah," the weasel deputy said.

"Well, hang onto him. He'll be wanting to go to town with the body."

I said, "I wasn't aware Trish had a boyfriend."

Alvin's head snapped to me, and there was a glitter in the squint of his eyes, as if I'd gone for the bait, fallen for a trap. "What do you know about it?"

My mouth snapped shut. He leaned a half foot closer.

"Go ahead," he encouraged, in an unencouraging way.

"Just that she's a family person, the thirteenth of thirteen kids, has a couple of kids of her own that I know of, Nina and Adam."

Alvin smiled—leered really. He seemed to be picking up more information than I was sharing. He tried hard to look relaxed and in control, but I don't know when I've seen anyone carry around as much tension as he did. His blunt hard fingers drummed on the table when he wasn't moving the clipboard and other papers from left to right. His head jerked around in birdlike movements. He looked intense and dangerous, and was just about the worst interrogator I'd ever met. He scowled at me. Flashes of pink shot across his cheeks like heat lightning.

Earlier I'd been thinking that it would be nice if people were taking the murder more seriously. Now I was getting serious with spurs on. You have to be careful what you wish for.

His head tilted a good inch to the left and he squinted at me. "You're not from here, are you?"

"Used to work out of New York City, worked a lot of places since. San Fran, Los Angeles, Seattle, but I've lived in Austin now for a few years."

"And you think if you eat enough biscuits and gravy it'll just natural make you a Texan, right?"

"I don't think I ever thought anything like that."

"Maybe there's something you should know. I have only time to give you a quick back sketch of this state, but I'll tell you this much. Was a time right after the Civil War when General Grant picked out his man and made him governor down here, name of Davis. There was a Yankee-leaning state police who kept people from the polls and fixed it so the carpetbagger was in. He used these state police fellas; half of them was nee-gros. Anyone didn't see it Davis' way he sicced those state thugs on 'em—picture that too, paying taxes to have some darkie thump you into line. Well, we had Injuns all over the place, and the Mex crowd here too, and if that wasn't enough, there were whole groups of people here that were Germans and every damn thing else. The Germans didn't vote to secede, so they were square with the Yankees who ended up runnin' the state back then after the war. Are you following me on all of this?"

I wanted like anything to glance at the other deputies, to see what they made of this digressive tirade. Instead I stayed fixed on the dark glitter of his squinting eyes. I nodded slowly, so he'd know I hadn't dozed off, or anything.

His flushed face stretched tight as a drum. There'd been a patterned lilt to the words, as if he'd heard them somewhere and memorized them. I'd heard that zealous sort of tone before, but didn't place it at the moment—understandable given the circumstances, which were tense. I believe everyone should have a passion, but I wasn't so sure about that in his case. "You see what I'm getting at here. True Texans have been having to fend off one bunch of yahoos after another who don't belong. You understand that?"

"I'm reaching hard to see how it applies to the young lady who's dead," I said. It seemed harmless enough, but from the small snap of his neck you'd have thought I hit him with a dead fish across the chops. His hands opened and closed into fists, and a darker red flush started up his neck toward his chin.

"Maybe you could answer me this. What brings a private detective all the way from the capital city out here to our sleepy little county?"

I didn't answer.

"Well?"

"I'm not at liberty to say," I said. "You'll have to believe me that it has nothing to do with your case." Eyebrows shot up on the other deputies.

"Why don't you let me decide that?"

"It's something I can't share," I said. "Feel free to ask me anything you want about what *you're* working on, though." I didn't mean or intend to be a smart ass. Truth was, I just didn't know.

I watched the amazing transformation of his face. The red line crept up from the collar of his uniform, passed his cheekbones, went all the way to his forehead before it hit the gong and I won a teddy bear. His eyes tightened to slits and his hands were slowly curling all the way into fists. I glanced at the other deputies. Winnick actually took a step back.

"You know," I said, "I'm getting the impression that Trish wasn't the one killed—that some fan got knocked off by mistake by getting into Trish's dressing room at a bad time." The surprised look on Winnick's face gave me some confirmation, but my attention was yanked back to Alvin.

21

"Can't share," he growled. "Not at liberty. Nothing to do with my case." His voice got louder. "Feel free. . . ." He leaped to his feet and swept the table to one side. Papers and the clipboard flew across the stage. Without seeming to bend forward he grabbed the lapels of my suit jacket in his fists and drew me close until my face hovered an inch from his own sweaty round one. I could see what looked like bands of muscle twitching in lines up and down his forehead.

"Now talk, damn you," he screamed into my face.

"No. I. . . ."

One hand let go of my jacket. His right shoulder dipped and a fist as big as a train rammed up and into my stomach. The top of me snapped forward in an accidental head butt that had to hurt me more than him. But, worse, the two or three beers I'd had back in the tent shot up my throat and onto Alvin's uniform. He dropped me to the floor. I landed with a soggy thump.

The other deputies were shouting. My head was ringing and it was hard to make out their words. I looked up at Alvin, and wished I hadn't. The black toe of his boot swung on its way to my head, and I was pretty sure the shouts of the other deputies weren't going to stop it. That was the last thing I remembered.

CHAPTER TWO

My eyes opened, caught a lot of white in the room—sheets, walls, and the fluffy hair on the man in uniform who looked a lot more like Mark Twain than I found comfortable. I felt reasonably sure Twain was dead. I wasn't so sure about myself.

"You took a lump or two," the man's voice crackled, a voice like over-starched sheets being tossed loosely by a breeze. "How many of me do you see?"

"One."

"Should be plenty." He was slim and stiff of back, wore the brown sheriff's department uniform as if he had done time in the marines, back in the Great War—WWI, that is. His hair stood out, crinkly white in Albert Einstein disarray. His tanned face had been mapped with weather and laughter wrinkles. Pinched eyes glittered out in black flickers from the cracked slits that were dominated by shaggy white eyebrows.

I looked around, caught the sterile white and square corners of the room. In a scratchy voice I said, "This a hospital room?"

"That's deduction. By damn, you *are* a detective. Just when I was having some doubt." He moved closer to the bed, picked up a glass of water with some kind of bent straw sticking from it. He lifted it over to my mouth and managed to poke the straw up my nose a couple of times before I reached for the glass.

"Give me that." I took a sip or two and put the glass back on the side table myself. Stretching that direction hurt my high ribs under my left arm. Alvin must have gotten off a couple

23

more kicks after I passed out.

"And you're Sheriff Cuthers," I said in a clearer voice. "Another deduction. No charge for that one."

He chuckled. "You bounce back better than most who've met Alvin," he said. He turned, dragged a chair over close to the bed and sat so that I wouldn't have to strain my neck looking up at him. He leaned near and gave me the benefit of his grizzled face above the neat uniform. "You mind telling me what brings you out to the Kasperville Folk Festival? They tell me they took a suit off you. No gun. But you did carry an active PI ticket."

"Guess I don't have the corner on deduction." The room smelled faintly of antiseptic. In the distance I could hear a dim siren headed our direction.

"That isn't deduction. It's observation. The question still stands." His voice crackled, but there was no missing the steel behind the words. His smile went all the way to his eyes and stopped.

"This is where Deputy Alvin and I fell out," I said. "I told him it was about an entirely different matter, one that had nothing to do with any murder. He differed. With his boot."

"For which I am truly sorry. It's why I stopped by to see you. To apologize."

"And ask a few questions."

"And that."

"Like why did I get in the way of Alvin's fist?"

"I'm not saying you should of worn a tie-dyed shirt and jeans," he said. "But if you had, you'd of fit in a sight better than you did."

I started to say something, but he held up a hand. "Oh, I know why you probably dress that way. Sure, a lot of folks in cities are all on the hip social bandwagon now that America did a terrible wrong by its native population. But out in the neck of woods where I live, there're still a smattering few who focus on the depredations and still subscribe to the unchallenged idea that Indians, like rattlesnakes, oughta be shot. Sound like anyone you've met?"

"He's *your* deputy."

He ignored that. "I imagine to someone who looks more than a bit like a leftover scrap of the Wild West shows, and I don't mean as Buffalo Bill Cody, that your wearing a suit seemed to be a good idea if you wanted to get any respect."

"A lot of my cases seem to draw me into prejudice of one kind or another. I'm no stranger to that." I reached to scratch an itch on my chest and found bandages wrapped tight there instead of skin I could scratch. "My limited wardrobe aside, have you made any progress on the murder investigation?"

He laughed, the kind of tossed-back-head laugh that made me think he would break into a cough when he came out of it. He snapped back to the intense and rapt attention he wasn't able to disguise. "Oh, I guess you haven't seen any of the papers. No. No, son. We haven't made a stitch of progress. But they *were* able to resume the festivities at the festival, if that troubled you."

I shrugged. Even that small movement made something inside me twinge in pain.

"That may have been what set Alvin off in the first place, knowing how little progress he was making. You sure that you're in no way involved in the murder, or in poking around about anything else?"

"Aside from me being still on the way when it happened, you mean? I do have a journalist and a couple or three other witnesses able to confirm the time he called me. You *were* able to fix a time of death, weren't you?"

His head tilted an inch to the right, and he gave me more of the gray-fox grin. "Jimmy said it back in the tent," I said.

"Who'd want to do somebody as sweet as Trish Mirandez? Was it a crime of hate? Passion?"

One shaggy white eyebrow lifted. "You don't know yet that it wasn't Trish?"

I sat up in the bed and was sorry. Pains shot through me. I looked down at where my chest was wrapped in tight white tape. A bandage covered my left cheekbone as well, and whatever was beneath that was throbbing now. I could see myself in a mirror that hung on the wall. The sight did little to reassure me. My black hair stuck out in many directions, my puzzled blue eyes peered back at me. "So it's not Trish," I said. I'd had that notion earlier. "That's good. Who was it?"

"We're still parsing that out. A fan maybe? Someone who got past security and tried to see Trish, got. . . ."

". . . killed instead of Trish?" I finished for him.

"Maybe. We don't even know that yet."

"I suppose the S.O.P. here isn't much different than in any other police investigation. You focus on family, friends, anyone close to Trish Mirandez, or this other person. Anyone who had any contact with Trish in the trailer, that sort of thing."

"Done that. Been there. Though there's little to follow on the victim until we get more on her."

"The boyfriend?" I said. "Wasn't someone from your staff going to speak with him?"

"Alvin did. Got little from him."

"He slip away?"

"Kind of." He looked down at the floor, must have seen little there. His head swung back up. "But we'll get more on her."

"And if all of the logical trails peter out, that leaves whatever improbable. . . ."

"You, for instance. You stick out a bit. If I was as young and impetuous as Alvin, I might've jumped to some conclusions about you myself. You show up late, dressed out of step with the event, and have a background that might suggest you're no stranger to violence."

"You making excuses for Alvin?"

"Checked up on your past, we did." The grin had a touch of menace to it. "You solved some nifty cases over to Austin, ruffled the feathers of a few cops as well. I spoke to a Sergeant Borster. . . ."

"No fan of mine."

"Exactly. I don't know what you've ever done to him, something bad, I reckon. At first he acted like we ought to give Alvin a medal for the way he treated you. He begrudged that you were good at what you do, got to the nub of things and scraped your busybody way to the right conclusion of a couple of cases that had them baffled."

"That was kind of him." I was surprised Borster had anything approaching a kind word for me. The last time I'd seen him he had thought out loud that Austin would be a better town without me in it—this after I'd been present when he missed out on collecting a huge reward, though I was not as responsible as he thought.

"And, as for Alvin, he's been suspended, without pay."

"I suppose Alvin's another fan of mine now."

"Oh, you won't confuse him for that should you run across him." He chuckled in a way that discouraged me from joining in.

He glanced toward the door, expecting someone perhaps. When he turned back to me, he said, "Look, I run a tiny department in a county of some forty thousand odd souls, the occasional emphasis on the odd. We have DARE, local crime prevention and gang awareness groups. We don't have some big department with an undersheriff, psychological services, and all of that. What we do have are patrol deputies as well as investigations people, some of them doubling up when it comes to our

Special Operations Unit. Alvin had worked his way up to investigations, had earned that, in spite of a mark or two against him."

A tap sounded at the half open door.

"Come in," Cuthers said, without lessening the intensity of the smiling stare he had locked on me.

Deputy Winnick slipped into the room. She held her deputy-sheriff hat in her hand, but her hair was down and loose for the moment, the blonde length of it contrasting with her dark uniform. She might have some Swedish roots in her background, I thought. Or it could have been some of the Germanic background that peppers nearby towns like Fredricksburg with German-style beer halls. In any case, she looked like the kind of woman who would make even the most tested of small-town clergymen start eyeing the collection plate if it meant getting next to her.

"Harmon," she said, nodding to Cuthers. "Sheriff," she corrected herself. "He's been spotted at. . . ."

Cuthers said, "Can you please hold that thought, Cassie?"

She didn't look at me. Instead, she eased back against the wall and went into parade rest, holding her hat in front of her with both hands.

Cuthers gave her a curt nod, came back to me. "I want you to know, I don't usually discuss an ongoing case with someone like yourself, particularly when you've been less than forthcoming. In this case . . . considering what Alvin. . . ." He was, for the first time, at a loss for words. "In this case," he continued, pushing himself upright and dragging the chair back to its place along the wall, "I'm under some adverse pressure. A lot of respectable people were in that folk festival crowd, Congressman Max Bolens among them. I wouldn't have wanted or expected things to have gone as far as they have." He cleared his throat, but it took none of the cragginess from his voice.

"I've authorized Cassie here to fill you in a tad, to the extent we can, when she escorts you back to get your car." The lack of expression on her face told me about what she wanted it to. "I understand they'll release you from here in just a while, if you've the notion to get up and go. And you strike me as someone who will. For your sake, as well as ours, I hope you'll take whatever business it is that brought you out here back to Austin without stirring up anything in this county. That clear?"

"The next bus leaves at five," I said. "Be under it. Is that it?"

He smiled, but didn't laugh. And his eyes didn't share the uptilted corners of his mouth. "Just think about it. Cassie will answer your questions."

He gave me a nod, turned and went over to trade whispers with Deputy Winnick.

"One thing, Sheriff," I said.

He turned back to me slowly.

"This has to be one of the busiest weeks of the year here in this county. You don't find it odd that you took a weekend right in the middle of all this to be off camping with your grandchildren, leaving someone like Alvin in charge?"

Deputy Winnick slipped into attention without knowing she did it.

Sheriff Cuthers stood for a moment, then moved slowly back to the side of my hospital bed. He looked down at me. I expected to see some unveiled menace. Instead, his smile was genuine this time. The corners of his eyes crinkled. "I mentioned that Alvin had a couple of strikes against him," he said. "We occasionally get one or two deputies with the same kind of mentality that makes schoolyard bullies want to be cops. Heavy badges, I call 'em. Alvin had such a leaning, and there's something else." He reached up to sweep back a wayward length of his thick white hair.

"You hear a lot out here about the passing of the Wild West, but there are a few out-of-touch types who aren't convinced it's over. They like the idea of those rougher days, like I said, where every Injun was a bad one, and when land, or anything else, could be had just by grabbing, if you were strong enough, or mean enough. We're living in some heady days, where the paranoia of the country has seeped all the way out here. People worry about terrorism, anthrax, and the same things they sweat over in the city, though out here some are used to fending for themselves, so they see this as opportunity to revert back to more basic rules of survival, though that may bring with it some of the old prejudices. Alvin had more of that in him than I realized when I hired him, and, I guess, all he needed was for someone who looked the part to come along on a bad day. That, and he'd been hanging around with some unsavory friends of a like mind. I'd a notion that sooner or later he was going to get his third strike. So I guess that makes me culpable here, or at least able to feel some old-fashioned guilt. His explosion, though, came from an accumulation of things that built up all day until he popped. I couldn't have predicted that. I didn't expect anyone to end up dead just because I gave Alvin a bit of rope to hang himself."

"I just happened to be that piece of rope?" I said.

"And a darned good and stringy length of it at that," he said. He turned and walked out the door, chuckling to himself as he left.

Deputy Winnick stared straight ahead.

I said, "You're going to have to turn your head, or leave the room if I'm to struggle into my clothes."

She turned to me for the first time. A spot of pink showed on her left cheek. "I've seen. . . ." She stopped herself. "I'll be right outside the door."

An hour later, after what was a much smaller flurry of hospital paperwork than I expected, I got into the front seat of the county patrol car beside Deputy Winnick. I'd had my share of backseat rides in these before.

The sun had taken over the day, no hint of yesterday's clouds. Plenty of blue sky and heat.

She pulled into traffic. We got half a mile from the hospital when she said, "You've made a real enemy."

"They say that a person is measured by the strength of his enemies."

"You must have the strength of ten."

"Because my heart is pure?" That got a grin out of her for the first time.

After another mile I asked, "How long's this Alvin been a loose cannon in the department?"

She kept her eyes on traffic. The profile of her blonde head and clean smooth face was very restful to the eye. She said, "How does one become a private detective?"

"When you're dropped on your head enough, or when the world peels away enough layers of skin, then the PI ticket just rolls your way like the prize in a box of Cracker Jacks."

Her head panned to me for a quick look, then went back to the road. Her eyes were a paler blue than my own, but full of suppressed sparkle. "You *are* a Gloomy Gus, aren't you."

"Oh, this is one of my better days," I said.

"No, really. How did you get into private investigating?" At least she said it without curling her lip like some officers of the law do about PIs.

"I got into this line of work for probably some of the same reasons you do the work you do. I had an aptitude for figuring things out, if not at first—eventually."

"You don't have any idea why I'm in my line of work," she said without looking at me.

We rode in a heavy quiet for another half mile.

31

There are a mere handful of women I have met in all my travels who generate an immediate chemical magnetism—call it what you might. I'd long ago learned to say no to doing anything about this rare epiphany of yearning. The women are usually married, spoken for, can see me in a clear light, or are in some other way unattainable. So I did some silent admiring of Deputy Winnick, but kept my mouth closed. She certainly seemed vibrant to me—I hoped the uniform wasn't any part of the appeal.

The traffic picked up as we neared the Laughing Burro Ranch. There were cars and people bustling about. As many or more tents were set up. It looked like life was going along fine after the business of death had been cleaned up.

"You didn't even get a name, or anything on the victim?" I asked.

"Oh, we got a name, all right. What Harmon said is that *Alvin* didn't get it. It's Marinda Selina, a fan, just like we suspected. Her boyfriend stood outside the trailer, waiting for her while she was being killed inside."

"How was she murdered, exactly?"

"Hit on the head, strangled from behind. We doubt the killer even looked at her face until she was dead and had been turned over. We don't even know that the murder was intentional. Someone could have just been trying to subdue an intruder, though the hit on the head should've done that. Anyway, the victim does look a lot like Trish Mirandez—enough to be mistaken for her."

"What did you mean Alvin didn't get her name from the boyfriend?"

Her lips tightened. She said, "After the little scuffle with you. . . ."

I must have snorted.

She went on, "Alvin went back to the victim's boyfriend.

Alvin hadn't gotten anything in their first conversation, something about his style of asking, I guess. While you were being tended to, Alvin might have felt a little desperate, thought that if he wrapped things up with the case everything wouldn't come down as hard on him. Hard to tell what he was thinking. In any case, he was rougher on the boyfriend than on you, which only made matters worse."

"The boyfriend's . . . ?"

"With his girlfriend, at least."

"So Alvin's not just suspended without pay, he's on the loose with a murder rap hanging over his head."

"And a picture of your face in his mental crosshairs for all we know."

There had to be something else, something I wasn't going to get from her or Cuthers. The sheriff had been keeping an eye on Alvin, and the publicity of handling a murder may have been what sent the deputy over the top. Murder doesn't happen all that often within the jurisdictions of county sheriffs and small-town cops. Even when it had, in my experience, I had yet to see any law enforcement officer act quite like Alvin.

The patrol car pulled into the ranch and wove through the tents until I motioned for her to stop. The tent where Jimmy, Dutch, and Johnny Gringo had bivouacked was gone. I stared for a moment at the empty spot.

"Your friends desert you?"

I said, "At least my car's around here someplace."

I got out of the car slowly, feeling each wrapped bruise on me. She gave a small wave as she pulled away, getting back to whatever business the department had today, like hunting down one of their own who had slipped off the deep end.

Most of the tents were empty. Only a few people moved about in the area. Everyone would be over near the music, catching up. The sun beat down on me, encouraged me to step up the pace. I walked the few hundred yards to the parking lot. As I got to my car, I saw Jimmy Bravuro slipping a note under my windshield wiper. He spun when I called out.

"Hey, we're packed and out of here like a herd of turtles," he shouted. As I got closer, he said, "The note says: 'Gig's over. See me about our case when you get back to Austin.' "

"Since we're both here, maybe you can . . . ?" I stopped myself. Over Jimmy's shoulder I saw two men coming our way. Both looked like they could be linemen for the Dallas Cowboys. Though they were in street clothes, I could see that one of them was Alvin. I glanced behind me. Another hulk closed in on us from that quarter.

Maybe they just wanted to talk, I lied to myself. That didn't explain why the one with Alvin stopped to pick up a short two-by-four that some fool had left laying around.

I shoved my car keys toward Jimmy. "Get in the car, Jimmy. Cut out of here fast as you can."

"Hey, I can't just ditch you."

"Do it," I snapped. I knew if we both scooted, there would be a pursuit. I wanted Jimmy out of the formula. It was me they were after.

He wanted to argue some more. But he caught the looks on the men as they got closer, and I gave him a short shove toward the car. Jimmy spun and opened the car door, climbed in and fired the engine. He peeled out of the parking spot, throwing a little gravel. I was too busy ducking to one side to worry about that.

Alvin glanced around the lot before focusing on me. Then he came up to me and stopped. His face shifted into a grin that I can only describe as raw evil. The equally large fellow beside him holding the two-by-four was tapping his open palm with it.

CHAPTER THREE

Two of them lined up in front of me. A third, who had slipped out from between two trucks, stayed around behind me where I couldn't get a fix on him even when I tried looking for his reflection in the nearest car's windows. I heard the soft crunch of gravel as he moved.

Though I try not to get in a fix like this, it has been my policy through the years to pick out the single individual who I think could do me the most harm and take him out first, if possible. In this case, though, they all looked an equal threat, including the one behind me, who was getting on my nerves the most by my not being able to see him.

"This is him, fellas, the asshole Indian, *cabrón*, who got me in all the trouble," Alvin said.

I could have argued with him about his logic. His voice had the tremor of one too far gone in anger to listen to reason. Not that he'd shown himself to be a reasonable person so far in my short acquaintance with him.

The fellow holding the lumber had a tattoo on the back of his hand, which at first hasty glance looked like two small lightning bolts side by side—the sign of the *Schutzstaffel*, Nazi blackshirt storm troopers. At closer glance, it was just someone's initials, maybe his, not a confirmation he was neo-Nazi. Such is the power of suggestion at a time like this, though his face *was* every bit as pit bull mean as Alvin's. He had a chew of tobacco

35

that made one cheek bulge out, and his hair was buzz cut just as short.

As far as I could see in any direction, there wasn't another person in the parking lot. The rim of the cloudless blue sky was edged with a band of pale rust as evening was sneaking up on the festival. I could hear music in the distance. Crowds would be gathering. I would be noticeably, to me, absent. The scrap of a song I could hear lilting out to the parking lot sounded like:

Track where you will, and despite all you do
The hounds of your fate will pursue and find you.

"What do you have to say for yourself?" Alvin asked, his eyes intense, dark slits in the muscles of his square face. He pulled a pair of black leather half gloves out of his back pocket and was tugging them on—didn't want to muss up his knuckles.

He said, "You sure you don't want to cop to the plea for doing the woman in Trish Mirandez's trailer? It'd simplify my life, and yours." He gave half a nod to the fellow behind me, which did little for my attention span. "At the very least maybe you might could answer some questions you felt too snotty about to answer earlier."

I sought to edge a step to the right, to bring the fellow to my rear into the corner of my eye. He moved as well to keep that from happening. What I did see, though, was Deputy Cassie Winnick slip around from beside one of the parked cars and stand up behind Alvin and his pal.

"You're in this too deep, Alvin, to get out even if you solve the woman's death now," I said.

"That's 'Deputy' to you."

"Not the way I hear it," I said. Soft gravel crunched closer to my back.

You ever see a person want to climb right out of his skin and come at you with everything he has, then you can imagine

Alvin's face at that moment. In some far cobweb-filled corner of his slow-ticking head perhaps he *did* think everything was going to be back the way it was and he was going to be out of trouble himself if he could complete the job he'd started. Or maybe he was just going through motions for which he'd been partially trained and knew little else. Time was running out for me to contemplate what made him tick. I had to deal with the ticking bomb he had become. The two of them in front of me started to move toward me. The crunch of gravel got louder behind me.

"Everybody stay right where you are. That means you too, Donnie. Step around where I can see you." It was Cassie's voice. She stood in stance behind Alvin, and her gun was out of its holster. I heard her draw the hammer all the way back.

The other two stopped, but Alvin didn't. The fellow beside him glanced Alvin's way. Alvin growled, "Ignore that bitch. If she had any balls she'd have shown them by now. She's not gonna shoot."

I sure hoped she was going to surprise them. I heard no shout or warning shot from her. She would go by the book; that or she was reluctant to shoot a former colleague in the back. I had my hands full concentrating on Alvin's progress when I heard the sound of an engine and tires spraying gravel.

I looked up and saw my car bearing down on us. Jimmy Bravuro sat tucked low over the wheel, his eyes squinted nearly shut. He had to be up to fifty miles per hour or so in the gravel parking lot and coming right at us. I heard the steps of the fellow behind me scamper as he got out of the way.

The fellow beside Alvin stopped and took a step back. There was no stopping Alvin. He put his head down and ran at me. I had about a second and a half to reflect again on how someone like him ever came to be a law officer in the first place. I had caught glimmers of a crafty intelligence shining out from that thick skull of his. I caught none of that at the moment. He had let his rage take over, not for the first time in his life.

I waited until his extended hands grasped at my suit jacket, then at the last second I ducked low and rolled in the gravel, using all the strength I could manage to kick out with one foot as he whooshed by. The edge of my shoe caught him square in the side of his left knee. I felt his knee buckle to the side as the kick landed. I kept rolling until I was out of the way of madman Jimmy and his auto-derby mentality.

Brakes squealed behind me. I heard the car skidding in the gravel. I spun, wiggled backward on the palms of my hands until I could tuck down close to one of the other parked cars. Alvin was just completing a somersault, the likes of which would have impressed the Flying Wallendas. Either from my kick, or in trying to stop, Alvin had somehow propelled himself into a mid-air flip. He landed with a dust-scattering thump I couldn't hear for all the noise of the car in a controlled slide. It skidded all the way to the prone Alvin. One wheel popped over an extended shin as if it was a speed bump. It rolled Alvin over onto his stomach, and I could hear him bellowing as the car's engine died. Jimmy leaped out of the driver's side door. He waved a tire iron.

But there was no one for him to take on. Cassie bent over Alvin's friend, snapping the cuffs into place. Alvin lay partially under the front of the car, screaming, but in too much pain to move. The third fellow, Donnie, was long gone.

"Thought I'd left you, didn't you?" Jimmy said as he came over to me. He was breathing hard, still pumped up. My breathing was labored as well.

Cassie stood up and came over to us.

"Better call EMS," I said. "I don't think Alvin's going anywhere on his own."

"He'll keep for a minute," she said. To Jimmy she said, "Hey, aren't you Jimmy Bravuro? I love your music."

"How do you like my driving?" he panted.

"Well, I'm not going to cite you *this* time," she said.

I drove on the way back to Austin. Night was slipping over the countryside like a pair of tight black nylons. Jimmy had missed his ride back, so he rode shotgun. I was, as usual, being too quiet, but that could have been because of the uncomfortable bandages and a rib or two that no longer felt all the way connected.

"You ever think you might have too much car here?" he said after a mile or two. He turned the radio knob, got nothing. He looked at the odometer. "Says seventy-nine thousand. How many times has that odometer been 'round the block?"

"Don't pick on the car, Jimmy. It got me out here. It's getting you home."

"No extra charge for the dents?"

"Hailstorm. Stones big as plums. Looks like a jealous husband with a ball-peen hammer found where I live." The car was a greenish June bug gold color I'd never seen on any car-dealer charts.

"More like a golf ball. Why don't you just paint 'Titleist' on the side and be done with it?"

"I'm told that the reason golf balls have those dents is to make them more aerodynamic. I'm pretty sure I get better gas mileage since the storm."

He fiddled with the radio knob some more, gave up on that and clicked it off.

The old heap, an '84 Pontiac Firebird, could take its knocks, but we'd been through a lot together. I'd had it since I first arrived in Austin. I knew its little quirks, like how to tickle it into action on one of our few frosty days. It had been with me on a chase scene or two as well, ones I wouldn't mind having a film of, if any was available.

He sat silent for almost a mile. Brooding and staring ahead at the rushing strobe of divider-line paint coming at us on the road in the headlights as the car wove out of Hill Country as I headed for Austin.

We climbed one hill, went down the side of another, the lush green of mountain cedar, live oaks, and mesquite at the outside edge of the headlight beams thick along the sides of the highway. People who have never been to Texas may picture it as some kind of desert, perhaps with those tall saguaro cactus plants that occur in Arizona but nowhere in Texas. The fact is, the center of the state, particularly in the western direction from Austin, has more ups and downs of green hills and valleys than many roller coasters. Socially the difference is pronounced too, since out of sight of the yuppie-filled and spotted-with-liberals capital, you're liable to run into Bubba and Leroy in a pickup truck with gun rack in the back window in front of a small-town convenience store, each with a lap full of beer and shooting aerosol cheese into their mouths while Jim Eddie leans his denim shirt shoulder against the truck and drinks from an open unheated can of gravy. Thus ran the line of my not-so-lofty thoughts until the twang of Jimmy's voice once again cracked the silence.

"Do you really think someone was out to kill Trish, Trav? I mean, it doesn't make any sense."

"Motive is one of the key aspects I seek." I eased the car around a curve on a hill and started down the other side, watching for deer or anything else that might dart out in our path. "At bottom, it's what most interests me, though opportunity's kind of handy too. I don't have near enough information to imagine why anyone would do what they did. It could be mistaken identity, or maybe the person wasn't even after Trish but was just surprised while snooping. None of it makes sense yet."

"You think the police in a county like that can't handle something like this? The egg or two of them I met didn't seem all the way boiled. But, if the cops everywhere were all that good, there wouldn't ever be work for someone like you."

"The police everywhere do a thorough and capable job in most cases," I said, "but their solution rate isn't one hundred percent. If it was, I guess I would have a broom in my hand about this time of day, as the janitor at some high school. I come in when their skills, equipment, and standard operating procedure have taken them to a wall—one where they're too busy with the incoming filth and effluvia of everyday crime and disorder to sort through—and find just the right pieces." Like any time when I talk at all, and especially when I talk too much or sound too preachy, I immediately wished I'd said nothing. Given a choice in life, I preferred being more of the silent type. Talk, especially honest talk, always made me feel embarrassed, and sad.

"There were far bigger fish out there than any of us musicians. The killer could have tried for any of them. Even Congressman Max Bolens was there."

I let out a slow, careful breath of air.

"What?"

"Max Bolens. Now there's a name to reckon with. Why do you suppose a man of his caliber and fame was at a folk festival?"

"Maybe he likes music. You do, Trav. It *is* possible, though I think in Max's case he was some kind of guest of honor."

"Oh."

"You don't think those fellows in the parking lot had some kind of militia backgrounds, do you?"

"How'd you make a leap like that?" I glanced across to Jimmy's concerned face.

"Well, one of Max's most recent claims to fame was his

41

daughter being tangled up with some sort of paramilitary bunch, wasn't it?"

"Right. I read about that. Girl named Donna, right? She went by some other name, didn't she? Friedya. That was it. Thought she was some kind of narc trying to infiltrate the far militant right, didn't she?"

"That's the story she sung loud and often after the FBI busted her along with her boyfriend in a small cell of some bigger militia bunch. Caught them with a handful of fully automatic weapons, just enough to make the story interesting."

"But they were just paramilitary, right? They weren't neo-Nazis, were they?" I said.

"Yeah, sure, I guess, just some fired-up citizens who halfway hoped our military's dabbling in the Middle East would spill over this way long enough to get to fire off a few rounds. Most of them think of themselves as patriots, wave the flag as much as anyone, they just usually happen to have a gun in the other hand. After those terrorist attacks in New York City, and then all the business in Iraq, some woodsy folks in Texas saw it as a call to arms like days of old. The ATF, FBI, and those homeland security people saw it differently. Donna just happened to get in the middle of some of that, thanks to a boyfriend who showed that different kind of spark that's often attractive to young girls."

I nodded, though he was looking away and perhaps didn't hear my head rattle. "It doesn't take too many sideways two-steps for a group of like-minded, gun-toting individuals with a 'locals-first' bias to slip to the xenophobic level of excluding anyone who isn't just like themselves. It must've felt like being rebels and patriots at the same time, from within. Without the automatic weapons it might've been okay . . . until people got hurt, and some did. All that must've been heady stuff to a young girl like Bolens' daughter, though. She's still on trial, isn't she?"

"Yeah, but now with all the threat of terrorist activities these guys don't look as radical as they did. Some people think they might have the right idea, action-oriented paranoia. Still, the feds seem to think they have a good case against the girl, I guess."

"That's bound to be tough on a father, no matter who he is."

"As if that isn't enough," Jimmy said, "not too long ago Bolens hears from some friend that he oughta check out the Web, that the friend found pictures of Max's wife Audrey naked with some other man. Imagine that. 'Naked on the Internet.' Now *there's* a song title for you."

"Does any of this have anything to do with this case you were talking about? The one you could have as easily shared with me when you got back to Austin, saving me a trip out here." The tussle with Alvin had been all the variety I needed or craved for a spell. All things being equal, I'd as soon not find that Jimmy's job was heading me toward any backwoods militia.

"Well, no, it doesn't, Trav. Sorry to send you into a snit," he said. "If my little problems trouble you in the least, you just say so."

I sighed. I'd been through a painful lot after being drug all the way out this way for something Jimmy hadn't gotten around to sharing yet. "We've got a few moments here, Jimmy." I gave him a quick glance. "Catch me up on why you called me out in the first place. I've gotten some heat about it. I stuck to client privilege. Please tell me that it was worth the hassle."

"Ya know, Trav, long as I've known you, man, you've been kind of on the edge of society, at best. You ever wonder if maybe . . . ?"

"Do you mind if we stay focused?"

"I mean, you're a lot like this car. Look at it. I gotta tell you, it's rusting, man."

"The hassle," I said. "Tell me it was worth it."

He sighed this time. "I hoped to get you cozied up to a

newcomer on the music scene, Johnny Gringo."

"We got along like brothers, don't you recall?" An ache low in my chest gave a twinge.

"I did notice your usual first-meeting charm wasn't in its best form. You guys weren't exactly soul mates from the get-go. What was that about?"

"My fault. I was tired, wet, too sober, and the guy was young enough to see the world as a bright shining path of opportunity. It bummed me, and I didn't flex enough. It's hard keeping after myself to respect everyone. Don't think it isn't. You know I'm hooked on the music business people, and that I love the music."

"That why you have a radio that doesn't work?"

"The people, like yourself, they're interesting and colorful folks, and about the only crowd I'd consider working for when not doing things for one of the tribes."

"I know, Trav. Even when we're pooped it's in the veins of all of us. I've seen your foot tapping." Jimmy turned back and spoke toward the road zipping at us. "Anyway, Johnny Gringo cut a CD deal with one of the local labels: Ruby Rhubarb. It's the imprint of a live music venue here, The Rubber Jungle."

"I'm not sure I want to know any more than that."

"Just drive. So, here's the skinny. The guy who owns the nightclub and record label is an ex-con named Bent Lenny."

"This just gets better." I'd heard of Lenny. He was the kind of small-timer who hints at mafia connections.

"Well, all Johnny Gringo wants is someone to release his first CD. You know what that can be like."

"Not firsthand."

"I'm warning you, Trav. Anyway, Lenny has Johnny Gringo in for a couple of gigs, then tells him he has tapes of the live gigs, and that Johnny's already halfway to a release. Next thing Johnny Gringo knows he's signing to do something like a subsidized release, where he pays part of the production costs.

He doesn't even have to lay any hard money down. He can pay some of the money spread over a few weeks. The rest'll come out of his royalties and residuals. It's a way around the Catch-twenty-two, so he goes for it."

"Let me guess where this is going," I said. "Johnny Gringo finds he's hooked himself up to a loan shark situation and has signed up for some ridiculous vig he can never pay."

"Not even close," Jimmy said.

We were approaching Austin. A warm yellow glow lit up the sky. We could make out the beginnings of the skyline, blue neon bars across the levels of one skyscraper, the white dome of the capital building standing out in the middle.

"It was nothing like that," Jimmy said. "What happens is, the CD comes out, is a small break for Johnny Gringo, even though it only sells locally, and in Europe. The clinker is that he owes Bent Lenny, who doesn't press him for any of the cash he owes, even though production costs ran over. Well, knowing Lenny, as we all do, it struck us as odd that Lenny doesn't press for the money. That's what's bugging Johnny Gringo, what he wants you to look into."

"Let me get this straight," I said. Traffic was picking up around us. I gave Jimmy a quick glance. "It's not getting hounded that's bugging Johnny Gringo. It's that he thinks he ought to be and isn't? You dragged me all the way out to Kasperville to lay that on me?"

"That's not all of it," Jimmy said.

"Well, I hope not. It's a pretty flat story as it stands after what I've been through."

"I'd buy that too if it stopped there. It doesn't."

I let Jimmy have some slack, kept myself busy weaving through traffic. It had gradually gotten less black around us out on the highway, was all bright lights now as my battered old car with my battered old ego in it eased into the edge of town. All the lights and activity gave my spirits a festive boost. Austin is the capital of live music in America—so I'm often told—and on a typical night you can go to any one of fifty to seventy-five clubs for a demonstration. Most of the venues don't begin their main show until ten P.M., so the early crowd was still shuffling from the restaurants to the clubs.

"Drop me off at the Constitutional Club," Jimmy said. "I promised to catch at least one set of Johnny Gringo's gig there. Tori Brice is doing the early show. Want to come?"

"I promised myself I would celebrate getting back to Austin by going to Hut's and wrapping my lips around one of their burgers," I said. "Go ahead with your story."

"So Johnny Gringo goes over to Lenny's house to see why he isn't getting pressured harder to pay Lenny the money. He's thinking, maybe Lenny isn't telling him everything and sales are better than he's saying. You know what I mean."

I mumbled something.

"Anyway, Johnny Gringo gets to Lenny's house, sees him down the street talking to some fellows. So Johnny Gringo decides he's going to wait inside. The front door's not locked. He goes in, and there on the dining-room table are piles of twenty-, fifty-, and hundred-dollar bills. He doesn't know what the total amount had to be, but he said there was a bushel or two of bills there. Then he hears Lenny coming back in the front way, so Johnny Gringo goes out the back."

I pulled the car into a parking spot on Congress Street, half a block from the Constitutional Club. It was as close as I could get, and I felt lucky to find that spot. We sat in the car. I left the motor running.

"You think Lenny's nightclub and record label are doing that good?" I asked.

"No way! At least not like that. Hard to tell how much was there."

"As a yardstick, two million in twenty-dollar bills weighs about two hundred forty-six pounds."

"That'd sure make a lump in my back pocket."

"Sure would."

"What do you say? Will you look into it?"

"And do what? Make Lenny put pressure on Johnny Gringo for money?"

"No. Just find out what's screwy about the setup."

"If Johnny Gringo doesn't have the money to pay Lenny, how's he going to pay me?"

"Whatever happened to that altruistic spirit everyone knows as part of the Blue-Eyed Indian's reputation?"

"I think it was Diamond Jim Brady who said, 'It's fun being a sucker, if you can afford it.' I can't afford it."

"Maybe you should give up this high lifestyle of yours."

"Jimmy."

"Okay. Okay. Just pulling on your coat. There's a pool of cash several of the area performers have put together. We can pay you out of that. Does that put you on the case?"

"I might look into it tomorrow. You'd better get into the club. I have to get hopping before Hut's closes at ten."

"Come on, say you'll take the case."

"Depends."

"On what?"

"A couple of things. One is what you want done with Lenny once I find out what he's up to. It doesn't seem logical that local musicians would want to eliminate a recording label. Seems like there are too few as it is for all the groups around here."

"The deal is, we just want to know if Lenny is clean. If he's not, any bad that sticks to him could hurt the careers of anyone having anything to do with him. If he's dirty, we need to know so that Johnny Gringo and any other local talent can steer clear of him. What's the other thing?"

47

"You mentioned guys Bent Lenny was talking to. You kind of skipped briskly over the description. Why?"

Jimmy looked out the passenger window, then back to me. "Fact is, Trav, some of them had pretty close haircuts too. It could be some of these militia types we just met out there, or it could just be a grunge band thing. But that's not the kind of people Lenny features at the Rubber Jungle. He leans toward folk music, and blues."

"You just thought you'd leave that part out?"

"Considering what you've just been through. I thought. . . ."

"Don't spare me details that matter."

CHAPTER FOUR

I sat in a black vinyl booth near the back of Hut's. Memorabilia covered the walls and the ceiling. The place had gotten stuck in time somewhere in the fifties. Near my booth the wall was covered with college pennants, pictures of Darrel Royal football teams, and a large ceramic dancing Mr. Peanut holding hands with Betty Boop. I felt particularly anti-social and had ordered lots of extra onion on my Arnold's Best. I nursed my second Shiner Bock beer while waiting for the burger. I thought Marcie was bringing it my way, then saw she carried no tray as she wove through the crowded tables toward me.

"Phone call for you, Travis. You can take it over at the bar."

"Go ahead, Jimmy," I said, when I picked up the phone. "It's your dime."

"You better get over here," he said. "Someone just tried to bump off Tori Brice."

This time I had to park three blocks up and two over from Congress Street to get near the Constitutional Club. Cars lined the street in every spot near the place, and a cluster of flashing lights from patrol cars in front of the club told me it wasn't going to be much easier to get in by the pedestrian pathways.

I clicked down the sidewalk in that direction. The night was black around me, the mixed colored glow of neon from across the street not quite bright enough to reach across the wide street. Where I would normally expect to hear the clang of a

49

drum set and thump of bass coming from down the street, it was quiet, just the wind whistling along the stone faces of buildings in the dark.

Near the club, a crowd had formed, packing the sidewalk to the corner curb. I pushed and jostled my way closer, weathering an occasional grumbled complaint. I saw a flash, then the camera lowered and Hal Jansen backed up a step and took a new angle of a policeman stretching yellow tape along one side of the building. That told me there was no longer any real news inside, or Hal wouldn't be out here getting insurance shots, the kind papers have to run if they don't have a body bag or someone crying on which to focus.

From the way the gendarmes were wrapping up, and even some of the crowd oozed away, it looked like most of the show was over. I could wait until later to come back and look for the spots where bullets had been dug from the wall, that sort of thing, or I could just talk to Hal, who probably knew as much as I could learn. I panned through the faces around me, just in case there was someone getting too much zealous glee out of the moment, the way some pyromaniacs stand around and watch at the scene of a fire they've set. The faces were just those of regular music buffs, as well as the South Austin sort of bohemian crowd that always hung around the Constitutional Club, and a few neighbors who had adventured out to see if there was anything gory to witness.

A hand like a claw grabbed me by the shoulder and started to turn me. I tried to duck away from it, but the talons tightened and made me wince all the way to my bandaged ribs. My head turned slowly, and I saw Borster, never a pretty sight.

I can only imagine that this detective sergeant had had a rough childhood. His face is pocked, long and squarish, and there is a jagged scar coming down from the corner of his mouth. The pale green and red neon lights nearest us weren't helping his oily complexion any either.

"Nice stuff," the claws of his fingers roughed my suit coat shoulder without letting go of me. "You're living well." A sinister threat came through in every word he spoke.

The people standing close to us might have thought his behavior strange for a detective sergeant sworn to maintain law, order, and peace. But, then, they weren't aware of what Borster lost out on when last I meddled in one of his assigned cases. A Houston oil billionaire had offered ten million dollars to anyone who caught the ones who had kidnapped his daughter and killed her—ten million alive, that is. Dead, the kidnapper was still worth one million. That kind of money might corrupt the most stable cop, and I would never have accused Borster of being that. A bounty hunter had beat him to the lower amount, killing a friend of mine in the bargain. Somehow, Bortser blamed me for his missing out on the reward. Given my long-established interest in the motives of others, you can imagine what conclusions I came to about him. Right now he looked at me like I was something that had backed up out of a clogged sink. His hard fingers tightened on the trapezium muscle along my neck. I winced, but didn't give him the satisfaction of collapsing to the ground, though he was squeezing almost hard enough for that.

"If you plan on staying in a town where you're not welcome, you'd better reconcile yourself to paying up," he said. He leaned close enough to my ear for me to feel the heat of his breath. His voice had the whispering rasp of a steel file being drawn over the point of broken bone protruding from a bleeding wound. "Otherwise, there're some swell reservations out Oklahoma way, I hear." He gave the nerve along my neck a final hard squeeze that made my eyes water and nearly sent me to my knees. Then he spun and walked off through a crowd that opened to let him have all the room he wanted. Faces turned and looked at me as if wondering of what perversion I had to be guilty.

I eased away myself to check out all the other angles I could get to without brushing against Borster. I had to weave through people no matter on which side of the building I went.

There are sure a lot of people who like to crowd in at the scene of an attempt like this. I try hard sometimes to think what it'd take for anyone to try to murder someone else, for whatever reason. That may seem odd, given the business I'm in, but it's always a stretch for me. Still, the evidence is there every day that hate, rage—maybe even whim—dictate actions beyond ready comprehension. Look at the way tiny events through a day, and perhaps a biased background, had sent Alvin out of the blocks. Then too, I'd seen the crime stats for Austin like any other interested person, and had to shake my head that most murders in the past year were committed by strangers, with acquaintances coming in second. Family, friends, and one isolated cab driver incident came in third. It was no wonder the Austin homicide detectives wrapped themselves into knots every time another seemingly random murder, or attempt, happened.

A hand grabbed at my jacket again, and this time I made a six-inch vertical jump before breaking into a jog and tearing away from the grip.

"Hey," Jimmy Bravuro said. "Slow down. It's me."

I wheeled and saw his grin fade when he saw my face.

"Who'd you think I was?" he said, when I'd walked back to him.

"Borster."

Jimmy gave a small shudder. "As fuzz goes, he's one of the fuzziest. What do you make of this?"

"Tori's okay?"

"She's fine. Three shots were fired, the closest hit the wall a foot from where she was standing. She and her backup band were done, just getting their stuff out to the van. But, Trav, do you think you could add these attempts on female musicians to that case we discussed on the way back here?"

I thought of how eager Borster would be to have me poking around. "You think they're connected?"

"I don't know, man. You're the detective."

It was close to three A.M. when I finally pulled up to my office-slash-home, a cozy kind of hole-in-the-wall ground-floor place with a doorway and window on Brazos Street. I parked the car around back, had hiked to the front and was fiddling with the door to my office when a car door opened on the street.

I eased back into the shadow of the building.

"Oh, come out of there, Travis. I'm not going to hurt you."

I knew the voice, but I didn't buy the getup. Deputy Cassie Winnick had changed into street clothes—a rather tight pair of jeans, a white blouse, and cowboy boots worn on the outside.

"What're you doing out at this hour, and in Austin?" I asked. The only people out roaming around at this hour were drunks weaving home after bar-closing times, and a few anorexics heading to the twenty-four-hour grocery for celery.

"We'd better go inside." She glanced up and down the street.

I unlocked the office, went inside and flipped on the light. The blinds that covered the window facing the street were pulled. The door was solid and new, the last one shot out in that situation with Borster and a bounty hunter a while back.

I put the small sack I carried onto the desk, slipped into the back room where I had a small cot pressed against the door of the tiny bathroom. I tossed my jacket onto the bed and rummaged for a reserve half fifth of one-hundred-percent blue agave tequila I had tucked beneath the cot for extreme emergencies, and this seemed to be shaping into one.

"You live here?" she asked. She had followed me into the

small back room. I could feel her breathing over my shoulder.

"Sure," I said, "it's not much."

"You *are* the master of the understatement."

In the space of the small room, where I slept, she seemed larger than life. I wasn't used to seeing her out of uniform. I caught a mixed scent of saddle leather and lilacs. That was certainly a swell white blouse. My eyes lifted to hers and she grinned.

I carried the bottle back to the front office, sat on the corner of the desk and reached for the sack. "You mind if I take some refreshment?"

Her lip gave a twitch, but didn't curl all the way into an obvious snarl when her glance took in the bottle. I chose to ignore the glimmer of insight and said, "Have you had dinner yourself?"

"Nothing since lunch."

"If you can stand cold burger and onion rings . . . that's the fare."

"That would be great." She eyed the tequila bottle.

"You want a drink?"

"I don't."

"No problem." I went to the back room, rinsed out two small jars, the kind dried beef comes in. I brought hers back with some water in it. I put a little of the cactus juice into mine.

I cut the burger in half and handed her a share. I divided the onion rings and gave her an equal portion.

"It's like a picnic," she said. She sat on the other edge of the desk.

"Whee," I said.

I started to pick the onions off my half of the burger. She said, "You'd better leave them on. I'm going to eat mine."

We wrapped up the moment of high dining. I let her have the napkin and went into the bathroom to splash water from the sink onto my face. As I pulled the towel away I caught a glimpse of my face in the mirror, never very reassuring. I didn't know what to make of the look on my face this time. The ring of a purple bruise ran around the edge of the white tape on my cheekbone.

When I came back into the small front office she still sat on her corner of the desk. She dabbed delicately at the corner of those lips with her napkin. Her clothes pressed against her at thigh and chest from the way she was turned, and I had to remind myself to keep my eyes on hers as I said, "Aren't you out of your jurisdiction?"

"We think our case may have moved this way, or at least part of it."

I waited, poured another squirt of tequila while I did. Her eyes were larger, and paler blue than I remembered. My handful of pals, like Jimmy and Hal, are always busting my chops about why there's no woman in my life. Truth is, I'd lived alone far too long to be any kind of bargain to anyone I might care about. I had too many sharp edges of rigidity to adjust to the kind of give-and-take of nest life that went into any working relationship, though I had only a rough idea of even that in my head since I'd never once made that leap.

"You remember Donnie?" she said.

You bounce around as much as I have and you begin to suspect your take on people. I mean, here was Cassie, somewhere between Swedish bikini team and Rebecca of Sunnybrook Farm—emphasis on the agrarian background. What did I know about her, other than her badge number? Yet I felt the intuitive respect and warmth I do when someone is going to be a friend, no matter how rootless my life may seem. I look back on the dusty trail that's taken me across most of the states in the union and I can see old friends, new friends, good ones, some not quite so good, but all left pretty much behind in the wandering before I dropped anchor in Austin. I keep in touch with so few of all those people that my life might as well be comprised of the handful of close friends I'd made since coming to town. Most of all, I wonder if I should be making more new friends if it is just to leave them behind, or if I'm here to stay, if this is the place where my own roots take hold, and if my future is tied to the open, honest Texas faces like the one I was looking at now.

"You remember Donnie," she said again, brought me back from wherever I'd been.

"Alvin's friend. I didn't get a good look at him. He was always behind me."

"He looks much the same as the others," she said. "Except he's missing part of his left ear."

"Met Mike Tyson, has he?"

"Well, he and a couple of other fellows got Alvin loose. They hit us at the hospital, where we didn't have as much security as we would've liked."

"He's loose?"

"And we think he might've come to Austin. There are a number of fellows like himself. . . ."

"Paramilitary types," I said. "Or militia. Take your pick."

". . . down here in Texas. Since the World Trade Center tragedy, there've been a few people who choose to ride the paranoia by banding together and emphasizing survival, maybe overemphasizing it. Most of them quietly do their thing in camps in out-of-the-way spots across the state—as quiet as firing automatic weapons goes. A mixed-up pod of them is in Austin now, for whatever reason. We think Alvin's been linked up with them all along."

"And you're sharing this with me because . . . ?"

"You might be in danger."

"Gosh. It's awfully kind of Sheriff Cuthers to send someone all the way over here to protect me."

"I'm not here to protect you. We think you might be good bait." Her smooth face was so youthful, so innocent. The flicker of light in her eye I had to write off to the blood lust of the hunt.

I reached for my glass and let the tequila roll down the center of my tongue. I suppressed a small shudder.

"But why me?" I said.

"Well, there's the Indian angle. He seems heated up about you being one, even if you're only part-Indian. And I like the way you handled Alvin. You had no respect, no fear."

I said, "Respect is something anyone has to earn, even with a badge. As far as the fear goes, I might have been better advised."

"You're sure you had nothing to do with that business back in Trish Mirandez's trailer? That you aren't working on a related matter?"

I cleared my throat. "At that time," I said, "I wasn't. Since then, I may have become more involved than I was. I didn't share what took me out to Kasperville then, but that was because I didn't know. I hadn't been hired yet. A group of musicians wants me to look into a local recording studio and nightclub situation where the milk might've curdled. And, in the talk about the owner, an ex-con named Bent Lenny, mention of people with military-close haircuts came up there too."

"Are they connected with Alvin?"

"No way of knowing that, or even if they're of the same type. A lot of college kids here wear their hair short, and grunge musicians in the punk rock circles almost all have a close trim. There may well have been some confusion, mistaking people for neo-Nazis who aren't. We shouldn't leap to conclusions."

"You're awfully careful not to judge people, aren't you."

"Few people," I said, "have the experience, patience, vision, and compassion it takes to judge. And for half of those who have all that, the robe don't fit."

She gave me a gentle punch on the arm. "Oh, lighten up," she said. The room sure seemed awfully small, with her in it.

"The other part," I said, "relates to what happened tonight."

"Which is?"

"Someone took a couple of shots at Tori Brice as she was slipping out the back way after a gig at the Constitutional Club."

"Not a very good shot?"

"Didn't seem to be. Now we have two female singers from the Austin area who've had attempts made on their lives."

"Connected?"

"No way of knowing yet. The Austin police will probably be in touch with Cuthers tomorrow, or you can talk with them. They know about that try on Trish out at the folk festival."

"Lucky I came to town, then. I can look into that."

"Maybe you can tell me more about the strangled girl."

"Strangled may not be the right word. Looks like whoever hit her on the head might've got a look at the face, realized it wasn't Trish Mirandez, and panicked. A handkerchief, one of Mirandez's, was shoved into the girl's mouth as a gag. That, and the way she fell, was what strangled her."

"So, her death could've been an accident."

"It's still a murder case."

"Just what's your role there in your department? I thought you were a patrol deputy."

"I was," she said. "But I'm also acting department psychiatrist. My degree in college was in psychology. Limited as we are in a small sheriff's department we all double up when we can. The criminal psychology stuff usually gets pushed onto my plate. I have the interest, even if I don't have the job title. Though I was next in line for the acting detective slot Alvin opened by his actions. I'd been away, just got back from training at the N.A. in Quantico. I got even more interested in profiling while I was there."

"The FBI's school, huh. Only two law officers from each state get picked to go to the National Academy each year."

"I wouldn't make too much of that, although Alvin did."

I said, "Those couple of strikes Alvin had against him. One was a link to the local militia types out there, wasn't it?"

"We didn't have enough hard data to act on that," she said, "until now. But Harmon, Sheriff Cuthers, had his suspicions."

"Cuthers seems a pretty sharp fellow," I said. "He hired you."

"He hired Alvin too."

I couldn't help sneaking glances at the rest of her while she talked. Part of it was her casual assertiveness, I guess. The other part was the oxymoron of someone as attractive as her being a sheriff's deputy. She could easily have been a model.

"Why did you become a deputy sheriff?" I asked. The pale blue of her eyes took on an additional sparkle at the question. "It's a leap from a background in psychology. Are you sure you aren't one of those people who seek to establish order where there's chaos?"

"If that's the case, I'd have a good starting place in here." She glanced at the back wall beside the door that led to the bathroom and small space where I pitched my cot. In haphazard fashion I'd hung up some of the various junk that Indian tribes had given me in exchange for my help when they didn't have money. I knew some of it was worth quite a chunk of change. I have trouble selling things given to me as a gift, especially when it's as payment for services rendered. So, that made me little better off than if I didn't have the stuff, although most of the pieces were scarce to rare. There was an Arapaho pipe bag, with bead work and a fringe along the bottom, a wooden Kwakiutl mask, a Nez Perce pair of porcupine quilled moccasins, an Iroquois wooden fetish box with bear designs carved on the lid, a Teec Nos Pos woven blanket, only two feet by four feet, with brown white, blue, and gray colors in the geometric design, and a Chippewa love flute.

When a Chippewa brave thought he was in love he had to go out into the woods and find a blooming Spiderwort plant and sing to the bright blue blooms, or play a flute, I guess. Maybe it was to make him feel ridiculous and get over the idea of being in love. Or, if he didn't feel ridiculous, then he *was* in love. I don't know. I looked back at Cassie Winnick and felt a warm flush on the high cheekbones of my face I hoped didn't show through the tanned-looking tint of my skin.

The randomness of the hanging was because I'd really hung them at all to cover the bullet holes from that time Detective Sergeant Borster and I'd been crouched low while someone shot at us in the tail end of that kidnapping case where Borster thought I'd screwed him out of the big bucks of the reward. I hadn't planned for an Indian motif in the office, but I'd had the stuff lying around and had been too busy to patch holes or paint.

"You see, you do have a penchant for order," I said.

"Maybe there's a side of me I'm scared of." She frowned, as if catching herself talking too much the way I often do. Somehow the frown seemed attractive on her.

"Like what?"

She lifted her head and looked right at me, maybe into me. The pale blue of those eyes had shifted to the gray of steel. Her voice grew colder too. "Back there in that folk festival parking lot . . . I really wanted to plug Alvin and his friends, to shoot them dead and see them drop bleeding into the gravel. Like they say here in Texas, he's a man who could use a good killing."

I'd been thinking of her as maybe too tender for the job. An icy finger ran down along my spine. Even that didn't keep me from feeling the long day I'd had. I stifled a yawn. "I'd better turn in soon. I'm past the point of turning into a pumpkin."

She grinned at me.

"Where are you staying here in town?" I asked.

"Here," she said. She glanced around at my tiny office and the open door to the back room. "Before I saw your place I was hoping you could put me up for the night."

"Here?" I said, and noticed a sudden rasp in my voice.

CHAPTER FIVE

Someone began whanging on my door at barely ten A.M., hard enough to rattle the plate glass of the office window. I tugged on my slacks. Barefoot and in a T-shirt, I went out into the office and peeked through the blinds, thinking Borster might be paying an early call. Jimmy Bravuro's bug-eyed face beamed back at me.

"I see you," he yelled. "Don't go back in your hole, you mole. Open up."

I cracked the door and he pushed it the rest of the way open. A wash of bright sunlight swept over me, and I recoiled from it like Dracula.

"Man, you've got to change your habits. Wrestling with the cactus juice again, eh?" He plopped onto the corner of the desk, left me standing there blinking back at him.

"What have you gotten on the case so far?" he said. I looked to see if he'd brought a sack with cups of coffee or anything that might help promote thought. He hadn't. "I mean," he said, "daylight's burnin'."

I looked at my watch. "It's been only a few hours since you guys hired me. You think you might be cracking the whip somewhat?"

"Have you called Kasperville yet? Seen if anything ties together between that and the bullets they dug out of the back of the Constitutional Club last night?"

"I suspect that the law over there is as fully up to speed on the Tori Brice thing as they can be."

"Where do you get that?" Jimmy said. "How can you know what some one-horse sheriff's department knows?"

"By listening." The female voice came from the back room. Cassie Winnick came out into the office, tucking her blouse into the top of her jeans as she did. "Didn't you see our department's one horse tied up outside?"

I don't know when I've seen Jimmy more taken aback. He visibly rocked back on the top of the desk. His head panned to stare at me.

"Why, Trav," he said, in as demure a tone as I'd ever heard him use. "I take all of that back about your wrestling with the cactus juice, sleeping the night away, and even the part about once voting Republican." His mouth hung open half an inch. He realized it, and clicked it shut.

"You mind sharing what has *you* up so early and being unreasonable about results?" I said.

"The paper," he said. He stared at Cassie while he spoke to me. "It had a front-page story . . . tied some things together."

"With facts or words?"

"Just words and a few pictures so far." He wrenched his stare away from Cassie and looked at me. "But they *did* have something else worth knowing about."

"And what's that?"

"Jayne Randall," he said. "She's not a musician, Trav."

"She's a senator," I said. "Yeah, I know all about her, Jimmy. She's one of the few who survived back when Ann Richards lost to George W. Bush. I haven't been living in a cave."

"Well, I don't know if we can verify that until we get a chance to talk to your interior decorator." Jimmy glanced around. It was all he could do to keep his lip from curling. "Anyway, it ties into what you're working on, or what you should be working on when you get around to working."

"Spit it out," I said.

"Someone made a try for Jayne Randall too. And it happened *before* the Trish Mirandez attempt. The story had been suppressed, but the paper decided that after the tries on Trish and Tori that it was front-page news after all."

"Does that change anything?"

"Like?"

"That it may not be just a music biz thing. Do your people want to back out of hiring me for that, and for me to focus just on the Johnny Gringo thing?"

"Of course not. Fact is, two singers still had attempts made on them. Besides, it was the Johnny Gringo thing we wanted you on first. This other just came along."

"We *are* getting one new aspect to the pattern, though," Cassie said. "All the attempts were on public women who have strong characteristics." She picked up the phone and was dialing.

"What're you up to?" I asked.

"Seeing if we can set up a lunch date," she said.

Give Cassie her due; she landed a lunch interview with a senator in far faster time than a PI ever could have managed it. Just before noon, that same day, a nervous maître d' of the Z Tejas restaurant ushered the two of us to a back table where not just one member of Congress sat, but two. I recognized Jayne Randall, although she no longer wore her distinctive beehive hairdo. Like the late governor, Ann Richards, she had changed with the times. These days, Jayne's hairdo looked like what I would call the dignified liberated senior woman's special. Its medium white length swept back in a way that implied motion. The person across the table from her was a member of the House of Representatives: Max Bolens.

Be calm, I told myself. Stay cool. I could see too what had

shaken not stirred the maître d'. A man in a dark suit leaned against one wall. Another, enough like him to be his twin, hovered over by the foyer. Both had the obvious little wires that went up out of their suit collars to an earpiece so you could tell there was nothing really secret about the Secret Service. Our tax dollars at work.

Jayne proved she was one of those people who miss very little. She caught something in my glance to Bolens and back to her. She laughed a hearty laugh. "I know. The two of us are hardly peas from the same pod. Yin and yang, more likely. We vote the opposite direction on nearly every issue, but we do share an interest in some of the same charities. Congress is in session, as you know, and I wouldn't be here if it wasn't to honor a request from one of my favorites."

Max endured the introductions and snapped his fingers to get a waiter. He ordered for everyone, which did not tell me anything I didn't already know about him. He liked things done quickly, and his way if at all possible. In half a shake of a cow's tail, as the ranchers are prone to say, the waiter was sliding plates in front of us. As near as I could figure, I was having the ruby smoked trout on a Caesar salad of tiny Romaine hearts. It was no burger from Hut's, but you have to take the rough with the smooth.

Jayne Randall ignored Max for the moment and leaned closer to Cassie. "Women are supposed to be so damn smart," she said, "yet look at the shoes most of us put on our feet to wear. Now, those boots of yours look much more sensible."

I still hadn't lost my awe of her. She held the same charismatic charm as the late Governor Ann Richards—whatever it was that made them both seem like the larger-than-life kind of people who had just stepped down from Mt. Rushmore to mingle with everyday folks. Yet, Jayne is the last person who would ever make you feel that way. She is the kind of person who acts and looks like she grew up with one foot on a ranch and the other in the biggest cities Texas and the U.S. have to offer.

Max Bolens, on the other hand, seemed put out by our presence. I had heard far more than I cared to about him through the years, but I had never met him face-to-face, nor had I been eager to do so. He lived up to my expectations and looked like someone who could sell used cars, or meet in the smoke-filled back room with a power-hungry caucus, or set up an arms deal with Oliver North. He had dark hair, combed back in an impeccable pompadour and wore a suit that probably cost more than I made last year.

I pushed some of the trout around on my plate with my fork.

Jayne handled her silver with the practiced poise of someone who had dined with presidents and queens. I suppose she would be as relaxed holding an ear of corn.

"You know," she said, "I supported Ann Richards when they tried to scoot that handgun law across her desk when she was in office. She just said no. This isn't the Wild West anymore." She bit off each word—polite, but she meant it. She spoke to Cassie, who picked away at a dish identical to mine. Jayne turned to me and said, "You think these attempts on women are connected?"

"It could just be coincidence," I said. "You know how quick the media is to jump on anything that smacks of a better story."

"Tori *was* shot at, am I correct? And the woman in Trish's trailer was strangled," Jayne said. "Do I have that right?"

"Right."

"What are we to make of it all?"

"If it's the same person," Cassie explained, "it's highly unusual to use such different M.O.s."

"Unless it's part of an attempt to throw off any investigations," I added. "Tell us about the attempt on you, and why you did what you could to keep it quiet?"

"You see those men in the dark suits?" Jayne nodded toward one of the secret service types watching over the room. "I always thought Ann Richards had it tough with all these types tagging along until George W. Bush became governor, and then went on to be president."

"The man Ann Richards called a 'shrub,' " Bolens said.

"She called him worse than that. That's so much water over the dam. He went out of this state's hair and on to become the nation's albatross." She turned back to me. "I did all I could to limit the coverage of my *accident* so I wouldn't have to endure these goons," she nodded toward the Secret Service men. "But these other stories nudged out any clout I thought I had."

"Accident?" I said.

"It *was* just a traffic accident," she said. "One with a bizarre twist, but an accident nevertheless."

"But now you're not so sure it was an accident?"

"The police were looking into it before the try on Trish. Someone from the press decided to pull the cork on the story. Suddenly, as I said, I'm surrounded by these . . . men, here to protect me. And don't think for a moment I find that pleasant."

I knew just about who it was at the press, too. I'd seen Hal Jansen's credit line on the photo. "Any detail left out of what was in the paper?"

"There were just one or two tiny details. The paper had the part about the truck rolling down the hill and hitting my car after I'd gotten into it. But I wasn't in it. I'd gotten right back out to go back into the drugstore, had forgotten some damn thing or other."

Max Bolens said, "Think you might be getting a touch of what haunted Reagan? You know, Alzheimer's."

Jayne let a puff of air out and ignored him. She said, "The part the paper's story left out was that when they opened the truck door, it was empty too. That was no accident."

My head panned back to Jayne. I had been checking out the other people in the restaurant. The place had filled up, a lot of people noticing the bodyguards and Jayne, or Max. I'd spotted one fellow who sat alone at a table near us, but the goons along the wall ignored him, so I suspected he belonged somehow to our group.

"So, how does that fit any sort of pattern?" Jayne asked.

"That's just the thing," Cassie explained. "It does and doesn't. The only thing we had was that two of the women were musicians. Now it looks like women in the public eye. That's all we have in common."

"After all I've done, too, toward seeing that women get more public opportunities," Jayne said. "I would hate to think success makes us targets as well."

"There's that," I said, "and the person doing this is one of the most incompetent people I've ever encountered. An amateur, I'd say, unless the object was to just make the attempts."

"How do you get that?" Max asked.

"The fellow hasn't been successful once in the three tries we're discussing here," I said, "except to kill some stranger he, or she, mistook for Trish Mirandez. And even that death might have started out to be a scare, with someone hitting harder than planned, then the victim being gagged just to cover up a getaway. That's if all this *does* point to the same person, not a copycat, or unrelated circumstantial situations."

Some of the confusion I felt reflected back from their faces now.

"How many people knew exactly where you'd be when the truck incident happened?" I asked Jayne.

"A lot," Max butted in. "It was a ribbon-cutting event. Battered wives and abused women were the focus. The public had to know Jayne would be there. Everyone of any note was there."

"Including you?" I asked him.

"Yes, even me," he said, "as bleeding heart as that may seem. The voters want to see a warm, fuzzy side now and again."

I looked at him, watched his eyes narrow into a competitive glitter, giving me the alpha-dog look, challenging me. Jayne caught the mood and changed the subject. She said to Cassie, "I wish you well in cleaning up your department's internal business too."

"Thanks." Cassie dabbed at her pink rounded lips with her napkin.

"You tell Harmon for me, Cassie," Jayne resumed, "that I hope he weathers this bit of rough water he's having. We go way back, Harmon and me. We used to dove hunt together."

"Good thing you never took Cheney along," Max said. When she ignored him, he turned to Cassie.

"Is it that militia business you're working on that brings you to Austin, Cassie?" He seemed to grab more from the air than had been said. The papers had covered the murder at the folk festival, but had said little, if anything, about Sheriff Cuther's deputy going rogue, or why.

"We tend to think of them as the far, far right," Cassie said. "But there isn't much more hair than a hedgehog on some of them. Still, we haven't made any firm tie to the neo-Nazis, supremacists, anything like that, if that's what you were hoping for."

With Max here I'd been hoping the whole issue wouldn't come up in conversation. His daughter Donna—or Friedya as she'd called herself for a while—had just been the subject of my recent chat with Jimmy Bravuro. She was the one who had been living with one of the worst of the militants, a maker of bombs. The ATF had coerced her into spying for them, but when the boyfriend began to suspect her she became suicidal, so the ATF decided she was far too flaky for their use and dumped her.

When the FBI raided the boyfriend's house, and found enough to put him away, they also blew Donna's cover. Instead of being any kind of hero, she ended up being indicted—prosecutors contending she was more genuinely involved in the militia activities than she had let on and had complied with the ATF only to survive. The case had made it into the courts and had been splashed all over the newspapers and media for the past few weeks like some minor-league princess Paris Hilton yarn. Public opinion ran to the surly side about the whole mess too, according to the summaries of blogs and E-mails I had seen in the papers, some folks going so far as to say it might be a good time to bring back public floggings. I tried to stay objective about the whole business myself. Maybe a public flogging went too far, although I felt a parental spanking might be in order, despite her age.

"The whole bunch of those asshole skinhead types . . . ," Max started to say.

"Are hard to tell apart," I butted in. "When I was a kid it was long hair. Not everyone with it hanging past their shoulders was a drug dealer. Now we have short hair, as much to signal a rebellious nest-leaving to parents as anything. I see far more buzz haircuts near the University of Texas campus than I do anywhere else."

Knowing what I did about Max, I had tried to make myself stay quiet. He seemed to know just how to get under my faintly red skin.

"You've been stung a time or two, I take it," Jayne said to me. I think I'm so damned subtle sometimes; but, I'm not. Women, in particular, seem to see right through me.

Max's eyes connected with the fellow sitting alone near us. The man rose and came over to our table. I watched the guys in suits. When they didn't leave their posts, I knew they had cleared him.

When the man got to our table, Max introduced him. "Don Briscoe. My aide." Don bent close. He and Max had a mini conference.

Jayne leaned closer to Cassie and whispered loud enough for me to hear. "Here's a conspiracy against women I uncovered. Do you know who owns Playtex, one of the biggest girdle makers? Sara Lee. I wonder if you honestly think *that's* a coincidence." Then Jayne tucked into her lunch, choosing to ignore Max's whispering with Briscoe, which I thought was gracious of her.

When Max had finished whispering, Don straightened, gave a curt nod, and left the table and the restaurant. Max gave us a twisted half smile, but didn't apologize.

As lunch trailed to its conclusion, Max started to say something. Jayne cut him off and said, "We can get to your agenda some other time." He looked as happy about that as the cat whose mouse was taken away. If I had to guess, I would have said Max was working on something about his daughter. From what I knew and had heard about him, he was the type who believes that justice is where you buy it.

Cassie saw something in my face and gave me a raised eyebrow. I shook my head.

Outside the restaurant, Don Briscoe hustled over and asked me to step over to Bolens' limo. I waved for Cassie to tag along, but Don said, "Just you."

"Just me," I said to Cassie and watched the pink tint form on her cheeks. I tossed her my keys, and she went over to my car to wait.

The windows of the limo were tinted so dark that the light was actually dim inside once the door snicked shut. Briscoe waited outside in the sun. Max sat in the back left corner. He peeled the wrapper from a short dark cigar with a glittering gold-and-red label. I wondered if there was some sort of magazine a man like him reads to help him become a cliché. He seemed far too aware of his own recent good fortune, and not above rubbing the noses of others in it.

"I'd like to offer you a job," Max said. He clipped the end off the cigar.

"I have a couple already," I said.

"You must be well off to turn down work," he said.

"What did you have in mind?"

"Some of the investigation by state, local, and federal police"—he picked words carefully as he held the flame of a gold Dunhill lighter up to the end of the cigar—"of these militia types has died down. Since the World Trade Center September 11 thing, some people kind of like the patriotic side of these folks, think they might have a point. Be armed and ready. Though the law seems to care less about them, I remain interested in these men, very interested. Do you have any reason to believe that what you are looking into might take you closer to their circles?"

"You'd better tell me more about where you're going with this."

"What I have in mind shouldn't put you in conflict with anything else you're looking into." He leaned his head back on the black leather seat, puffed his cigar, then watched the clouds rise to the limo's ceiling before they were grabbed and tugged out in a whisk by air-conditioning. "If you feel it creates a conflict, it'll be up to you to decide what you can share."

"What is it you want shared?"

"Anything you can find out about these militia folks. And before you go off on some bleeding-heart tangent, I mean the legitimately bad skinhead, neo-Nazi, supremacist sons-of-bitches."

"This about your daughter?"

"The feds have worked over the issue. You don't need to

know what's already been said in court, or what's going to be said next. We're looking at a serious situation here—one that might, that probably *will*, involve my daughter going into the witness protection program. If you can find anything, anything at all I or my lawyers can use, I want to have it. Is that something you can do for me?"

On the face of it, it wasn't such an unreasonable request. If I hadn't been just a little off balance at meeting him face-to-face for the first time I might have followed the policy that has worked best for me through the years, of keeping my stupid Indian/Irish mouth closed—just give him a polite no and a stupid but obsequious look. As it was, I snapped.

"I don't like to make judgments, Mr. Bolens," I said. "And I resent even more the people who stir me up enough to share them when I do. I know you clawed your way up to becoming an industrial giant, the CEO of a Fortune-Five-Hundred company and that you left that behind to enter politics. But I want you to know that no matter how much money you have you damn sure can't buy my time."

His mouth opened, then closed.

I reached to open the door. Before I stepped out, I said, "You were awfully fast leaping to the militia issue back there in the restaurant. Maybe you have some inside connections—big shot like you probably does. I'll bet you follow everything you can that might help your daughter. At least that's how I hope you know about Alvin and his ties to any of those types. Otherwise, you know enough to be a suspect."

He bit down on the cigar, but said nothing.

"I'll tell you one more thing too." I could have been frothing for all I knew. At least that's how I felt. "When I do find whoever's behind this, I hope for a change it's someone as rich as you, not some petty everyday gazoony fed up with being the little guy. I really want the villain to be rich this time, and just like you. In fact, I'd be pretty damn tickled if I'm able to prove it *was* you."

His mouth opened and the cigar fell out and onto his lap, started burning a hole into his mega-expensive suit.

I got out of the car and slammed the door, hard. The heat slapped into me. Briscoe stepped closer and held out a check and a slip of paper on which was Bolens' address and numbers. A sheen of sweat made his face glisten. A phony smile spread across his strained face. I reached for the papers, tore them to small bits in front of his widening eyes. He glanced at the limo window, but the deep black tint made it as empty to him as to me.

I hiked across the now-crowded parking lot to my car. Cassie waited inside my car and steamed, as much from finding my air-conditioning didn't work as from being excluded from the meet.

She started to say something, then caught my expression. I hopped in, twisted the key, and jammed the car into gear, pulling out of the lot with a small squeal and pop of hot tires.

"Whoo-eee," she said.

"Just call me stupid," I said, once we'd gone a mile or two and sat at a red light. "Men like Max get to me. I'm usually pretty good at hanging in the corner of the room and keeping myself from saying too much. Now I come off like the biggest bigot ever to be born with lips."

"Okay, spill."

"No. I've said way too much already." The light changed and I eased off the brake and flowed with the traffic.

"There's no way you're getting out of this after that buildup. What is it? You don't like Max because he's *nouveau riche?*"

"He doesn't get up my sleeve just because he's rich. I know of plenty of people who earned their way to a better life and I have no problem with that. My issue with Max is that he thinks being well off means he and his family, especially his daughter, deserve a different brand of justice, privileged treatment, by the law and everyone else." My voice grew louder and I tried to tone it down. "His thinking that way shouldn't surprise me, or vex me mightily. If I take a bias about him over the way he thinks, then I'm no better than he is."

"This really bugs you. Doesn't it?"

"Look. I grew up poor and the folks I pal around with, like Hal, Huff and Jimmy, come from the same stock. I don't mind other people being rich, unless that involves them having an unfair sense that the system should be stacked their way, and especially if they happen to be the kind of people who enjoy kicking sand in your face about it."

"A lot of people get upset about that."

"Yeah, but it's not okay for me. Detective work is supposed to be objective. I blew it. It's a weakness I admit to, or at least can't deny."

"It might just be one of your more endearing features, though. Ever think of that? That and caring for your friends, however few there may be."

She was quiet for a few blocks and finally said, "That Max. He's sure used to getting his way, isn't he?" she said.

"His daughter must be a real tribulation to him then," I said.

Cassie grinned for the first time in a while. "I hope to hell she is."

Chapter Six

We headed from there to the offices of the newspaper. On the way, windows open and our hair streaming back, I asked her, "How long do you plan to stay in Austin?"

"I can find a motel, if that's what you mean. Sleeping on your cot was no day at the beach."

I could have said that the floor wasn't an improvement. Much as I would have hated to burst Jimmy Bravuro's bubble, my night spent with Cassie had been only talk and a little of my partaking of the tequila sleep tonic before we had landed in our respective and platonic sleeping arrangements. My wrapped chest still ached and throbbed after spending a night on the hardwood.

"No. That's not it," I said. "I just thought, with your interests in psychology and profiling, you might be able to help me. I'm a cause-and-effect guy who can go a ways with a clue or two. So far, this case has been coming at me in bits, like snowflakes at a windshield. I'd be glad for some of your wisdom about personality here."

She didn't say anything for a block or two. I suspected she was replaying what I'd said to make sure I wasn't being patronizing.

"Sure," she said. "I'll help. But just remember, I'm here on the case myself."

Inside the newspaper building, I asked the receptionist to page Hal Jansen, from their photography staff. The paper publishes each morning, so only some of the people were in the building. I could count on Hal being around, though, unless he was on assignment somewhere. His social calendar was more spotty and wide open than mine, if that's possible.

He came down the hallway rubbing his hands together like some kind of happy cricket. He may have caught the irritated expression on my face. Hal, after all, had been the one to call me and send me off in a lather to Kasperville to help with Jimmy's problem, when I could have been staying home and dry, and off the injured list. He chose to roll right past that.

"Those jerkwater cops back in Kasperville told me *nothing*, Trav. They just heaved me out. Did you get anything?" Hal was thin and full of energy, or caffeine. He was leaner and an inch or two shorter than me, had thinning grayish, mid-fifties hair, and was always hopping about, wired with antic bounce, like one of those little springy dogs that hop all over the place, even when they have a few white hairs on the muzzle.

"This is Cassie Winnick," I said. "She's one of those official jerkwater cops from the Kasperville Folk Festival end of this."

"Hey, I'm sorry," Hal said, giving her a glance that was awfully brief for as good as she looked. "That big guy, though. Whew. It didn't surprise me to hear he'd gone off the rails later. I wish I could've gotten some snaps of him. He was some piece of work. What happened to you? You've got lumps and bruises everywhere on you."

"Thanks for noticing, Hal."

"Travis here was the one Alvin went off the rails onto," Cassie said.

Hal just shook off that. Too bad for me, I guess. He instead looked focused and eager to get back to whatever scoop was in any of this. I had promised myself I would chew on his ear for calling me when I ran into him again, but this puppy eagerness from a man in his fifties shamed me out of it.

"Tell me you got something," he said. "Something hard that ties all these together."

"I haven't got anything yet."

"Oh, damn. You're onto something, you keyhole peeper you." He gave a curt wave to Cassie without looking at her again, which summed up Hal, far more interested in a big story, something he really needed, than someone as attractive as her.

"You have anything else on the Tori Brice shooting?" I asked.

"Nothing you didn't see in the paper, Trav. The cops are playing this one close to their vests after the Senator Jayne Randall attempt was made public."

"By you, Hal."

"Well, sure, I landed the story on that one. My editor sat on it for a day or two, which isn't like him. Someone sure must have put the vise grips to him. The stories on the other two women broke it free or it might have never made it past galleys to the light of day. I've had my precious time wasted before that way. What else brings you here?"

Yeah, right. You take a job as a reporter and you know the pay's not the thing, unless you own or manage the paper, or unless you're a syndicated award winner. Hal's circumstances were even more unusual than most reporters, so I knew he made very little. But I have yet to know one of these news hounds who doesn't delight in seeing his name there on the byline or the credit on the cutlines below the photos, and Hal was no exception. "The story" becomes the driving thing too, and once that nose got honed, a reporter's blood might just as well be ink, even though he'll never retire rich or drive the hottest car in the lot. Just a job. I'd seen him work hundred-hour weeks standing on his ear for a story, his eyes lit up because he was on the chase, as full of passion as a cub reporter on his first beat.

"I need some stuff from the morgue, Hal. Think you can . . . ?"

He spun and was off to the races, with the two of us struggling to keep up.

"What files will you need?" He leered back over his shoulder at me.

"Anything you have on Texas militia groups, paramilitary, the militant right, Bent Lenny Coggins, Ruby Rhubarb, The Rubber Jungle. And, of course, anything on the Mirandez, Brice, and Randall attempts."

He screeched to a stop and spun to share excited wide eyes. "Man, what *are* you up to, Trav?"

"You know I can't share anything yet, Hal. Now, do we get the files?"

"Sure. Sure." He turned and started off again, his pace slow enough at least to talk this time.

"Hal's the journalist who stuck me with that 'Blue-Eyed Indian' handle, by the way," I told Cassie while we walked. She knew how little I enjoyed carrying a tag like that.

She reached to turn my face toward hers. "Yeah, they're blue all right. The first time I saw you and your high cheekbones I knew you had some Indian blood in you." Her fingers on my chin were soft, and warm.

"I think you caught Alvin's response to that Indian blood, too," I said.

"A guy needs a hook if he's gonna make it in any business, especially the PI one," Hal said. "I was only trying to help. And haven't you practically become the PI to Austin's music stars?"

This was another tag Hal had tried to lay on me. He was a big believer in reputation and a person's story line leading to success.

He glanced at Cassie. "I owe Trav large," he confided. "He got some really nasty loan-shark types to leave me alone."

"You have any more problem from them?" I asked.

"Nothing. Nada. Haven't heard a word. I don't know what you said or did to them, but that coast has been quiet since."

Cassie's puzzled look, and frown, shifted to me.

I shrugged at her. "Not right now," I said. "It's simpler than Hal makes it sound, just the right kind of leverage applied at the correct moment."

"That must be why they call it 'private' detective, huh?" Cassie said.

Hal ushered us into a small room with a metal table and chairs. Along the walls were bookshelves, a microfiche reader, and a copy machine. He darted off. In ten minutes he was back with the files.

"Took a minute," he said, "because a couple of the files were out in the newsroom. Some of the staffers are putting together follow-up stories."

The files were thick, some with clippings, photos, and even notes torn out of reporters' notebooks. A couple held cassettes of taped interviews.

"There's a lot of data here," Cassie said, as she pulled one of the files over and opened it.

"We'll just copy the parts we need," I said.

"Yeah," Hal said. "We get tons of info; can't begin to use it all. Everything we do's pretty boiled down, some of it run past lawyers before it goes to print. Everyone's got both hands on their ass these days. Folks think we're like some tabloid, print every little rumor we hear. But I could tell you. . . ."

"You know if anyone working on the stories here has found anything 'hard,' as you put it? Something that, as you said, ties any of this together?" I said to slow him down and get him back in focus as much as anything.

"Depends on which story you're talking about," he said. "Your interest in Bent Lenny kinda hit me by surprise, though he may well be up to something. He's been trying to keep a low profile. You'll probably find some stuff that overlaps with your other files, though. In spite of running a blues and folks place, he may have been linked to the supremacists when he was doing six hard at Huntsville, paying his debt to society."

Cassie was over at the copy machine, making copies of some stuff from her file. I continued to sort through the file in front of me.

"I thought most of the militia guys these days liked to hole up in backwoods retreats, waiting for the big terrorist invasion," I said. I culled a few articles from a file and went over to the copier while Cassie sat back down and grabbed another file. Over the sound of the machines whirring and clicking, I asked, "Is there someplace they're hanging out here in Austin?"

"No place *you'd* want to go," Hal said. I looked up in time to see him shudder.

"Come on," I said. "Spill it."

"Look, Trav. You don't know what you're asking for here. Let me tell you a story."

I sighed, but it didn't slow him.

"Not too long ago, a couple of these guys—call them militia or just over-patriotic—went to a convenience store here in town and tore down an American flag off the front of the store. They say the franchise owners were Islamic and didn't deserve to fly the flag. These were Islamic people, all right, but people born in America just like you and me. Worse yet, people who saw this happen cheered the militia guys. These are mixed-up times, and no one seems to know who's on the right or wrong side. You see what I mean?"

Cassie looked up at us now and then as she dug in the files. I kept the papers going through the copier, but said to Hal, "Why don't you let me decide? Spill it, Hal."

He watched what we copied, taking mental notes. His hands

went into their brisk rubbing drill again like they had a life of their own. "You guys are gonna owe *me* large this time. You know that, don't you? When there's ever a story here . . . well, you know I could use the break, Trav."

"Hal," I said.

"Way out on East Seventh," he said. "There's a warehouse, name says 'Mokey's Movers.' But you didn't hear that from me. You're as likely to get plugged in a drive-by shooting there as to mess with any militia types if you go late at night. So, be warned."

I nodded, and, as always, was glad when nothing rattled.

Cassie and I worked well and quickly together in our hasty research. We churned through the files and had quite a lump of paper assembled between us. Hal sat and watched, licking his lips and rubbing his hands until I wanted to grab his wrists.

"The cops have nothing so far. You gotta know that," he said. "If any of this ties together, I'd sure like to be the first. They've held out on us often enough."

"You know I've got to share anything solid with the cops," I said. "It's as good as my license if I don't." My eyes flicked to Cassie, reminding him she was official. He knew of a case or two firsthand where I had shared less than I might have. He steered clear of mentioning that.

"The thing about any of this," he said, "is that if it's random, and unconnected, it's gonna be a real nut to crack. And even if it's some kook, the motivating cause is going to be the tough part. You got to remember that this is a country where a guy who didn't get reinstated as a Boy Scout leader killed sixteen kindergarten kids and their teacher."

"That happened in Scotland, didn't it?" Cassie said.

"Same difference," Hal said.

Cassie's eyebrows tightened, but she didn't touch that.

In a crude way, Hal did have a point. For each of the cases

for which I'd been hired, including the one I'd turned down with Bolens, I was on a fishing expedition. I had only visited the Tori Brice crime scene, had not seen the first bit of hard evidence related to any of it. The police, and Cassie's department, had the jump there. It didn't matter to me if they solved what they were working on. I still had my little jobs to do, such as they were.

Hal ushered us back to the door after returning the files to their places. He stood by the door, the same eager look on his face of a newshound catching a scent. He said to me, "You be careful where you go on this one, Trav. You may find you do a lot of work and it takes you nowhere. And worse, you might find yourself way to the other side of nowhere."

Back at my office we put the piles of paper on the desk.

"Your friend Hal is an odd duck, isn't he?" Cassie asked while sorting the piles.

"What do you mean?"

"I mean he's kind of . . . not young enough for all the cub reporter eagerness."

"Hal's in a funny position," I said. "About three years back he thought he saw a brass ring and grabbed at it—turned out to be a bad idea."

"What do you mean?"

"He had been a newspaper photographer since getting out of high school. He never got much higher, since he'd never gotten a college degree. He finally realized that if he was ever going to get a break it wasn't going to be at the newspaper. There were a couple of directions he could go, he figured. One was to the magazines, where he had a few connections based on some breaking stories of his. The other way was to start dogging the local stars that make Austin such a live music capital."

"Let me guess."

"Yeah," I said, "he went for glitz. Trouble was, he found that the pictures that generated the most cash were the ones people *didn't* want taken: someone coming in late and drunk, a woman with her makeup on sideways, a guy just getting out of a drug rehab clinic—you know, that sort of thing."

"He became one of the paparazzi?"

"Only in the small-town way Austin represents. This is no Hollywood, after all. He sold a few snapshots—ones that only got him into trouble. Some he put on a Web page, trying to drum up some fame and momentum for himself. He even got punched in the beezer by Betty Sandler, a blues singer who'd had a few shots of tequila before having Hal's flash go off in her face. He hit bottom when he crashed a private party for Sue Ball and Marcie Foley out at the Oasis and took some photos he thought would be cute. They heaved his camera and a laptop over the cliff onto rocks a couple of hundred feet below. He sued. They countersued, and they won."

"So, Hal went bust?"

"Yeah, then had to come crawling back to the paper when that was the only thing for him to do. But they'd yanked his seniority. He was back to square one. So, now he thinks that a good story—one good enough to win an award or two—will get him back square." I shrugged, having heard better, as well as worse dreams.

"I don't know." Cassie shook her pretty head. "He should probably stick with what worked before, what got him all the way to where he was. Quick fixes rarely work."

I nodded. "I'm thinking Hal suspects he's getting too old to be patient. Besides, he burned a lot of bridges when he tried to go out on his own and failed. I think some of the resentment from that's coming back to slow him now, or at least not let him crawl back to where he was. That's why he might seem overeager and gets that 'all or nothing' gleam in his eyes about a big story."

"He's not going to be a problem because of that, is he?"

The really sad thing about Hal's case is that, like myself, he is drawn magnetically to the robust Austin live music scene, for many of the same reasons. Yet, even more than myself, he loved it. I mean he loved it. But he had tried to use it in the wrong way. So, the thing he loved came back to bite him in the butt. The musicians rallied against him, and they eventually drove him from his freelance trade and back to the newspaper at a much-reduced salary.

"He's a friend," I said. "He's not out to mess us up, just ride on our coattails to get back in the game. What do you say we do some work."

I dragged the other straight-backed chair over and we sat to start the paper end of our chase. Tiny beads of sweat soon showed on Cassie's forehead. "I should have guessed," she said, "when that deluxe car of yours wasn't air-conditioned that your office wasn't either."

"No one said that the detective biz is all . . ." I stopped myself, then finished with "iced tea and air-conditioning." She was starting to sweat through her white blouse, and it wasn't helping my thought processes.

I got out the house entertainment bottle. I had a little tequila to fend off the heat, while she stayed with water.

We pored through the papers for another hour. Sweat dripped from both of us. I was down to my T-shirt and slacks. Cassie abruptly put down the paper she held and said, "Lock the door, would you."

I got up and did so. When I turned back, she tugged off her blouse.

"I don't think we. . . ." I got close to a stutter.

"Oh, sit down and get back to work," she said. She kicked off her jeans and sat back down.

We got back to it. But I'm here to say, I've worked under

some adverse conditions in my checkered career, being shot at, thumped on, staked out for nights, all of that sort of thing. I don't know when I've had a harder time working than when sitting across the desk with the better half of Victoria's Secret revealed to me.

It had gotten darker in the room by the time we got through reading everything and making some notes. She went back to my small bathroom, splashed around, and in a relief to me, came back with all her clothes on.

"Do you think we have enough for any kind of personality profile yet?" I asked.

She rubbed her hands together. I hoped she hadn't picked up a permanent habit from Hal. She tilted her head and those blue eyes were a'twinkle.

"You know what envelope you're pushing, don't you?"

"What do you mean?"

"The 'S' word. Serial."

"You think some serial killer's out there? It's bad enough the media's fishing hard for that, but you?"

"Give me a day or so to do this right. I'll look up a few things and give you as much to go on as I can. Until I write something down you can mull over what we have so far. If the attempts on Trish, Tori, and Jayne *were* all done by the same person, we have a very unstable personality on our hands. You're probably right that the person is new to this kind of thing, is an amateur. It's my guess that the person is uncertain, or deliberately trying to mask his or her identity."

"Her?"

"Can you think of any of the attempts that couldn't have been orchestrated by a woman?"

"The truck that hit Jayne's empty car was a big one. I guess that made me think male. But there's no reason, I guess, a woman couldn't get one started and rolling down a hill."

"The bigger issue is the motivator," Cassie said. "Whoever is behind this—what makes them tick? What's sending them off the blocks? What it looks like so far is we have someone who resents women who have prominent reputations and are respected. It's the kind of thing makes me want to get on the phone to other Austin area women and tell them to watch out."

"What causes someone to . . . ?"

"Causes is a good word," she interrupted, "but it's hard for me to get a handle on motivations yet. Wait until I dig deeper into that profile you want. As far as looking, I think we'd better start casting a net in places the police aren't likely to go."

"Which, as far as I know, is every place outside of a doughnut shop," I said. "You know I don't have many supporters on the local force, don't you?"

"I wish you wouldn't talk about food," she said. "But maybe I can trade a favor or two for some information."

"Okay. Okay. Why don't we take this discussion over to the County Line. I'll buy you some steak on a stick."

"What?"

"Beef ribs. Some of the best around."

I didn't have to argue that, though she did insist we take her car. I had no problem with her driving.

The streets were dark when we went out. I climbed into the passenger seat, glanced back as she pulled away from the curb. A pair of lights clicked on as a pickup pulled out into traffic behind us.

I did have a problem with that.

CHAPTER SEVEN

The pickup stayed half a block to a block back for the first mile. As we left the lights of the city and drove up along the darker winding road with the down side of a cliff looming off to our left, it got closer.

A lot of people think Austin is flat as a fritter. But we have hills. The Colorado River, which becomes a string of lakes leading down to and through town, has carved steep rocky cliffs. We rode high up on the edge of that valley. The headlights behind us surged even closer.

I wasn't sure at first that Cassie had picked up on it until I saw her eyes flicking to the rearview mirror.

"Alvin's pickup?"

"Donnie's probably. Alvin has a bum foot for driving a stick shift. Remember?"

"Should certainly help his attitude along."

"There's a gun in the glove box. Maybe you should get it out. Just in case," she said.

I didn't reach that way. She leaned forward in her seat, and her hands slipped to the nine and three position on the steering wheel. We moved faster. Her head swept to me for a moment before returning to the road. "You don't do guns?"

When I didn't answer, she said, "You're a hell of a private detective to have along in a fight."

"I didn't say I wouldn't fight," I said.

We zipped along, making good time on Bull Creek Road. I

didn't want to turn this into an all-night chase. I said, "Up ahead on your left will be the County Line restaurant. Go past that. Your next left will be the area fire department station. Turn in there."

"You planning on a fire?"

"That might also work," I said. "What I want is to be near people inclined to dial nine-one-one if the mood strikes."

We passed the restaurant, its parking lot already filling with cars. The truck was up to our back bumper and accelerating. When Cassie hit the breaks for the turn, the truck jerked back as its driver braked too. We spun into the lot. Cassie drove toward the big arched doors of the fire station.

"Pull up and stop. I'm going to jump out. Then get ready to take off again."

"You don't think I'm going to leave you behind, do you?"

"Just do it."

We skidded to a stop. I hopped out and ran back toward the truck. I could see the eyes of the three men in the truck pop wide. It was the last thing they had suspected of me. But the surprise lasted only seconds. They opened the doors and started to tumble out.

Alvin had climbed halfway out the passenger door as I got to it. Running at full speed, I leaped into the air and kicked the door. It would have closed if Alvin's head hadn't been in the way. The door slamming on his head made a noise that I thought could have been heard in San Marcos, twenty-five miles away. To be sure my point had landed home, I kicked the door shut on his head a couple more times. When it did swing open, it had Alvin's weight behind it. He tumbled out of the truck onto his side and lay there.

Donnie slid out from behind the steering wheel. The fellow in the middle decided to use that side to get out as well. Cassie climbed out of the car, though she had taken the time to get out her gun.

Neither Donnie, nor his friend with the equally porcine squinting face, seemed to pay her any mind. They squared off against me and rushed forward.

Cassie fired twice into the air and they froze. They had to look to confirm there were no holes in either of them, that she wasn't aiming right at them. But the warning shots did get through to the fire brigade. I saw a light flick on. If we had roused the off-shift crew, perhaps the awake crew had already called for help. All we had to do was last until then.

I rushed forward, dove at the ankles of one of them, felt him tumble to the asphalt as I rolled past, then scrambled back to my feet. Donnie still stood. He lowered his head and charged. I don't know where he and Alvin picked up that technique. Surely they had seen or heard of bullfights.

I stepped slightly to the side, looped both arms under Donnie's chin while still facing him, and lifted. I had done this before with lighter men and their whole momentum had lifted them clear through the air. Donnie just kept running. His head stayed tucked down and pressed against my lower chest. My arms had to be cutting off his air. But he ran. I hung above him, like a hood ornament on a truck being whooshed along. His arms arched up and punched at my head. One ham of a fist smashed against my ear. The other clipped off the front of my skull. After a dozen more steps, Donnie's knees buckled and he fell forward, then rolled over onto his side, completely out.

I fell with him. But I was able to get up and dust myself off, though my throbbing ribs were reminding me why I had been in a hospital bed. Cassie stood over the other fellow, who also wasn't moving. From the way she stood, I gathered she had rushed forward when he fell and hit him with her gun.

She waved cheerily. I walked toward her. In the distance I could hear a siren getting closer. Blue and red bits of lights flicked up against the side of the hill coming from town.

The local cops were on their way, and it didn't look like Alvin and his buddies were going to offer much resistance. I watched Cassie's expressions shift as she wrestled to snap decision. I knew she wanted this collar, and wanted it now, but we would be several hungry hours explaining *our* situation, her out of her jurisdiction and me having to make what is always a shaky case for self-defense. I nodded toward the car. Staying seemed like a bad idea. Her lips tightened and she nodded in agreement, decided to leave Alvin and get him through official channels in the morning. Without a word, we scrambled to the car, got in and pulled out onto the road long enough to swing right back into the County Line parking lot.

As we were being led to a table, someone asked a waitress what all the hubbub was about down the road. A man sitting at the bar, who looked like he'd been there for hours, said with authority, "SWAT team had to be called out to a domestic dispute."

We got back to my office at nine-thirty or so, having both eaten more than we should have, which I believe is one of the rules in going to the County Line. We had barely waddled through the door and closed it when we heard a knock.

I peeked, then opened the door and let in Don Briscoe, Max Bolens' flunkie.

He stood just inside the door, looking apologetic. If he had worn a hat, he'd have been holding it in his hands, looking like the kind of sycophant he was, out on a mission to do what his boss had already failed at. You have got to love a country where career paths like his open for those who in some other incarnation spent their days attached by a sucker to the belly of a shark.

"Do you have a moment?" he asked. His eyes darted around the tiny room, swept over the haphazard array of Indian bric-abrac hung on the back wall. He registered that Cassie had made herself at home. She slipped around and sat in the chair behind the desk.

"Before you start," I said, "I wish you would apologize to Max for me." I caught the snap of Cassie's head toward me.

"Then you'll take his case?"

"I didn't say that. I'm just genuinely sorry for my lousy attitude."

"But . . . but. . . ."

"Look, what I'm admitting is that I'm human enough to have irrational prejudices myself. One I've only realized and been able to talk about recently is this thing I have about Volvos."

One of Cassie's eyebrows rose slowly. She wrestled against a smile that wanted to show. Don's lower lip dropped at about the same rate.

"No, I mean it. They really bug the crap out of me," I said, "and the people who drive them. I know. I know. It's stark prejudice and it doesn't make a damned bit of sense. Maybe there really is more to it. Perhaps they're bought by conservative and careful people who as a collective group drive in an awkward style that doesn't jibe with my own darting about. Could be I'm just arrhythmic with them. I've struggled with it. I know, it's silly and it's stupid. I admit I have a problem with it, and someday hope I'll be a better person for my struggles."

"I can see that I'm wasting time for both of us."

"Convey, if you will, that it's an irrational thing. I admit to it, and I am working on it. I'm just not there yet where Max is concerned."

Once he was out the door, Cassie looked toward the back room.

"Go ahead," I said. "I'll get some of my things."

"I don't want to run you out of your own home, even such as it is," she said.

"It's stakeout night for me," I said. "I want to get a fix on what goes on over at Bent Lenny's place. It's a case unrelated to your business here, I hope. So you might as well catch a few winks." If I did doze off in the car myself, it would have to be more comfortable than the floor. My ribs didn't feel like they wanted another night on the hardwood, especially after my brief bout with Donnie.

I drove out into the night, my small cloth grip on the seat beside me, the sound of tequila sloshing lightly against the insides of the bottle to comfort me.

The streets were dark all over town, even darker in the narrow two-lane streets of Clarksville, a section just north of Sixth Street and to the west of Congress Avenue that bisects the city down the middle in that area.

Clarksville had once been a predominantly black section of the city before it gentrified, with the yuppies gradually taking over the homes and apartments that were near so many desirable things, a brisk walk away, for instance, from the dozens of live music venues of Sixth Street. The houses ran to the small side, mostly wood, like little boxes of biscuits lined beneath long-established live oaks and the occasional mimosa tree, but all of them pricier than the average person can afford, much less someone with limited income. The area's only hat tip to its past these days is an annual blues festival, and not enough people knew or cared about Clarksville's past to find that even faintly ironic.

Alone and squeezing down the dim quiet streets, I began to hear, as I often do, low breathy saxophone notes lifting and falling in my head to some sonorous sad song that only I hear. I gave the old skull a rattle and eased the car up the street, looped around the block to the left, then right, finally took a narrow bending turn to the right up a hill before I could start down a steep alley.

It took just that long for me to do inventory. One tan sedan with tax-exempt plates and spotlight on the driver's side. Two guys inside, windows cracked open, smoking cigarettes. Down the street half a block, a dark van with tinted windows. Numbers on the plates matched those I'd memorized from an earlier case. Local field office of the FBI.

Whatever was going to happen to Bent Lenny had been already set in motion. Now wasn't a good time for me to hang around. I took my time driving back to my office. Once there, I eased the front door open, then snicked it softly shut. The room was dark. I couldn't hear any soft breathing coming from the back, but could imagine that I did. I slipped off my shoes by the door, and in socks went over and sat behind the desk. I took out the bottle, realized I didn't have a glass handy. Oh, well. Sometimes in the PI game you just have to rough it.

CHAPTER EIGHT

I woke up to the phone ringing in one ear and hammering coming from the door in the other direction. My face pressed against the wood surface of the desk. I could feel lines from the grain of the wood streaking my face as I raised my head. I got up, opened the door, then went to answer the phone while Dutch Hitchcock and Jimmy Bravuro tumbled into the office. I held up a finger to calm down their shouting while I lifted the receiver.

Jimmy wore a T-shirt with "Oklahoma State" across it. Dutch had a black vest over something that looked like a short-sleeved lumberjack's shirt. They grinned, jostled and pointed at the empty tequila bottle that lay on its side on the desk. I held a finger to my lips. It was like having kids.

"Go ahead," I said into the phone. "Yeah, Hal, I do have something for you. I'd get your materials together on Bent Lenny. Looks like he's half a step from a tumble. Laundering, I'd say based on some piles of cash Jimmy's friend Johnny Gringo saw at Lenny's place. Sure. Make it this afternoon. I've got chores that should take me till then." I put the receiver back.

"Laundering?" Jimmy said. "Hell, I doubt if that man changes his clothes more'n once a week, much less launders them."

I sighed. "You know exactly what I mean. Both of you have seen scores of businesses that open and close here in the revolving door of Austin entrepreneurship. People don't always put together a sound five-year business plan. Lenny, on the other

95

hand, is probably in no risk of going under. He can spend whatever he wants on furnishings."

"You could never tell that from looking at the place," Dutch said.

"Or booze, talent, the recording side of the business," I went on, ignoring him. "The reason he probably doesn't worry about amounts the size of what Johnny Gringo owes him is because he needs to lose some money."

"We should help him," Jimmy said. He plopped onto the corner of the desk. "Where's he get the money?" he asked.

Dutch tried to peer into the back room without seeming to peek.

I said, "Could be the mob, or some Columbian drug connection. Or it could even be from the paramilitary militia types Johnny Gringo says he saw talking with Lenny. There're lots of money laundering schemes. You figure that as long ago as back in the nineties, Americans averaged spending of over a hundred billion dollars a year on illegal drugs, all in cash, then you get some feel. The way a business launders any kind of cash, whether from drugs, guns, or whatever, is to have a business with legitimate expenses that records a hefty income. The business has to pay taxes on its income, but the money that's left is clean. Once the snoops start going over books and comparing gate receipts with actual attendance at shows, or start looking for CD sales figures that don't match with distribution channel numbers, the end approaches. Lenny's under local and federal surveillance right now. If he's the least bit dirty, he's going to fall. It's just a question of time."

"So Johnny Gringo had better be hunting up a new label?" Dutch asked.

"But you'll keep working on the Trish Mirandez, Tori Brice thing won't ya?" Jimmy said.

"Right to both," I said. "Why are you two up so early? Don't you work evenings?"

"I had a gig last night," Jimmy said. "Dutch didn't."

"Does that mean you're the better singer?" I asked.

Dutch said, "I'd like to see the money his poor mamma wasted on singing lessons."

"He's just mad because his last CD got stopped at the airport by the bomb-sniffing dog." Jimmy stuck out his tongue at Dutch.

"Guys. Guys. Much as I enjoy your always festive and educational company, there're still a lot of things I have to get done today."

Dutch worked his way closer to the back room. He finally cut right to it and said, "Where's the squeeze Jimmy says you have stashed here?" He slipped to the door to the back, and I got ready to call out and stop him.

The door to the street opened. Cassie walked in. I expected her eyes to be red and her clothes wrinkled. They were not. She looked dapper in her uniform, and carried a small bag.

Jimmy and Dutch traded looks.

Cassie plopped her bag onto the desk. "I know . . . ," she said, ". . . where the hell were you, honey?"

They turned to her, but Jimmy and Dutch's eyes connected again.

To me, Cassie said, "Since you were going to be on stakeout, I slipped back to Kasperville to sleep in my own bed and get a shower and change of clothes. I thought it'd help to be in uniform today to visit the local P.D. and pick up Alvin unless they have him in one of the hospitals after the way you worked him over."

She came over and bent close to me, pretended to give me a peck on the scratchy cheek and whispered, "Does that fix your *cojones* with the guys?" Something else was in her whisper, an edge.

The guys, Dutch and Jimmy, had stunned looks on their

faces. Jimmy said, "You beat up that Alvin guy? He was a tank."

"And his two friends," Cassie added. "They were big as he was. Only thing is, the cops were supposed to hold them so all I'd have to do is pick Alvin up this morning. But he was gone from the scene and there was no paper out on the other two." Her eyes flicked to me, then panned away.

Now I understood her look and tone. Cassie was steaming inside like an overheated boiler room about Alvin getting away, but she wasn't going to show that in front of my friends.

"Lordy. Lordy," Jimmy said.

Dutch said, "Jimmy said how he was sorry he got you into all this, now that it was getting rough. Sounds like you're equal to anything they throw at you."

"Don't get cocky, fellows," Cassie said. "It starts to get dicey from here on. You saw Trav's car."

"My car?" I said, close to shouting.

"Oh," she said. "You didn't know?"

The sun was up and the day was easing up to the regular Texas boil of early June. We stood in the alley behind the building, looking over what remained of what had once been my car.

All the tires were slashed, the windows broken, and the seats pulled out and stacked in heaps after being cut open. The glove box hung open and empty. The trunk and hood lids were up, but I couldn't bring myself to look in there. Bits of shattered glass from the windows and windshield lay in a circle around the car like odd-shaped diamond crystals. It wasn't pretty.

"You know," I said to no one in particular, though Jimmy, Dutch and Cassie all stood close, "I got that car when I moved to Austin. I don't think of myself as materialistic or sentimental, but I'm sure going to miss it."

"Maybe you can get something with air this time," Cassie said.

"Or one without dents already built in," Dutch said.

Jimmy was shaking his head. He squinted at me. "Hey, old buddy, maybe we *did* get you into something here. If you want to. . . ."

"I'm not backing out. If that's where you're going with that."

Jimmy said, "Well, you know our musicians group can cover the routine expenses. But. . . ."

"And that's a big but," Dutch added, then shut up when he caught a glance from Jimmy.

Cassie stepped in front of me, stood right in my face. "Trav, you've got to face up to it. You've had your once."

"My what?"

"The one time you can take them on face-to-face in a little group. From now on it'll be a gang. Alvin's going to be forced to link up with the local people like himself now. And they'll be coming at your back as much as directly at you."

I dropped my eyes from hers and stared at the car.

"Really, if you want to back out, Trav . . . ," Jimmy started to say again, stopped when he saw my face.

"No one's going to fault your courage if you do back off, Trav," Cassie said. "You've just got to compare your own motivation with theirs. You are against prejudice, while they're fueled by it. They're the physical realization of all the small-scale, everyday hate you battle against. I've seen hornet nests I'd rather poke up than stir up one of these militia groups. They're willing to be active openly about their hate." She nodded toward what had been my car.

Cassie took a breath. Dutch was fiddling with the side-view mirror, which hung by part of one screw, its mirror broken and bringing someone bad luck, I hoped. "Get these kind of guys in a group and a pack of wolves or hyenas seem civilized. If it weren't for being caught sometimes, they would drag people to their deaths behind trucks all the time for entertainment. You fell into this side of things by accident. The cases you want to follow are the ones you were hired to solve. This is a hive of hornets you accidentally opened, and you don't have to poke at it anymore."

Dutch and Jimmy paid close attention.

"Thanks," I said, and it came out as more of a sigh, "for pointing out a big EXIT sign you'd be willing for me to follow. But there *is* a thread or two that ties them to Bent Lenny, even if the whole world of cops, local and federal, is about to land on Lenny's head."

"Please," she said. "Don't be bullheaded."

"No. Sorry." I looked at the faces of Jimmy and Dutch, usually over-chipper when in range of each other. Now both were as serious and somber as I had ever seen. "These guys will tell you, Cassie, that when I take on a case, bullheaded is exactly what I become. It's a kind of commitment. I'm surprised you discourage it in a man."

I meant the latter as a half-joke, to ease some of the tension. It fell as flat as my hopes and dreams of peace for the next few days.

"Well, Trav," Jimmy said, "looks like. . . ."

Whatever he was going to say got stopped by the look on Cassie's face as well as the one I wore.

"Trav," Cassie said, her voice low, close to a whisper. "There is someone I haven't told you about, someone we might call on if things get rocky."

"Someone tougher than these militia?" Jimmy asked.

"*Way* tougher," she said.

"You don't mean . . . ?" Dutch slipped off the fender of the car and stood upright. He was from out of that part of Texas, knew some of the characters.

"Yeah," she said.

"Joz Brosche," Dutch said in a whisper, like it was a name

you were not allowed to say out loud. Some of the color washed from his face.

CHAPTER NINE

Cassie closed the blinds, blocking out any but a few razor-thin slices of daylight. If ever there was a moment at the home front where I would not have been least surprised to hear a crack of lightning and see the door slam open and Vincent Price walk in, this would be it.

Jimmy and Dutch were long gone, and Cassie and I sat down around the desk, me with no bottle or glass in my hand. The single ceiling light sprayed the desktop in a swath of pale yellow in the otherwise dim room, highlighting the folder in front of where she sat behind the desk.

"You sure you want to do this profile thing right now?" she said.

"You're not just trying to get my mind off Alvin and his friends, are you?"

"Don't get me started on Alvin just now. I get to start all over on that myself. Besides, you think pointing your way toward a possible serial killer is an act of kindness?"

"Hit me with it." I sat on the straight-backed chair like a lump of clay, wanting to scratch myself or cross my legs or anything. I just sat, thinking about the bits and pieces of what had been my car. Guys like that start with something outside that's vulnerable. Next they'll move inside. After that comes the bats and boards or whatever else they have to use to adjust your dental work or noggin.

Outside a car went by, its tires brushing the street like wire brushes on a snare drum. If it had backfired just then I don't know that I'd have cared to see a replay of how I might have responded.

"I know it's hard not to think about Alvin and his friends, but you'll be doing yourself and your music pals a favor by sticking to the attempts on the women for now."

"If you say so."

"I do, and you know you think so too. Don't be such a grump. It wasn't all that great a car. Be honest, Trav."

Maybe I thought the car was a lot more like me than I let on. I gave her a curt shrug. "You said you had something toward a profile. Why don't you share that?"

"First of all, we need to agree that the police here will be following the usual S.O.P. on this, so we don't need to focus on the same things they do."

"That is, if we believe they're fully competent and locked onto this."

"Speaking on behalf of all the law involved here, I'd say you can assume that."

"Sorry."

"You saw the media out there, scurrying around like so many rabid weasels. The heat's on. Believe that."

I repressed a sigh and stared at the folder in front of her, hoping she'd open the damned thing and get with it. I glanced up at her face.

"Don't give me that look. You know why everyone's in a flap. You probably do have a serial here. The worst thing about a serial murderer or rapist is that there is usually no connection with the victims. The police will be checking all the usual serial aspects, that the perp is probably a white male from an upper-lower-class background who had a rough childhood, possible abuse or personal trauma of some kind that has been activated now by a precipitating stressor—whatever event or series of events set the person off again. That is, if this wasn't all done on purpose by someone for whatever reason. Still, there's too much clumsiness to make any of this premeditated. Whoever tried to kill Trish Martinez and got a fan instead may have only meant to scare Trish, but bungled until it was murder. There are more indications of that than not. Then there's the fact that the attempts on Tori Brice and the senator both failed. Still, it smacks of serial—a series of related actions by the same person—no matter the results, and that's why the media is giving law enforcement the hot foot."

She paused. And she had a determined steel edge to her words when she spoke again. "I'm telling you this only for the part of it that relates to your work for those music fellows. Okay? *Alvin is still all mine. Understood?* I should have grabbed him and held on when I had him instead of trusting that to the locals. Don't think I'm not kicking myself now with both boots. It's what I should be doing right now instead of helping you. But I promised. Got it?"

I nodded slowly.

"For anything connected with the possible serial events, the cops will be checking with VICAP, the centralized data information center over in Quantico where similar patterns for multiple murders are stored. The fact is, that almost all serial events are similar in some ways but quite different in others. There's never been anyone quite like Jeffrey Dahmer before or since, thank goodness. After all, a profile is just a profile and nothing more—a starting place to help the looking. Some perps purposefully shift from knife play to strangling, anything to toy with or throw off the law after them."

All this coming from a smooth wholesome face surrounded by a fall of blonde hair. Who would believe it? You might expect to see a face like Cassie's on the side of a package of butter, not spouting murder modus operandi details.

She opened the folder, looked down at a page of notes, then her light blue eyes lifted to search my face before starting. I don't know why she supposed an old piece of shoe leather in the detecting business might have anything about which she need be cautious, and she seemed to come to the same conclusion and let her focus drift back to her notes in the folder.

"Some of the general traits of anyone prone to serial murders include a difficulty in establishing long-term relationships. That doesn't mean the outward behavior is noticeably odd. Many serial killers could be outwardly personable, even charming. Some have even been married, though it didn't usually take."

"You could be describing me," I said. It gave me a jolt when she didn't look up, just nodded and kept going.

"The perp is usually a white male who fixes on female or homosexual male victims. The victims most often come from a stratum of society where they won't be missed—prostitutes or men who cruise parks and gay bars. That's an area where our case differs dramatically. The targets here seem to be higher-profile ones. That's what has the media boiling more than usual."

"So far, it sounds like things could be left or right, that these instances could fit with a pattern or be random. What're you saying?" I knew I was letting my irritation poke through, but my just having lost my sole mode of transportation explained some of the angst.

"Hold on. I'm getting to that. I'll skip the different schools of thought on profiling and just say that the FBI take on it is that the personality traits of a person show through in a way that can be more or less identified. A person whose behavior is abnormal enough to do anything like this is most likely to be even more ritualized than usual."

"You think the police are going to call in the FBI on this?"

"Probably not. The ones I've spoken with seem disposed to solve their end of this themselves. Speaking for the department

I work for, we'd also like to do our own laundry, which means me bringing in Alvin and you staying out of that. I'm okay with you doing your thing for those musicians. Just know your part of the turf. Okay?"

She had been hammering that particular point in too much, but I hesitated to point that out. I looked deep into those staring pale-blue eyes, and saw no ounce of flinch in them.

She took a breath and relaxed, looking back to the folder. "Sorry. That just needed to be said."

"Like I haven't heard it from a thousand law officers before."

"I'm not sorry for saying it again, just ticked at myself for letting the bastard go. I was venting. Okay?" She gave her long blonde hair a toss and caught a glimpse of me from the corner of her eye before she went on.

"One of the chief problems with all serial cases is the reluctance of one level of law to work with another, the FBI with locals, or vice versa. Here that will be even more the case, because you've got only one accidental death so far, and that was out in our county along with the mess Alvin made."

"Serial killers kill strangers," I said. "That's a normal part of that. How's that tell us anything?"

"There are a few things we can learn from previous instances, Travis. You go back through the past and there are the likes of Henry Lee Lucas, John Wayne Gacy, Jeffrey Dahmer, and the one most like we have here, Ted Bundy."

"You think Ted Bundy did this?"

"Not unless it was his ghost. He was executed in Florida back in eighty-nine. The point is that it could be someone as outwardly normal seeming as Bundy, but who has deeply repressed feelings, the way he did."

Outside the distant sound of thunder rumbled . . . that or a large truck was busy turning its transmission inside out. I noticed all the cheer went out of Cassie as she dealt with this business. It was nothing to chuckle about. With her, there was something almost personal about all of this.

"Why Ted Bundy?"

"Listen. He had a high intelligence and none of the usual traumatizing influences during his childhood. He had no serious physical defects, had sufficient interest in hobbies and recreation, like skiing, and he had no previous history of mental illness. Yet whenever anyone got close to understanding him he got evasive. While he wasn't psychotic or schizophrenic, he did have some features of antisocial personality disorder that led him to compartmentalize and rationalize his behavior in a way that led to callous guilt-free behavior outside what we would call normal. He had a strong dependence on women, yet had an equally fierce need to be independent, probably because he feared being hurt by women. Either because of this, or in spite of this, he gravitated to his serial crimes. Beneath what seemed to be a normal-enough person was a great deal of general anger, in particular, a near rage against women."

She stood up and looked down with a touch of disgust as she closed the folder, then picked it up the way I'd seen an ME remove a malignant lung from a corpse once. She started toward the door.

"That's all?" I said. She kept going. "You think the person we're after is something like that?"

"I do." She paused, opened the door. The light poured inside. She looked back at me.

"Are you sure you aren't trying to tell me something?" I said.

"No. I don't think you're a woman hater. You just don't always know what to do with them."

CHAPTER TEN

The Copper Spoon's a little breakfast and coffee place tucked in a nook between the shadows of two of the newer high-rise buildings off Congress Street, not too far from the newspaper offices. A Starbucks had opened on the corner just down the street. But the Spoon still had its loyal patrons, addicted to the mediocre fare and the cheaper coffee—still just twenty-five cents, with free refills. I found Hal on the next-to-last stool, all by himself, huddled over what didn't look like his first cup, given the number of empty tiny half-and-half containers near the small huddle of loose change by his chipped white cup.

"You reporter types really know how to live." I slid onto the stool on the end and waved a dollar at the guy scraping at the grill who had three days' growth on his chin. He put the long spatula down and headed for the glass coffee pots in a row on the warmer.

Hal waited until I had my coffee, and the short-order cook had made change. When it was just the two of us again, Hal leaned closer. "I made up a short list, but are you sure about this?"

"No," I said. "But it is a different spin than Borster and his department will take."

"Could just be a waste of your time. Probably is." Hal took a small folded sheet of paper out of his pocket. He slipped it across the countertop to me. His pinched narrow face had a tingle of gray to it, and his expression made me think he was carrying far more of the world's problems than he needed to be lugging for such a guy his size, and with his mileage. "This may give you a starting point or two, if that helps. Something might come of the busywork if you have no other leads."

I unfolded the slip and looked at the names and addresses, each with a short explanatory note.

"This idea of hers. . . ." He hesitated and looked down at his cup, then back up at me. "You really think much of the profile pointing at some woman hater?"

"She majored in psychology in college."

"Back in J-school, we always heard that those who headed for that major had problems themselves they were trying to work out."

"I've heard something like that too, but I spend most of my life talking myself out of a lot of the things I hear that relate to other people. She has an interest in profiling too, and got a boost on that in her stint at Quantico."

"But, still. You've always worked so well alone."

"We all have to learn to take help now and then, Hal."

"You might be headed all wrong from this kind of help."

"I don't mind, Hal, if it gets my feet moving in *some* direction. Sure, I don't buy the woman-hater profile either. It's not anything I'd go on myself. Some good might come of it, even if it's just to get me thinking clearer on some of this. Sometimes, when I go through the motions of anything, let myself get caught up in the busywork, I stumble onto an answer where I didn't expect it. It's like people when they do everyday things, like showering, shaving, doing the dishes, driving a car—that keeps the motor cortex busy and frees up the rest of the head to focus on dusting out the corners and maybe seeing things more clearly."

He nodded to the scrap of paper I'd folded up and left by my cup. "Well, that should keep you busy."

"And that's not a bad thing." I finished the coffee in my cup, reached for the bit of paper, and waved away the guy who turned and hurried toward the urn. "My feet are barely on the ground right now," I told Hal. "There doesn't seem to be any sense or pattern to any of this. That's about par for my life."

Hal leaned closer, with that gray-tinged face of his, and looked up at me, as intense as he can get at times. His voice was low, and he spoke clearly, though rapidly, without ever seeming to take a breath, and he stared right at me with wide unblinking eyes.

"You know, Trav, long as I've known you I've always admired you for going it on your own. You and maybe a little tequila. You . . . um . . . were good by yourself. Tough as nails. Remember, Trav? You were good. Alone. Remember?"

He looked embarrassed. Blinked. Then he got up and left, and I sat there for a few more ticks, warming the stool and reminding myself all over again what I needed to do that day. I finally pushed off from the counter and, in spite of that little cloud of gloom from Hal, headed out into what was shaping up to be another sunny and hot day.

The house, slightly bigger than a cottage but with all the cuteness, sat at the back of a cul-de-sac in the Hyde Park area. The lawn was an impeccable green, while other lawns in the neighborhood were showing yellow patches. The house had been freshly painted. Tight, hunter-green shutters framed each of the windows against off-white sides that looked tastefully like ostrich eggshell.

My usual sense of urgency was doing battle with the notion I'd shared with Hal, that I really didn't have much of a starting point.

The door opened. The man who stood there was tall and craggy; the features of his long pale face were etched in deep lines. His hair was gray and going white. He wore a light charcoal suit, white shirt, and a plain red tie. From what Hal had told me, I guess I had expected a mauve silk shirt with big sleeves, unbuttoned halfway down the center of his chest to his tight jeans, with a golden pendant hung in the curling white hairs of his chest.

His first words were, "Don't ever be gay and get old."

"Okay," I said.

"Come on in." He spun on one foot and glided off into the cottage. I didn't know whether to expect lava lamps and cushions on the floor or what. The inside was very white and spare. Each room held only an item or two of black furniture. The walls and ceiling were white. The floors were polished hardwood with no rugs.

"Are you gay?" he said, as I came in and sat on the sofa to keep from sitting in what looked like a beanbag chair.

"No. Just cheerful." This was going well.

"I don't get many callers at home."

"Where do you get them?"

"Oh, you scamp." His voice was husky and low, but had no lisp to it. It also had little genuine humor. "Hal said you'd be stopping around."

"Do you know him well?"

"Not in the biblical sense, if that's what you meant."

I sat still and felt like humming, or twirling my thumbs. That must be why people give you coffee, so you can have something to do with your hands when you're feeling awkward.

His head lowered and he looked up at me through thick, shaggy eyebrows. "Hal said you asked him where you could find the head queen bee of our community. I must be that person in Hal's mind."

"How do you know Hal?"

"I ran into him in Saint-Tropez, of all places. I was wearing a

T-shirt for the capital ten-K run and he seemed surprised to see another Austinite in France. He tagged along with a little group of ours to Martinique a year or two later. He had a good time, too. That is, until he found out what kind of group we were. Now he just calls on me as his local lavender expert about whatever goes on in this dark world of ours. Maybe you can share why *you're* here."

"I'm working on a case where we don't have much to go on. The police are checking the regular trails, family, friends, contacts, enemies, that sort of thing. We have three women who've been attacked—at least there've been tries. I'm doing what I can to follow any thread to someone who might be a woman hater."

His lips pursed and his eyes narrowed. "I can see you don't know all that much about our culture."

"I'm here because of that."

"Well, there are societies, organizations, gay bars sprinkled through town, a few of them that lean to the lez crowd, and there's a bathhouse or two. If you started now and haunted them all, I doubt if you could turn up a woman hater. It's not how it works."

"Kind of make love, not war?"

For the first time, his dour face made a scramble toward something resembling a smile. "As you probably know," he said, "this town is enigmatic in Texas. Austin itself, according to those who should know, is close to twenty-percent gay, perhaps higher once some of the closets swing open around town. Yet, if there's any hate going on out there, it's directed *at* the gay community, most often by those who have the most reason to fear they might be a secret part of it."

I tilted my head at him. "And, do you think Hal had any of those kind of fears?"

He came close to sharing a brief gargle of a laugh. "Oh, our dear Hal has many fears, and as a result, a few hates. But, in recent days, he seems far more caught up in the vortex angst of his own atavistic entropy, if you know what I mean."

Know what he meant? I wasn't even sure we were speaking the same language anymore. I shook the old coconut in what I hoped was an expressive way.

He seemed to catch on, and gave me one of those professorial looks of someone who realizes that his erudition has bowled you over when he thought you were equal to the task of keeping up. He said, "If there is one thing motivating Hal these days, it has to be his obsession to get back to the position of comfort, and perhaps of power, which he once held and enjoyed."

"Hal's little quirks aside, will you let me know if you think of anything else related to the possible hate crimes I mentioned?"

He gave me a tired sigh. "Of course."

As he ushered me to the door, he asked, "Where do your travels take you next?"

"A whorehouse, I believe, is next on my list," I said.

"My," he said, "I'm in good company today, aren't I."

"I didn't know there really *were* places like this," I said.

"There aren't," the woman leading me down the hallway said. We turned into a library, or parlor. It was mid-afternoon. Business didn't seem at its peak yet. The room was empty. An overstuffed sofa sat near the fireplace beside a wall of books and knickknacks. I eased down onto the sofa. She sat in a matching chair facing me, said, "And when you leave, I want you to do your level best to forget about this one."

"I don't look the potential customer type to you?"

"I'm a better judge of character than most—clergymen, writers, and bellhops included," she said. "And no. You don't look the type."

"Can we talk?"

113

"Oh, come now," she said. "You can just imagine how that is in my line."

"I'm after a killer . . . of women. All I have to go on right now, that the police aren't already working on, is that the person might hate women."

"And you think the men who come to me *hate* women?"

"I don't know about that. I know some like to be tied up, or to tie up others, all that crazy sort of thing."

"I see where you're going. But I'd have to say that anyone who comes to me *has* an outlet to play out the kind of fantasy you're talking about, to release those hostilities. What you're probably really after is someone who has those feelings but is repressed, who has no such outlet."

I glanced around for a bookshelf of self-help books. She spoke the same pop-psych lingo as Cassie. I said, "You don't know of anyone . . . no one's ever acted up in here, done something unspeakably hostile."

"Not here. Oh, we've covered up a thing or two. I imagine the girls standing too close to the curb could tell you better stories than I could ever come up with. That's the thing about a house. Men don't come to a house with the same attitudes they carry into a situation they start with someone they meet on the street. We have bouncers and, for all they know, films."

"You really have films?"

"Now that would be telling, wouldn't it," she said. "You don't look satisfied."

"I've used up the contacts I was given," I said. "You have a fix on what I'm after. If you were me, who would you speak to?"

"If I was in your shoes, I'd be talking with Carol Myller. But don't you dare tell her I suggested it."

Carol Myller's place, if she had been the old woman in the

shoe, would have been a glass slipper. She lived and worked in the penthouse of a building that had a direct view of the Capital Building. I don't know when I've seen as much glass in one home. Eighty percent of three of the walls were picture windows. As if that was not enough, the coffee table was glass, as were the bookshelves, and there was an aquarium in the center of the room. Along the wall that faced away from the white dome of the Capital Building, a glass desk stretched along the wall. At least the computer wasn't made of glass.

The woman seated across from me—leaning back in a brown-with-white-spots cowhide chair with the fur-side of the hide on the outside—wasn't made of glass, though. She was a top-heavy brunette in her forties who looked as in control of her kingdom as anyone I'd ever met.

"You sure you don't want to take a leap and try my services for a day or two?" she pressed. She was grinning past the cigarette she lifted from her face. She sent a stream of smoke up toward the white ceiling.

"No. I don't," I said, "even though I'm not even sure how it works."

Her smile was sly. Woman of the world. Mona Lisa with the inside scoop. "I got the idea when I was in New York City," she said. "I brought it down here and thought I'd run it a while, see if it could hold up in this population. It does."

"How does it work?"

"Oh, it's nothing illegal. I hope you weren't steered wrong about that. It's just that my clients might not want any publicity." Her round face, beneath the dark hair, had an oriental cast to it, which she emphasized with a tilt of her head.

"This isn't about your clients. It's about the women already threatened, and those who might be next."

"Oh, I'm going to tell you." She bent forward to twist her cigarette out in a glass ashtray. "It's just that, you know what people say about people who live in glass houses."

I sighed. It was getting to be a long day. I had skipped lunch and had been forced to take a cab from place to place.

The phone rang. She jumped to her feet. Spry for her years.

"I'll take that in the next room," she said. "You understand."

I pushed myself out of my chair and walked over to peer down at Guadalupe Street. At least it was cool in her apartment. It looked very hot down below. I wandered along the wall, heard Carol's mumbling, then laughter coming from the next room. At the desk I glanced over the paperwork. Nothing showing except some spreadsheets that meant nothing to me. The computer screen was blank and dark, turned off. A small stack of disks had been piled at the back corner of the desk. Each said "ZIP" on one end. Carol had penciled in some kind of abbreviated acronyms that meant something to her. The bottom one on the stack was marked "Bkp." I slipped it out and dropped it into my suit jacket pocket. By the time I heard Carol hang up, I sat in the chair waiting.

"Sorry about that," she said, glancing around the room as she came back in. "But opportunity knocks."

"That how it works? They call up? How's it advertised?"

"It's just like the hooker trade, and at least as discreet. Men hear about it word-of-mouth. Then they call."

"I still don't understand?"

"The mechanics of it, or the psychology?"

"Both. Especially the psychology."

"It's simple, really. The old clearinghouse or want-ad approach. I find someone in need of a service and someone else who needs to serve."

My patience had worn thin and it must have shown in a glimmer across my face. She picked up the pace, "I got in it by having houses cleaned. I'm a former trophy wife who found herself single once it was time for my ex to marry young again.

I had to build a trade, or career, from scratch. This is what I ended up with. Like I said, it started with cleaning houses. I built up a clientele of folks, a lot of women, who preferred their places cleaned by men. Then I got onto the spin. There are men out there in positions of high authority who need to do something that brings them back to earth."

"And that's clean houses?"

"Exactly. And they pay to do it. Imagine some three-piece-suit guy who's a senior VP or CEO by day. He comes to me and I have him scrubbing a kitchen floor with a toothbrush. Some of them even like for me to have them work naked."

"They pay for that?"

"What they're paying for is expiation. These are men of authority. All week long they ride their troops, are probably firm with their wives at home. They need some release. Getting on their hands and knees, scrubbing, cleaning out toilets—there's nothing like that to bring you back to earth."

"I've always suspected that janitors have the inside track on life," I said.

"You don't buy into it?"

I shook my head. "I must be missing something. Men *pay* you to be debased by cleaning houses and apartments, in the nude, while being yelled at the whole time?"

"That's how it works."

"But it doesn't make sense."

"Not to you. I doubt if you've ever been in that position—an authority figure, the top guy in a company, king of a castle at home. Jobs like those can be unrelenting. They wear. And some men feel they need to reverse the roles. They would never dare to do so at home or at the office, or they would forfeit their control for all time, not just for a day grabbed now and then."

"And they feel better after scrubbing and scouring toilet bowls with toothbrushes?"

"Most do. Absolutely."

"None ever spin out, lash back, resent the treatment instead of enjoy it?"

"It's just like bondage," she said. "Some people experiment and find it's not right for them, that appeasing the guilt isn't a good enough reason for the pain. Sure, some guys try it and don't come back. That's what works about it—it's their call. This is just another business—a legitimate though discreet one. They don't like the service; they don't have to come back."

"But a lot of 'em do?"

"Most of them," she said. "And the higher their stress at the office, the more often they come."

I shook my head. I think I've seen a lot of things in the snoopy kind of business I do. Every now and then I realize I'm not above getting shocked at some new twist.

"How's this help you with what you're working on?"

"Adds to the confusion," I said. "Just adds to the confusion."

"This isn't something you can just let the police handle?"

"They've got their slant. On something like this there's an element of randomness that defies the logical approach."

"Which, I guess, explains why you're here."

I stood up slowly. Sooner or later I was going to have to spend a night in my cot if I was ever to get over the thumping Alvin had given me.

"Come back some time," she said as I left, "when you feel like cleaning up."

CHAPTER ELEVEN

I rode in the back of a red-and-key-lime-pie-green Roy's Taxi on the way to my office. The cabbie tried and failed to stir up a conversation, speculating how the Longhorns were going to do in the coming college football season. The windows were up, but the heat of the afternoon beat through the glass, as we passed through the downtown traffic and structures of Austin. Some of the buildings looked as bleached to me as bones lying in a desert sun. I rolled my head from side to side, worked the tension from my neck and fought to stay awake until I got back to my office.

When I had paid and climbed out of the cab, a car door opened on the street. Cassie, still in uniform, waved to me. I opened the office and we slipped inside. It felt only slightly less warm there than on the street. Cassie turned on the overhead fan and lights.

"You find Alvin?" I asked.

"He wasn't in any of the hospitals on his own, morgues either."

"I don't think I conked him that hard, or at the least his skull is thick enough to take it. These guys probably do their own first aid . . . goes with the tough-guy image," I said. "Hey, you mind if I grab a quick shower?"

I sat on the corner of the desk. She came over and lifted my chin and looked into my face. Her pale-blue eyes were very large. I hadn't noticed how large before. Her lips were full too, and unencumbered by lipstick. I shook my head from where that seemed headed and pushed myself up off the desk. She stepped aside as I lumbered toward the back.

"Sure," she said. "Just pretend you're at home."

Over the sound of the shower I didn't hear anyone come in the front office. When I turned off the lukewarm water, I went out to sit on the edge of the cot, a towel around my waist. My head was lowered as I contemplated the soggy tape wound tightly around my chest. I debated whether taking it off and letting the ribs flop around would feel better than the itching. Soft footsteps at the door made me lift my head. Cassie stood there. She held one of the small jars I use for glasses, and what was inside glittered with an amber charm.

"Where'd you get that?" I asked. The office medicine chest, even the emergency jug, had been empty when last I'd checked.

"Hal's in the outside office, and he brought you a gift." She shook her head at me. "Man, you're shot, aren't you?"

I reached for the glass. "I'm okay," I said. "Now give me a minute to get back into my clothes."

Hal and Cassie both sat on the desk when I came out. A familiarly shaped brown paper bag stood between them. "One of these days I'm going to have to get some office furniture," I said. "A few more chairs, maybe."

"A recliner would be nice," Hal said.

"Or psychiatric couch," Cassie said. "Or a couch, period," she added.

Empty glass in hand, I honed in on the bottle and helped myself to another jolt. "Thanks." I saluted Hal as I took a sip.

"No. Thank *you*," he said. "I went through the files and got ready for a photo spread on Bent Lenny, if and when that goes down. I even slipped over to his club and got some shots of The Rubber Jungle in good light. There're only a few more shots I need to round out what I have. Then I should have enough for a fold-open double-truck. . . ." He stopped himself. "Two side-by-side pages," he explained, "with a full pictorial story."

"Any of it tied to our militia pals?" I asked.

"You should see the photo of Lenny I dug up from when he stepped out of stir. My sister's Chihuahua has more hair."

"Hey," I said. "I'm being a lousy host. Can I get you a glass?"

"Not my thing," he said. "But, hey, Trav," his voice quivered, "you don't know what working on this means to me. This could be the big one. Dare I say the word 'Pulitzer'?"

It seemed to have taken his mind off his worries and given him something positive on which to focus. I hated to poke at his bubble, but I said, "You really think there's *that* much to the story?"

He nodded energetically. His hands started to rub together fast enough to start a fire. I glanced at Cassie.

"How about what *you're* working on?" he asked. "Get any farther with that?"

I shook my head, asked Cassie, "You get much from the police?"

"I talked with a fellow you know—a sergeant named Borster. Man. What'd you ever do to him, kill his pet or something?"

"Doing this job doesn't leave one loved by all," I said.

"Anyway," Cassie said, "all they have are a couple of bullets they dug out of the wall at the Constitutional Club. You were there. They don't have any more than they did then. No witness, no motive. While I was there, I looked over the traffic report on the truck that squashed Jayne Randall's car. No fingerprints. No witnesses there, either."

"We had random before," I said. "We still have random. That's the hardest kind of trail for police to track, even tougher for someone like me."

"If we just had something . . . ," Cassie said.

"Hey." I jumped off the corner of the desk, went over to my

suit jacket. I pulled the disk out of the pocket. "What do you know about a computer disk like this?" I asked.

Cassie shook her head. Hal came over to look at it. "It's a ZIP disk," he said. "It's like a recordable CD-ROM, only you can write, erase, everything on one of these. Some folks use them for backup, though they're not as current as jump drives and such. Where'd you get it?"

"At a woman named Carol Myller's place," I said. Hal gave a start.

I asked, "How do we look inside it?"

Hal took a step toward me. "I think there's a machine at the office linked to one of the computers that can read it. We could. . . ."

I shook it off. "Naw. I've got to go out and see Dirty-Fingernails Huff anyway. It'll be child's play for him."

"I can do it, Trav," Hal said. "Come on. We can go down there right now."

"Won't it be busy? Maybe we'd better wait until tomorrow."

"No way, Trav. The Bent Lenny bust is going down then. I can't miss that."

"What do the police do? Send out engraved invitations?"

"I'm on the inside track, that's all. Can't we do it tonight?"

"Well," I said, "maybe in the wee hours, when the staff has cleared out. Can you make that?"

"Sure," he said. "But we don't *need* to wait."

"Later tonight will be fine," I said. I went over, slipped the disk back into my pocket.

"I could take it down," Hal said, "and print out the contents, bring that back here."

I waved it off. "I'll just hang onto the disk," I said.

"At least let me drive," Cassie said. "You've had a couple. And buckle up, too."

I made quiet grumping noises as I slid in and buckled up.

"Where's this Huff person live?" she asked. She started the car and flipped on the lights. She had changed out of her uniform and into a red blouse with jeans and cowboy boots this time.

I told her how to get on the road heading up into Hill Country toward his place. She drove no faster than the speed limit all the way to the edge of town. A car swooped across two lanes in front of us in indecision before weaving back to the right and taking an off-ramp. Cassie slowed and gave it a wary eye.

"See," I said. "Another Volvo from hell."

"That wasn't a Volvo," she said.

"It's an honorary one, then." She gave me a quick, sharp glance. I slumped in the seat, thinking strong thoughts about grabbing a nap.

"My god. You weren't kidding Don Briscoe, then," she said. "You really *do* have this Volvo thing."

"I'm not proud of it. Sure, I was using it to get under Briscoe's skin, but the bias is really there, and a failing in me. That's the thing about prejudice. It creeps in, and you can only stop it by thinking it out. I just haven't had the time to pursue, wrestle with, and purge this Volvo thing from my system yet."

"How did it get started?"

"Hard to say. Maybe Volvo owners watch too many of those safety commercials and believe they really are safer than in any other car. At any rate, a lot of Volvo drivers seem conservative, thoughtful. Those aren't necessarily positive qualities in the flow of traffic. All I know is that with a lot of Volvos the drivers seem to be pondering which lane they should be in, whether they should use a turn signal or not, and whether they really want to make the turn they're halfway through."

"That *is* stark prejudice."

"So, what's your issue with that. I've already admitted to the problem."

"Tell me about this Dirty-Fingernails Huff we're going to see," she said. I began to reduce my chances of catching that nap.

"Huff's what some people would call a techie, or nerd or geek."

"Hey."

"He'd be the first to admit it," I said. "He hasn't answered the phone since JFK, and he gave up on living around people earlier than that."

"How's he make a living?"

"Oh, projects here and there. He's a whiz with electronics and computers. You can make a pretty good income working at home these days if you've got some marketable skills. Huff was the kind of guy building oscilloscopes in his garage as a kid, tapping main power lines and nearly killing himself as an adolescent. He did a stint with the air force. Tore up the instructions and put together a radio in half the time it'd ever been done before. It was a cakewalk for someone who used to put together crystal radios out of junk in his pockets during school."

"Sounds like a genius."

"In the sense that all the talent is focused in a narrow area. Huff's social skills pay the price. If you see him wipe his nose on his sweatshirt sleeve, don't be alarmed. We can only hope he's changed it within the past month."

"Ugh."

"Oh, and there'll be a few animals around. They're more forgiving than people to hermits like Huff."

"You trying to scare me?"

"No. The badgers'll be in cages. So will Tippy, the fox. But there should be a flying squirrel loose in the house somewhere. There used to be a raccoon that lived on the porch and would never let me in. It got so I'd always have to go around to the back. The last time I was out there, the raccoon was gone, but there was a deer fawn that ate the buttons off one sleeve."

Her hands had shifted to the nine and three position on the steering wheel. I could see her grow tense. So I asked, "You're law enforcement in Texas. What have you heard about any real paramilitary groups, white-supremacist groups, and outfits like them?"

"Turn here?"

"Yeah," I said. We still had a good fifteen minutes of back road left before going up the long drive to Huff's place.

"First of all," she said, "you've already pointed out that a militia person isn't necessarily a skinhead, and that someone with short hair isn't always a skinhead. I get your drift. Some folks just wear their hair short 'cause the fashion's swung that way. That doesn't make them racists. With the racist groups there are a handful of other distinctions to make. The skinhead movement itself got going strong in the seventies in England. They had their 'oi' music, the slam-dancing, the heavy beer drinking, the tattoos, the wearing of boots. The American part got started in neo-Nazi and white-supremacist pockets in the eighties. Some skinheads aren't racist, but those linked to the Aryan Nations sure are. On another front, you have some militant, and by that, I mean armed so-called Christian movements, which share some of the racist views but do so because they say God and Jesus tell them to be that way. Then there are at least half dozen other brands of racist, resistance, or revolution groups who just want to hang out in the woods with other guys and play with guns."

She took a breath. "It just happens that the group we're looking at now is probably a group of local patriots gone heavy-handed in the heady aftermath of terrorism—no more than that. That doesn't make them less dangerous, or, in cases, less bigoted. I don't know that I'd put them quite in the league with the small supremacist groups that splintered and ran after the Oklahoma City bombing, folded in with some other militants who had axes of their own to grind."

"The Oklahoma City bombing was done by supremacists?"

"None of that's proven, and stands as much of a chance of being proven as who was really behind the JFK hit. The ATF, DEA, and FBI all had informants sprinkled through various skinhead groups. One of the people undercover who penetrated the skinhead scene was whooshed away right after the bombing, and he was assisted in getting away by the GSG-Nine, the German counterterrorist unit."

"It's a mystery to me, with all those informants, how there ever *was* an Oklahoma City bombing," I said.

"Yeah, well the World Trade Center disaster came as a surprise too. You don't want to buy into any conspiracy theory too quickly, Trav. Fact is, all these agencies worked with varying degrees of informants who were often kooks to begin with. Information was compartmentalized and undependable. The competition between agencies may add to the confusion instead of help, but after September 11 and all the other terrorist news all of them are hyper on the alert now, and I can't say that's all a good thing."

I listened to the rhythm and tone of Cassie's words. There had been a change, a subtle one, the same as when she spoke to me about serial killers. I'd heard Bureau agents talk like that before. It could be the FBI association she'd recently experienced. After all, she had just gotten back from Quantico.

Sometimes I can get to be a bother to myself. Earlier I was having twinges about the goose chase on which Hal had sent me. Now I felt the familiar shadow of paranoia about Cassie. No wonder I spend most of my time alone.

"Let me know when the dirt road turnoff to Huff's place

comes up," she said.

"It's ahead after this next bend to the left and back to the right. There's a gate." My chances of grabbing a nap had pretty well slipped by. "Right there."

We wove back through Huff's long lane. Something barked as we pulled up and stopped, but it didn't sound like a dog. Cassie gave me a quick glance as we got out of the car.

"It's me, Huff," I called out. There was no answer from the house. An armadillo scurried past in an alarmed waddle.

I stepped onto the wooden porch, watched for loose boards, and rapped on the door. "Huff?"

The door finally cracked. Huff's small voice came through the crack. "Is that a woman with you, Trav?"

I looked back at Cassie, who hovered near the edge of the porch. It was hard to miss the distinguishing features. "Sure looks like it, Huff."

"What's she doing here?"

"Is this an all-men's club?" I asked. "Some of your critters are female. She's not here to bug you, and I'll vouch for her."

"Oh, all right," he said, but there was a quiver to his voice. He swung the door open, reached down to grab a ferret that tried to make a bolt for the great outdoors.

I watched Cassie to see how she would respond as we went inside. I'd been inside many a time. She rolled well, her eyes widening only slightly. The dim light came from a television from which I could make out Jay Leno's voice. Huff must have been once again between any efforts that demanded his focused thought. He slips to television when not helping out on a case or working on one of his own high-intensity projects.

He stared at Cassie, shook out of that and reached for his holster belt, where he wears at least three remote devices in homemade holsters. He drew one, clicked it, and the television went off, leaving us in darkness.

I heard him mess around with one of his remotes. Then the lights came on, very bright, but dimmed as he pressed a button. His thumb slid over the remote and music came on, some of the Peruvian panpipe music he claims his critters like.

"Have a seat," he said, once again the perfect host, except there was no place to sit. Piles of technical magazines filled every table and chair in the room, except the ratty and patched overstuffed cloth recliner that faced the television. It had worn impressions of where Huff had spent far too much time, and it would have taken a stronger constitution than mine to sit in it. "Or stand, if you like," he added.

"I just came to borrow some night-vision goggles if I could, Huff." I hoped to speed things along. I saw Cassie looking around the room with some obvious horror. Something moved over behind a pile of magazines, and she didn't look like she cared to know what.

"Sure, no problem. You want the AN/PVS-Five model that the marines use, or the SV-Seventy-Three MPN Thirty-Five-K-One? I think the SV-Seventy-Three works a hair better in total darkness. I mean, the PVS-Five is fine where you got some light, from stars, streetlights, that sort of thing. But when it's dark as the inside of a cow, then I'd go SV-Seventy-Three. If it's distance you want, I've got one of the SV-Seventy-Four Panteras that'll really get you out there."

"Maybe just the SV-Seventy-Four will be fine. There. You see, Cassie? A lot of people wouldn't even know what I was talking about, and with Huff I get choices."

"Good lord," she said. "What do you do with that kind of hardware? Our department can hardly afford them."

I saw Huff tighten into a frozen stance. So I said, "Little sheriff's department, west of here. She's with me, Huff. I vouched for her. Remember?" Defending her felt awkward. I'd been having my own doubts about her as recently as the ride here.

He gave me a nervous look, then slipped off into the other room. An opossum came strolling out of the room, as if it'd been disturbed.

I held a finger to my lips at Cassie.

She shrugged.

Huff came out carrying a small case, which he handed to me. He cast an apprehensive look at Cassie again.

"I'm off duty," she said. "Just helping Trav with a little problem he's having." She grinned.

It was enough to charm Huff. He moved closer to Cassie and said, "I watch critters at night. Most of 'em get moving around best when it's dark." That didn't explain why he had something like the piece of work he'd handed me, which cost in the neighborhood of three thousand dollars. Cassie let it slide. I saw her rock back on her heels and figured she'd gotten a thorough sample of Huff's famous halitosis problem. His breath is rated somewhere between Vietnam-level napalm and swamp gas. Being close to him is part of the price one pays for his techie insight.

"Huff," I said. I pulled the disk out of my pocket. "Any chance of getting you to make a copy of this?"

"Not even a problem, Trav," he said. "What'cha got there is a ZIP disk. Holds a hundred megabytes of data. I installed an Iomega one when the prototypes came out years ago. I'll have it in a jiff." He wove a path through the dusty carpet and stacks of magazines and took the disk off into yet another room. I'd been in one or two of the other rooms before. Each looked like a peek inside the guts of the Starship Enterprise. I'd never seen so many beeping lights and gadgets.

As soon as he was out of the room, Cassie waved a hand back and forth in front of her face and acted like she was going to swoon. I waved the flat of my hand at her to get her off the subject before Huff rejoined us.

She started to sit down on one cluttered chair, forgot how dusty it was. Something furry turned around on it to get more comfortable. Cassie reeled away from that as Huff came back into the room.

He held out two copies of the disk, each in its clear jewel box container.

"Keep one copy here for me, if you would," I said.

He had moved over closer to Cassie. "You wanna see some more of the critters?" he asked. He saw her stare down at the chair. "There's a roadrunner's been bringing me baby rattle-snakes in its beak each day. But it's too late in the day for him. I got some bats out in the barn you won't believe."

I watched her try to take a step back and hold her breath without seeming to. She shook her head.

"Some other time, Huff," I said. "I've got work to do back in town."

Huff and the possum escorted us to the car. A deer stuck its head out of the shrubs, but moved away when it saw Huff wasn't alone. Cassie stepped lively to get back into the car.

"You two serious?" Huff asked Cassie. I shook my head to him, trying to steer him off where he was going, but his focus was on her.

"What do you mean?" She stopped, halfway into the driver's seat.

"Well, bringing you out here's kinda like Trav taking you to meet his parents, ain't it?"

"How do you get that?" Cassie asked.

" 'Cause he don't have any, what'd you'd call real family. So it's just a few of his close friends matter. Right, Trav?"

I nodded. What else was there to do?

Cassie had the car in gear and was heading back out the lane before she said, "I suppose he'd take it wrong if you were to give him, say, a fifty-gallon drum of Listerine."

"He might," I said. "Besides, animals go for that sort of thing. You know, scent and all that. He told me once that it's easy to open your heart to animals, because you can trust their genuineness."

She thought for half a mile, then said, "You don't really have all that many friends yourself, do you?"

"I have lots of friends."

"Have any of them ever let you down?"

"Lots of them have," I said, my voice fading as I slumped in my seat, headed for that long-awaited nap.

Cassie woke me when we were on the outskirts of Austin. The lights flickered in waves of yellow sparkles across the hills and through the dark trees of the city. The skyscrapers lined the horizon. I looked at my watch. Barely midnight.

"Thanks for letting me catch up. I may have another long night ahead of me."

"What's your big rush?"

"I don't know a timetable, but I sense one," I said. "If the bust of Bent Lenny goes down tomorrow, it may heat things up."

"Heat what up? If you look at all there is so far, there are a few missed homicides and one accidental one."

"An accidental strangling?"

"You know what I mean. The wrong person got killed, and the gag choking her to death instead of just keeping her quiet might've been an accident. As for the rest of it, there's not that much serious going on just yet."

"It was humorous about my car getting trashed?" I said with no humor.

"At least you weren't in it."

We threaded the Austin streets, bright streetlights and neon fading to black on the smaller streets. Cassie turned off onto Brazos. Half a block down was my office. I could tell, because that's where the crowd had gathered.

Cassie glanced at me and pulled over far enough away for us to have a parking space. As we got out and walked, we saw police cruisers, an EMS vehicle, lights, and yellow tape stretched around the area.

CHAPTER TWELVE

"There he is," an authoritative voice shouted as soon as Cassie and I got to the yellow tape.

Thick arms of a couple of the uniforms grabbed me, lifted, and rushed me through the swirl of lights and the crowd gathered around my smashed picture window. Bits of glass crunched under my feet when they touched the ground. My arms being pressed against my sides did little good to my ribs beneath their wrapping. The light of a television camera crew swept to me and blinded me for the next few steps. Someone shove a microphone toward my face, and I swear they asked, "How do you feel?"

Inside my former luxury digs it was quieter and less bright. The uniforms set me down firmly and stayed attached, as if I might bolt.

I blinked as my vision returned. The man standing beside the overturned desk and the body was my close and personal friend, Sergeant Borster. The human scab beside him taking notes on the pad he held was Findlay, Borster's partner. It was the first time since the bounty hunter case, where they missed out on the reward, that they had visited my office. The office was not at its best, but it matched their moods.

"Well, well, well," Borster said. His voice still sounded like gravel being poured out of a tin boot. "You *do* have your nerve coming back here."

"I live here," I said.

"Answer when you're spoken to," Findlay snapped. "Why are you here?"

"I live here," I repeated.

Findlay dropped his pad and took a step toward me. Borster extended an arm and stopped him, but not because he wouldn't enjoy seeing Findlay play handball with my head for a spell.

"You want to identify the body?" Borster asked. His long, square face looked, as it always had, like it was chiseled out of stone on a sculptor's bad day. My poor lighting wasn't doing much for the jagged scar that runs down from the corner of his mouth, or his lightly pockmarked face, with its oily sheen. He reached up and ran his calloused hand over his short hair. I could hear the hair crackle.

I looked down. Don Briscoe lay partially on his back, and partially on his front. I know that's not normally possible. His face was twisted up enough for me to make out what features remained. I could see that someone, or several someones, had stomped all over him with boots. The distinctive marks that boot heels make had left their imprint around him on the wooden floor. Briscoe wore a dark suit like the one I had on, only his cost more. All of the Indian relics that had hung on the back wall—each one also worth more than my suit—had been tugged down and smashed to small bits. Even the scattered porcupine quill beads had been squashed after they'd broken loose from their strings. Someone had found a small Pima vase and a Coushatta basket that'd been tucked away in one of the desk's drawers and had shattered them, spreading the shards among the rest of the debris. My eyes swung to what had once been a nearly new bottle of tequila. Broken glass poked out of the bag, and there was a wet spot where a pool of it had mixed with some of Briscoe's blood.

"Well?" Findlay said.

"Don Briscoe," I said. "He works for Max Bolens."

"That's Congressman Bolens, asshole," Findlay said.

"What did you just call a congressman?" Cassie said. She stood in the doorway, flashing her gold-star badge. The uniforms who had escorted her to the door stepped back outside.

"You're still out of your jurisdiction, aren't you?" Borster said.

"I'm his alibi," she said, and stared back at him with as much intensity as he shared.

It was a little after two A.M. when we got to the newspaper office. I used the phone in the lobby to call Hal's desk while Cassie tapped the toe of her cowboy boot.

"Wow," Hal said when he swung the door open for us and waved us inside to the newsroom. "You're tomorrow's story."

"Today's," I said. "It *is* tomorrow."

"He's a little grumpy," Cassie explained.

By way of worldly possessions, I was down to the borrowed nightscope in Cassie's trunk and the suit I had on. "Let's just get to it," I said. I held out the disk I had snagged at Carol Myller's place.

He led the way down the hall past his own desk to a layout room where an IBM desktop computer had half a dozen extra slots in its tower.

"They use this for graphics," he explained. "This machine's got about a gadzillion gigabytes of memory, but they used to store stuff on these ZIP disks and still have the hardware. I think it's this slot here." He popped the disk into the slot and started to peck away at the keyboard.

I moved over to a table where a copy of tomorrow's front page lay. The shattered front of my office spread square across the middle of page one, above the fold. Congressman Max Bolens' name was prominent, as it would be with his assistant being the victim.

"It's a sad day when the wiping out of everything I own crowds out headlines about terrorist suicide bombings and the doings in the Middle East," I said.

"The story's about Don Briscoe," Cassie said, "not about you."

I mulled over what a paranoid country we'd become in such a short time. What made it hit even harder, I realized I'd begun to worry about Cassie maybe having ties to the FBI. On top of that, I had started to see a pattern to the stories Hal was sharing with the public.

"Eureka," Hal said. I could hear the keys of his keyboard clicking away.

"What?" I said. I had been catching up on what the cops had so far, which was nada. The paper had gone into a brief replay of Bolens' daughter's recent involvement with local militia and automatic weapons, though. The story let the reader form conclusions. In Hal's story he casually mentioned how Max Bolens had been present at every one of the attempts on Mirandez, Randall, and Brice. He left any conclusions out there too, though they weren't hard to come to if you had other than warm feelings for Max. Cassie had moved closer and read the story over my shoulder. Something soft pressed against me, which I struggled not to notice.

"You should see the names on this client list," Hal called over. "And Bolens' name is on the list, too. Man, if this ever got out, there would be dozens of divorces, with CEOs heading for the hills all over town."

"It doesn't look good for Max," Cassie said.

"No, it doesn't," Hal agreed.

"Do you have routine back files on the stuff on Bolens' daughter?" I asked.

"Sure."

"And the wife?"

"What about the wife?" Hal's voice sounded pinched and far away.

"Never mind," I said. "Just some stuff I heard about. It wouldn't have made print."

"Like what?"

"Internet stuff, Hal," I said, looking up from the paper. He stared at me.

I said, "I could have heard it wrong. Those morgue files on the daughter. Can I look at them?"

"Sure," he said. "Sure." He headed out of the room.

"What was that all about?" Cassie asked.

"I don't know," I said. "But the spot seemed tender. I heard something about Bolens' wife being naked on the Internet with another man, thought Hal might have something like that in one of those files he's always talking about that he can't use. I guess I was wrong."

Hal came back in with a couple of files. The three of us took them over to the little cafeteria, where we were able to get some very bad coffee out of a machine.

"You like motives, Trav," Cassie said, looking up from a clipping she held. "What do you make of Bolens' daughter, Donna-slash-Friedya."

I'd just been hashing over her story with Jimmy Bravuro, and I knew Hal was up to speed on the story, but I let Cassie tell it again. I wanted to watch Hal's face. She went over the same ground, then wrapped up saying, "The ATF didn't let her have her Patty Hearst dream and call her Donna or Friedya. They called her C-one-three-seven. Once all the feds had dumped her for being too flaky she starts to fear for her life and takes on a new tune: 'Where's that Witness Protection Program? I hope I don't get an ugly new name.' "

Hal's face looked like he'd just eaten a lemon.

Cassie turned to me. "What do you think, Trav?"

"I don't know what to think." My voice was scratchy, and the words came out slow. I watched Hal, wondering about him in a paranoid way that would have done those militia folks proud.

Cassie dropped the file she was holding and said, "Sounds like a spoiled brat to me. More to be pitied than scorned."

Hal stared off at nothing. I shook my head, having years ago given up on knowing the reasons people do some of the wacky things they do in the name of having a more exciting life.

We got Cassie settled into a La Quinta motel room. I might not have told her everything. If she thought for a second that I had any chance of running into Alvin she sure wouldn't have stayed behind, tired as she might be. When I took the car out it was going on four in the morning. Most of Austin had curled up like an earthworm on a hot sunny highway. The parts that were still moving were squirming. I saw two pairs of police cars, lights going, each pair with a vehicle pulled over along I-35—almost always a DWI.

I stopped at a twenty-four-hour convenience store and bought two large coffees. I thought some memorial thoughts about the bottle of tequila that had given its life defending what had been my home.

This was an hour when a number of drive-by shootings happen in the neighborhood where I was headed. It made me anxious, but not to get there.

The breathy saxophone that has a time of it in my head now and again had begun squeezing out a string of notes that drifted up the scale and dipped into low, agonizing notes.

I made the turn to the east and kept a careful eye on the curbs and side streets as I drove Cassie's car out toward Mokey's, the warehouse Hal had mentioned. Two blocks away from it, I pulled off onto a side street and parked half a block back. I got out of the car with the nightscope tucked under my jacket. I eased up an alleyway, slipping from shadow to shadow without making any sound. The Indian side of my ancestry would have been proud.

By a row of Dumpsters I slid over near a building and got close enough to peer over at the warehouse. A car or truck pulled in every now and then. Guys went in or came out the side door of the warehouse that faced the gravel lot. There was some loud talk, and once in a while I heard a kind of music I'd never heard before. I could tell some of the fellows had been drinking. A few had women along, or girls for all I could tell from where I stood. I focused the nightscope but was only able to confirm that most of the guys had fairly short hair. Nothing too new there.

For an hour I watched the occasional traffic. My legs were close to cramping and my arms were getting tired of holding up the scope. I swept the surrounding cars, rooftops, then spotted a small movement on a covered set of stairs on a building a block away. I swung the scope back and fixed on the spot. A good five minutes later, a head popped up again wearing night goggles. It made the guy's head look like a Martian. The head looked around, pivoted my way and froze on me. The glasses lifted, and there was Hal.

I slowly lowered my scope. Those two large coffees were really beginning to call attention to themselves. I put the scope down along the base of one of the Dumpsters and looked around for a dark corner. There was an indented doorway a few feet along the building from me. I walked that way. I wondered about old Hal out busting his butt for his "Pulitzer" scoop, up as late as me. Maybe that *was* all there was to it. When he got wind of a story he could be a real ferret.

It was very dark back in the shadow where I stepped. I unzipped and was partaking in one of the oldest rituals known to man. I noticed something odd about where I was peeing.

There was a boot there, an army boot. I followed the boot up and there was a leg in it. I didn't like where this was going.

I panned all the way up to the face, past the folded arms that cradled a baseball bat. The face I saw wasn't a happy face, but it was a very intent one, and it stared at me. The head had hardly any hair at all.

CHAPTER THIRTEEN

He leaped out of the shadow, and probably would have grabbed me if I had taken the time to zip up. I spun and raced down the alley. The whip through the air a baseball bat makes when it narrowly misses sounded close behind me as motivation as I whooshed down the dark alley. I ran through the gravel and broken glass, spun around a light pole at the corner and shot up toward the bigger street where there were a few more lights. Suddenly, between me and the lights, four guys popped out and stood in front of me. I heard the pounding clomp of boots near me from behind.

I skidded and darted left—straight, as it turned out, toward a fellow I'd seen before: Donnie. He stood beside two other bulky fellows, one who wore biker's black leather and had long dark hair. The other had white tape around his head and a cast on one leg: he waved a crutch at me—had to be Alvin. There sure seemed to be a lot of them up at this advanced hour. I spun and started back the other direction so quickly I ran right under the arms of the fellow with the wet boot who was swinging the bat.

The alley I ran down had no lights to welcome me. Many boots crunched behind me now as the whole militia jogging class kicked into high-gear pursuit. I huffed and felt an alarming pain settling into my chest. There was no time to slow down and baby the stitch or I would be feeling far more pain. I picked up my pace and squeezed more speed out of myself. I bought a little distance, but had no confidence that it was going to any more than tease fate. These guys were younger and in much better shape than me. The only advantage I had was that they had to have been sucking up beers all night.

Parked cars and the backs of dark houses were along one side of me. To my left was another long building. When I came to its end, I churned my tired feet in a wide arc as I turned the corner and almost ran into the back of a dark van. Its doors swung wide. Arms reached out and yanked me up off my feet and inside. I sailed and landed with an ungraceful thud; the doors slammed shut behind me. Tires squealed and the van surged away—all this with lights out.

I rolled onto my back and began to struggle to my feet, but one of the men in black held a foot on my chest. "Stay low," he commanded. I could make out the silhouette of his black ball cap. I lay panting like a fish just pulled from the water as the van zoomed up the alley and slid out onto a street, picking up speed. The headlights came on.

The inside walls of the van held equipment. I couldn't make out what kind yet in the dark, but the picture began to come together. The guys on either side of me got up off their knees onto low seats. They wore dark flak jackets and gun belts. I heard the low chatter of voices on a radio coming from the front. The two guys up there stared at the road and into the van's mirrors. The van made two more right turns, then a left until we pulled out into the brighter lights of the lit street. I could make out the white ATF letters on the ball caps now. I began to get that "out of the frying pan into the fire" feeling. I was going to have to have it on my own, because no one in the van wanted to talk.

The van ran silent and dark, except for the headlights, as it wove back to the heart of Austin, through the night streets and down a ramp into an underground parking garage beneath one of the federal buildings. It slid into a slot near the elevator. The driver turned back and spoke for the first time. "Let's go. And bring Jesse Owens there with you."

One of the guys in black opened the back door and turned me. "Zip up, would you. The boss's probably already had his Oscar Mayer moment."

I rode up in the elevator with this somber crew, a long-established apprehension about guys like these welling up in me. The thing about feds is that lots of them are brought up on old movies where they watch De Niro say, "You talking to me?" into a mirror. They're lousy with officious attitude.

The field agent I met seemed no exception. He sat behind a desk, talking to someone in a time zone that cared. His navy blue Armani jacket hung on a polished cherry-wood valet beside the desk. He wore a white shirt that had been dry cleaned. It was set off by dark suspenders and a Di Santis shoulder holster.

He hung up and spun to me, saying, "What the hell are you trying to pull?"

My mouth opened, but the question was rhetorical, I found.

One of my flak-jacket buddies brought over the night-vision scope and placed it on the desk. I hadn't seen them carry it in, but I was glad Huff's toy hadn't been lost.

"He left this behind, Gareth."

Gareth looked up from the scope to me. "I'm sure you have a very good reason . . ."—he had to pause and look down at a file he had open on the desk—". . . Travis, for having a state-of-the-art covert tool like this out there at this hour."

"Bird watching?" I said.

His already stern voice ratcheted up a notch. "I hope you don't think all this is some kind of mother-the-humping joke," he said. He wasn't a very good, or a native cusser, but he put a lot of raw feeling into it, in spite of saying each syllable of every word too carefully and distinctly.

I thought about how they hadn't checked me for identification or a weapon. They seemed to know way too much about me.

Old habits fought their way through whatever had put sand in his shorts. He reached to his jacket and tugged out the little leather folder they all carry. "I'm Special Agent Gareth Fields," he said, "FBI."

The last part was unnecessary—I could read the big print just fine. I had met people like Fields before. You wouldn't have to scratch too deep to get to what put the fire in his belly—raw ambition. I stayed with the silent program, which I suspected was going to work better for me.

It was none of my business, but I wondered where the agent in charge was. Maybe it was past his bedtime. Or he could still be pitching in up at Fort Worth where there had been an arms heist at a warehouse three months back. A huge inventory of assault weapons had been taken. I could've been the first to tell them that most of those had probably slipped over the border to some South American buyer within days, perhaps hours, of the hit.

"We're engaged in a cooperative operation with our colleagues at ATF, and I shouldn't have to explain in over-much detail that you're compromising us." He had hazel eyes, which were big and open wide. There was nothing innocent about them. His reddish-blonde hair was as short as it could get and still hold a part. "You know which end of the need-to-know basis you're on, and will understand that I have now said as much as I'm going to say. Am I understood?"

I nodded my head. In case he missed the rattle, I added, "Sure." Then, "Understood."

The ATF guys spun me around and started tugging me back toward the door. "Hey," I said. "My scope."

One of them went back and got it. Then they moved me in

brisk steps to the elevator and soon we were on the streets of Austin again, this time in a sedan. I sat in the back.

"You can drop me off at my office," I said. I figured I could catch a cab to the motel.

Neither of the guys in the front seat said anything. They drove me to the La Quinta where I'd left Cassie. I climbed out, holding the scope and what scraps were left of my dignity. The car pulled out with a little chirp of tire rubber and had soon moved out of sight.

Either I had been tailed earlier, or someone sleeping inside had shared the location with the feds. It did little to alleviate the growing paranoia I felt about Cassie.

I had a key to the motel room, but I hesitated to wake Cassie. It was five-thirty A.M. But I couldn't just stand out there. So I opened the door softly and slipped into the darkened room. I put the scope down and tiptoed around the two beds to the bathroom. Once inside, I flipped on the lights and took a shower. It wasn't until I was done that I realized I had no toothbrush or razor. Cassie's stuff was there. I used some of her toothpaste on my finger, had a little mouthwash as rinse. Then I turned out the light and in T-shirt and boxers started for the empty bed. The light snapped on.

"Aren't you going to tell me what happened?" Cassie said. She sat up in her bed with the covers pulled up around her, but not very well. Far more of her soft skin showed than I felt ready to see. I focused on her face and tried to ease into the covers of the spare bed.

"Just stay put and tell me," she snapped. The authoritative tone of her voice froze me for a second. Then I reached and pulled off the coverlet and wrapped it around me. I moved over and plopped into the chair beside the desk.

"I had a run-in with Donnie," I said, "and Alvin and some more of his militia pals, then with the feds."

"You found Alvin?" I watched the whole gamut of emotions gallop across her face, ending in a flash of anger that I was on her turf. "Alvin was mine. I screwed up once by not just hauling his ass in, and I won't let that happen again. I thought I was as clear as I could be about that." There was that steel icicle tone in her voice.

I could have said that the seed of some overlap here was sprouting in my so-called brain—that Bent Lenny's having a lot of cash at hand at the same time that these militia guys had temporarily moved into downtown Austin seemed more than a coincidence. The needle of my record player was still stuck on the FBI agents dropping me off at the motel. How had they known that?

She stopped when she saw something in my face. "You weren't hurt?" Her voice was softer, more concerned this time.

"Just my feelings," I said, thankful that she hadn't first asked, "How's my car?" and that she seemed to have said all she wanted to say about the Alvin issue for now. "It was close there for a few seconds, and much as I hate to be pulled from the fire by the feds, I'm glad they were there."

"That worries me," she said. "You may be taking on far more risk than you know. You've been lucky so far, but maybe it's time for me to get in touch with Joz Brosche."

"Not while I have the U.S. government as my good fairy," I said.

"The feds," she said. "How much do you think they know?"

"They know a lot, Cassie." I looked at her long blonde hair, the pale-blue eyes and wondered how much I dared share, or if there was anything she didn't already know.

"Like what?"

"Like who I am. Where I'm staying. That I don't carry a gun."

"And you think . . . ?"

"Well, you know."

"Oh, Trav," she said. "I'm not one of them. I have far too much farm girl in me for their taste. I could never be that much of a prig. You really thought I was an FBI agent, or even an information source to them?"

"It crossed my mind is all," I said. "So, what's their thing? They pick me up, give me some kind of warning, but don't tell me squat."

"You must have crossed their path with something you've done in the past day or two."

I thought over everything as best I could. I was far too tired to make much sense to myself. I felt my eyes close then snap open. "Well," I said, "I'd better get some sleep."

"You were just going to crawl into bed and not tell me anything?" she said.

"I . . . well, I. . . ."

"Oh, come on," she said, and threw back her covers.

My eyes snapped all the way open and awake. There was lots of her, all in top shape.

"Don't just stare. Get in here," she said.

I stood slowly, because, well, I had to. I blinked once and started slowly forward. I might still have paranoid doubts about her, reservations. Maybe she worked for the feds, maybe she didn't. She could have been in the pay of the FBI, or the al-Qaeda, for all that, or she could have been Osama bin Laden for all I cared at that second. All I knew was that the Indian who never got the girl was going to get into that bed with her.

CHAPTER FOURTEEN

By nine the next morning, Cassie dropped me off at the place formerly known as my office. Les Bettles, the often-testy fellow who owned the building, had hammered plywood into place to cover where the picture window had been. He had put in a new door, too. This one was solid oak, with a slot for mail, no window this time. All of this, he assured me, was going to have a negative effect on my rent, which, by the way, he said, was a month late. As I started inside the office, Cassie called out after me, "And wipe that goofy smile off your face." She pulled away, heading back to Kasperville for the day.

I opened the door, which wasn't locked. There was nothing there to steal. As the door slid open, it pushed an envelope on the floor that had been dropped through the mail slot. I bent, scooped it up, and opened it. There were keys to a rental car and a note from Jimmy Bravuro: "This is to help you work in mysterious ways your wonders to perform."

I waded through the rubble of what had been my office. It's always a disappointment that cops no longer leave the tape-lined imprint of the corpse on the floor anymore. That would have added to the decor.

Someone had set the desk back upright, but one of its legs was gone. It tilted to one corner. The telephone was shattered and pieces were spread along one wall. The scattered small bits of what had once been handsome—and valuable—Indian relics littered the floor in small smashed piles.

People with any Indian background like to bring up the famous Trail of Tears every now and then—when the remnants of Native Americans who survived the Indian Wars were forced to march to reservations in Oklahoma, many dying along the way. The path I made through the debris that had been my office and home had many parallels. I thought I might be able to salvage a razor and a toothbrush in the back, but it was, if anything, worse back there. I did find a broom that still worked. I took off my jacket, rolled up my sleeves, and started sweeping up the broken glass of my bathroom mirror and everything else that had been destroyed.

I made several trips out to the Dumpster with loads of broken stuff until the inside of my home was empty except for the scarred desk with no drawers, which I was able to prop upright with a few bricks. Then I got into the rental car and drove to the Banana Bay Trading Company, our local army surplus home decoration center, where I was able to pick up a new cot and a couple of army blankets. I stopped at a drugstore on the way back, where I got a small mirror to hang on the wall to facilitate shaving.

I showered, shaved, lay down on my cot for ten minutes to initiate the homestead. Then I got up, dressed, and drove toward the Bolens' residence.

Max Bolens had done well for himself in the matter of putting a roof over his head. I passed through wrought-iron gates, through a flower-lined sprawling lawn on a paved lane, and pulled up in front of a home that could have housed one of the members of England's royal family.

Audrey Bolens answered the door herself, which is always a surprise in a home that had to have more than a dozen bedrooms. She might have been a mousy little woman once, but after a few makeovers she looked pert and attractive. I had watched her evolution in the newspaper clippings I read as I'd progressed in the datelines through the Bolens' files. It seemed that the more money Max made, the better looking she became.

"What is it?" she said, giving me the hairline to shoe-strings eye sweep that sized me up. She relaxed when she dismissed the possibility of my being a cop, perked up as she figured me for a salesman of some sort.

"Come on in," she said before I answered.

I followed her in. The air felt cooler and pleasant inside. The foyer had been designed to overwhelm—it was a vast opening that led to a spiral staircase that went up three floors. Audrey veered left, went past open rooms that looked like a library, billiard room, and a room that opened into a glass-encased area with plants and its own pool that connected with the outdoor pool. Outside I could see someone's wet tanned arms lifting out of the pool in precise sweeps. Looked like a bikini and goggles from here—probably the daughter, Donna.

Audrey sat down on a cushioned wicker sofa. A glass end table separated her seat from the chair I sat in.

"Come over here," she patted the seat beside her. Her smile was playful, a little sultry.

She had pixie-short blonde hair and the face I'd called pert. In the pictures of her with her daughter, she looked like the younger of the two. The daughter had always managed a photogenic moment where her mouth hung partially open. She looked barely sharp enough to put in a light bulb with good clear instructions in hand.

"I've just got a few questions."

"Okay," she said. "I'll come over there." She rose and walked to me, spun and dropped into my lap. She felt lighter than I expected, and even up close she was very attractive. She smelled good, though from a perfume I didn't know on a first-name basis. I can't say that I felt comfortable with the arrangement.

Her eyes were radiant blue, her nose slightly upturned, and

her complexion smooth. She may never have been a cheerleader in school, but she made up for it by looking and acting like one now. Behind the giggling exterior there were years of knowledge. She was measuring my discomfort.

I couldn't just push her off, nor could I ignore her squirming. I left my hands on the arms of the chair.

She twisted around to look close into my face. Over her shoulder I could see her slim twenty-five-year-old daughter Donna step out of the pool and reach for a towel. When she stood, she stared at us.

I watched the daughter shake her head, wrap the towel around herself, and start for the house.

Audrey got off me. She stood in front of me and looked down at me. This time her laugh was genuine.

"Okay," she said. "You pass."

"I didn't know it was a test," I said.

"All of life is a test," she said. She walked back over to the wicker sofa. Before she sat, she said, "Can I get you anything? Coffee? Brandy and soda?"

"Coffee and brandy would be great," I said with a voice too scratchy to be my own.

When she came back to the sunny glassed-in room, she still chuckled to herself. "You'd be surprised the number of people who've been surfing the Internet and think they come across some compromising pictures of me. I've heard a lot of different pitches. Most of them, the ones from men and even a few from women, have me pegged for easy or in an awkward position they can take advantage of. You're a refreshing and different package."

So was the brandy, I could have said. I put down the whole snifter load and added a sip of coffee to it.

"Most people sip brandy," she said.

"Probably have more time than I do." That got another

chuckle from her. Everything I said struck her as funny now.

"You want to know if the pictures were real, don't you?" Her eyes glittered.

I usually ask most of the questions myself, but I was going to have to get cracking to take the lead. "Were they?"

"Of course. How they got out of my keeping, into someone else's hands, and onto the Web is another story. As for why Max and I are still together, relationships have to weather more than that these days. Most people know that, though you may not. You're not married, are you?"

She was one of those extroverted people who feel they can bowl strangers over with intimate detail. Maybe I seemed like the kind of guy who would be uncomfortable with that. Well, I was.

I said, "That's not what I came to talk about. I'm a private detective."

She shrugged, as if I had said I was the brush salesman after all. "What does bring you here? The militia business, or Don Briscoe's untimely demise?"

I nodded. "Both. Briscoe died in my office. The cops tell me he was stomped to death by men wearing boots." They had confirmed my initial impression. "That suggests something to me. Does it to you?"

"I guess it's supposed to. Could someone have faked that part of it?"

"Maybe. But it'd be a lot of bother, and for what? A guy like Briscoe wasn't going to hold still. He was twisted like a pretzel and jumped on by, like I said, more than one pair of boots. You know anyone who would want to choreograph that?"

"When you put it that way. . . ."

"Who's the hunky fresh meat?" The voice came from the doorway.

Donna stood among us. Her wet blonde hair lay pressed

along her neck and back. She had wrapped her towel around herself like a sarong. Even in person her mouth hung open— another of life's open-mouth breathers. She looked pretty, in the way that the young and not-so-innocent can, though she was no match for her mother. Perhaps that's the way mom wanted it.

A small dog tiny enough to be a hairless rat followed her into the room, stayed at her heel for a moment, then sprinted across the room and sprang into Audrey's lap.

"It's the private detective, dear. The one in whose office Don Briscoe died. He's here detecting."

"I could tell, Mom. You didn't pick his pocket or anything, did you?"

Audrey ignored that. To me she said, "I don't know where your investigation's going, but I gather you think Max is a suspect. I want you to take one thing with you. Max is a lot of things. But he's no killer. Not a good one, anyway."

"Oh, Mom." Donna threw a pout Audrey's way.

I had come here with a lot of questions I wasn't getting to ask. But the answers were floating around.

"You can imagine that by now we've been grilled by all manner of people. You would think that Max's position would ensure cushion from all that. It seems to have only made matters worse. You've heard that Donna may end up in the Witness Protection Program?"

"Have there been any attempts to stop her from talking by the . . . the people with whom. . . ."

"Skinheads?" Donna said. "Paramilitaries? Neo-Nazis? Aryan Resistance? Is that what you were going to say? Like everyone else. They're just militia, good country folk keeping honed to protect their homeland. That's all." Her voice had gone up an octave to what might be able to cut glass.

"Have any of these . . . militia tried to get to you?"

"Of course they have. You may not have noticed it, but this place is crawling with goons—you know, the cop type. Oh, I know, you can't see 'em. But they're all around here like termites." She had a way of sounding like she was chewing gum even when she wasn't.

Audrey looked at her the way a mother will, one who is sorry about the way Donna turned out, but sorrier that it may mean she will no longer be able to see her or be around her. "Donna, are you sure you don't have more swimming to get in?"

The girl shared a bemused frown as she watched her mother twist in her chair a couple of times until she was comfortable.

"Come on, Mom. Look at you squirm. What's the matter with you? Is your thong on backwards?"

"My thong is just fine, dear." Audrey turned to me. "You can't imagine all the various kinds of people who've talked with us in the past few weeks about one damned thing and another. It's turned this whole thing into something of a game for us."

Some game.

Donna had more to say. "Yeah, I make one lousy call to Dial-A-Racist, next thing I know I'm courted into joining the feds in the great fight against the White Aryan Resistance—that's WAR, not the folks I was with at all. Oh, Mom, don't give me *the face.* This stuff's already come out in the trial. Anyway, this guy I kinda had a relationship with for a while wasn't really interested in being in a relationship. But he *was* sexy. First time I meet him he's shoving his hands down my dress. I think, well, he's up to something else. It don't hit me till later he's looking for wires."

She, like her mother, was uncomfortably forthcoming without much encouragement. The acorn had not fallen far from the tree.

"Well, young lady," Audrey said, "that's thirty on that. I think Mr. Whatever-the-hell-his-name-is has gotten all we should share." She turned to me with a bright smile, "Don't you?"

"Sure," I said. "I've got to go peek in some keyholes."

Audrey let me out the front door, and when I turned to go to my rental, Max Bolens was getting helped out of a limo. He spotted me and came striding over to me.

"I heard you were here," he said. "Does this mean . . . ?"

"That my investigation is going on?" I said. "It sure does. I still have plenty of clients."

"But, Don Briscoe. . . ."

"Is as dead as your hopes of hiring me." I climbed in the car and pulled out of the drive. I could see him standing in the driveway staring after me.

It had been so long since I'd been in a car with all of its parts working that it didn't dawn on me until two more blocks to turn on the air conditioner. I knew what bugged me. All my life I've gone out on a limb for cases where prejudice was the bottom line. But there was no other way for me to identify the way I felt about Max other than I had judged him in advance. I may well be as big a bigot as the people I most often worked against. I was going to have to work on my thing about Max; that and this little thing I had going against Volvos.

I decided that the last thing my restored office needed to bring it fully back up to speed was a new office bottle, so I stopped on the way home and splurged on a fresh liter of one-hundred-percent blue agave. I hummed to myself as I pulled up to the office in my frosty cool car. I may have been nearly broke, and getting nowhere visible on the case, but I had a new cot at home and had made a nice ride through the city getting home.

It didn't hit me until I had pulled up near my door to wonder what pretty, airheaded, and potentially racist Donna would have thought of me if she had known I was part-Indian. I guess my blue eyes had gotten me past finding out.

155

I got out of the car, and blinked in the sunlight.

"What you need is a fistful of cigars," a voice said. I turned, saw Hal climb out of his car. Nothing like a friend to bring you back to earth with a bit of wooden Indian humor, especially one who you're halfway thinking is involved himself. He walked toward me, rubbing his hands briskly together.

"How long have you been waiting on me?"

"Let's go inside," he said. He looked up and down the street.

Once inside, he said, "I like what you've done with the place. Neat and Spartan."

I put the bag holding the new office bottle on the desk. "Sorry to say, your last gift didn't make it through the little excitement I had here."

"They hit Bent Lenny's place today," he said, getting right to it. I could tell something was crawling under his skin. I gave him the chance to share it.

He said, "After sitting outside his place for days, the feds finally pop the warrant on him. He's not there, but they go tearing inside, find the place clean as a pin and empty of anything they can use against him."

"Don't they have a paper trail?" I asked. I unscrewed the top off the bottle, then realized my good crystal—in my case, former dried-beef jars—was broken and gone. Hal gave me a shake of his head, so I had a sip out of the bottle.

"They needed the money that was being laundered," Hal said. "Without it, their case isn't nearly as good."

"Any ideas?"

"I don't know. Someone could've gotten the money out of the house by a second-story window," Hal said. "They found the end of a steel cable clipped into a bolt that looks like it was shot out of some kind of crossbow, or something. Everybody watching the place was focused on the front and back doors. None of the 'how' of it matters. The money's been removed."

"You think Lenny's militia pals helped him get the money and any evidence out of there?" I said.

Hal patted his jacket pocket. "After you distracted the feds staking out the warehouse," he said, "the rest of the deal went down. I followed some of them out to Mt. Bonnell. They use it as a meeting spot when it's very late. Bent Lenny was there. He must've slipped away from the feds, maybe the same way that whoever helped him got the money out of the house. Who knows? Anyway, I have pictures of the meeting."

"Nothing you can run in the paper, huh?"

"Not just yet. But here's the ticklish part. Neither the feds nor the local cops have been able to locate Bent Lenny. The pictures I took document the last time he was ever seen."

"You've got to share those with the cops," I said, "or the feds. It's withholding if you don't."

"Right. And have every one of the militia in Austin and this part of the state gunning for me." He trembled as he pulled an envelope out of his pocket. "I'm right on top of a really big change in my life, Trav. This is the story that's going to make me. Be with me on this, old pal. These are the negs. Do you think you can hide them somewhere for me?"

"Sure, I'll just put them in my office safe. Are you crazy, Hal? Look at my place. Anyone with a crowbar can pop my window and come in."

"It doesn't have to be here. Somewhere else, maybe. Please?" His eyes darted back and forth to each corner of the room. His head made restless birdlike motions. I'd known Hal a while, but had never seen him this nervous, not even when his world fell apart after his paparazzi dream crumbled.

There was a lot I wanted to ask Hal, but wired as he was, this was not the time. I reached for the envelope. If I could hide them anywhere, he could do the same, unless he feared he might not be around to find them again later. "You think they're onto you?"

"I don't know, Trav." His voice quivered. "Let's hope not." For once he forgot to rub his hands. His arms hung down loose at his sides. He stared ahead with blank eyes, like a deer just before the pop of the rifle.

CHAPTER FIFTEEN

It took me all of thirty minutes to hide Hal's negatives. I drove to the Post Office building on Sixth Street, bought a pre-stamped envelop, addressed it to Huff, put in the negs and dropped the envelope in the right slot. On the short drive back to the office I pondered why Hal hadn't done something as simple.

Cassie's car was parked outside my office when I got back. I went inside and found her sitting on the corner of the desk.

"Lock didn't slow you down, or anything, did it?" I asked.

"Credit card," she said. "You might think about a dead bolt. But none of it matters much if someone thinks to put a boot to that plywood. That's all that stands between you and the great outdoors."

"I've thought of just having a screen put in this time, let more air flow through," I said. I eyed the bottle in its sack sitting on the desk. I didn't want to be too obvious about slipping over and putting another dent in its contents. That was the homecoming chore that preyed on my mind most.

"I saw the new cot and toiletries," she said. "You aren't thinking of staying here, tonight, are you? You're wearing a bull's-eye on your forehead right now you wouldn't believe."

When I didn't answer, she said, "What are you thinking of doing? Checking out what's going on at that warehouse later tonight? I know you still have Huff's nightscope in my trunk. Well, you're not going there unless I go along. Alvin's my case," she said. Her mouth was set tight. She gave me an unflinching stare.

I sighed. "I've got a couple of chores you can help with this afternoon, if you want."

"Travis, I swear I don't know what you're up to. All you were hired to do is find out who's trying to kill Texas women with strong characters. Why don't you leave finding Alvin to me, and the rest of his militia pals to the feds?"

I ambled to the desk, kept it casual as I reached for the sack. She moved the bottle away. "Answer me," she said. "Hey, you. Anyone in there?"

I felt a blank look settle onto my face. I turned and sat on the other corner of the desk. I looked down at the stained and scarred floor.

"You know or suspect more than you're saying. Why is that?"

I blinked, but didn't answer.

"Don't you think that for just this once you could work as a team?"

"When I was in the service," I said, "it was my job to go in and get others—the wounded ones. That's all I did, whether they were hanging from some cliff, washed up along a stream, or in the middle of a firefight. Guys who did what I was doing didn't always last long. But I was lucky, I guess. I worked paired with a fellow named Spence. The two copter guys were Jason and Augie. I thought they were lower life forms, all three of them, when I got there. Back then I still had a lot of edges. We went out on a dozen missions before I relaxed with knowing what each of them would do, what they could be counted on for . . . that they *could* be counted on. It hit me at about the same time that I was as much of a ticking bomb for them as they were to me. Once that soaked in we all relaxed, did our jobs; went out, came back in—spattered blood on the inside of the copter and on us. Sometimes the guys we pulled out made it. I don't even know what our final count would've been for the year and a half we worked together."

"Do you miss them?" she asked. "Do you keep in touch?"

I could see me carrying one guy, running down the hill from the copter. He hung from my arms, flopped around, legs and arms swaying far too loosely. Spence had just run up to get another out. He was even worse, so Augie and Jason were helping. The explosion was so big it blew me flat to the ground where I was running. I didn't come to until later that evening. The guy I'd been carrying hadn't made it. Neither had Augie, Jason or Spence.

"Yeah, I miss 'em," I said. "But no, we don't keep in touch." Did that make me think everyone I would ever work with on a team would die? I don't know. I just knew I had always sought to work alone since.

"Man, you're strung out. Let me find you a glass somewhere."

"You'll be a long hunt finding a glass. Everything here's been trashed." I went the route of a shortcut and slid the bottle over and unscrewed the cap.

"So, what's your daytime plan, Trav?"

"I want to go talk with Johnny Gringo," I said. "I don't feel good about this whole mess. It's tangled and is hopping all over the place. I can't get a feel for anyone in it, or even those helping. I never talked with Trish Mirandez, spent only a minute or two with Tori Brice. I've had to read secondhand reports, for the most part, and I never got near Bent Lenny. I have had some contact with the militia, and I don't mind telling you that they scare me."

"They should."

"I just need to get a better handle here. What about you?"

"I'm here to find Alvin, to deal with a homicide that *does* belong to our department. There's not much mystery to mine. It's just roundup."

161

"We might as well go together," I said. "I seem to draw these guys like flies to the sugar bowl."

"Oh, geez, Trav. You can't go out there with those sad eyes and tiny violins in your head."

"Saxophone," I said, "or sometimes a muted trumpet."

"Whatever. Come here." She reached over for a hug. The next thing I knew, buttons were being opened, pale smooth skin was coming to light, and I was being led to the back room.

I'll say this for the U.S. military. They make one sturdy cot.

I drove the rental car down into South Austin. Cassie sat in the passenger seat. I glanced at her from time to time, still not sure what to make of her. She never wore makeup, or needed to. Her face was so round, so clean, so wholesome. She was the kind of person you could imagine growing up, being a young girl once, excited about Christmas, all that. When you've bounced through life the way I have, appearances are the starting point for wrong conclusions.

Everything I had seen, heard, and sensed so far told me it would be very easy for her to be a fed. What the hell kind of cover would being a deputy sheriff be? Would her infiltration be to know more about Alvin and his crew? I'd seen how that had gone. I saw her glance in the mirror on her side a few times. I'm pretty good at spotting a tail, and didn't cop to the hint of one.

Johnny Gringo's place was a trailer hanging close enough to a creek that the next big rain, if it ever came, was going to sweep the young singer in the direction of the Rio Grande. I beat on the door a couple of times.

The door finally cracked open, and Johnny Gringo, with tousled hair and wearing a T-shirt that had more holes in it than some alibis I've heard, stuck his head through the crack. Though it was mid-day, it was clear that my visit had served as a wake-up call. That's what I expected of someone in what Jimmy Bravuro calls "the biz."

"You're Travis, the something-or-other Indian," he said, with all that charm I recalled from the tent so well. "I remember you." He eyed Cassie, but didn't ask.

"Can we come in?" I asked.

Johnny Gringo glanced back over his shoulder, then back to us. "She's still asleep. Flew here all the way from Nashville to catch up, and I didn't get home from my gig until four or five in the morning. I better come out there. Just a minute."

He came out into the sunlight wearing a faded light-green corduroy bathrobe. He carried a pair of boots and sat on the step to shove his bare feet into them. He hadn't bothered to do a thing to his hair.

"I guess I owe you some thanks," he said to me. "Dutch and Jimmy said you were looking into my situation with Lenny. What d'you think's up with that now? Anyone seen Lenny?"

"The cops haven't," I said.

"What happens to the money I owe if he never shows?" Johnny Gringo looked down, let his eyes roll slowly back up to mine. "I mean, you know, I wouldn't want anything to happen to him, but if it did. . . ."

"That depends on the paperwork and who would handle it, if we're talking about an heir here. You have any reason to believe he might not be . . . alive?"

"No. No, I don't. And don't think I still don't think I owe him. I mean besides the money. You know, a European label liked one of the cuts on my CD so well that they want to cut a release for distribution there. That's for those who don't just download it onto an iPod or something. You don't think I'm going to be in a tangle about the rights, do you?"

"You better ask your pals in the music biz," I said. "You'll let me know if you hear from Lenny, won't you."

"Sure," he said. "Sure thing."

I started to turn away, but there was something else in his face. "What?" I said.

"Oh, it's this whole music business *thang*. You can't imagine. Night after night, gig after damned gig, singing the same music over and over. Tell you the truth, I thought it'd be more . . . well, different. Then to be so close to breaking through and have Lenny come up missing. It's just, you know, hard."

I almost told him that I could feel for him but that I couldn't quite reach him. He'd already spun and clumped his way inside the trailer.

Back in the car, Cassie said, "You think Lenny's dead, don't you. Why?"

I realized I hadn't told her about the negs of the pictures Hal took. I shrugged, concentrated on driving.

"Why'd you want to see Johnny Gringo?" she asked. "Is it because the case involving him got you into all this? You thought Johnny Gringo might be involved in a setup somehow, didn't you?"

"Maybe I kind of hoped that. He has no particular reason to like me, and that cuts both ways. But he's not involved. I know that now. It's a comfort to have at least one small thing that I can eliminate from the confusion at this point. I don't believe Johnny Gringo has any way at all of knowing what I'm in now, or why. I'm not so sure myself."

I drove west out of the city, heading back out to the Hill Country.

Cassie leaned back in her seat, looked out the window. Halfway to Huff's place, she said, "You've done the detective thing a long time. And you've been on this for a few days. What's your gut tell you about who made the tries on the women?"

"You mean if I had to make a bet right now?"

"Yeah, with just what you have."

"My money would have to be on Max," I said.

She snapped upright in her seat, looked at me. "Max Bolens? The Congressman, Max Bolens?"

"The same," I said. "It's been almost too obvious from the first."

"How do you get that?"

"I'll share my five-cent version of detective hypothesis: when you've exhausted all the logical solutions, try the next possibility, however illogical."

"That's a cheap paraphrase of Sherlock Holmes. And your hypothesis is thin. What'd you do, grab it from the air?"

"There's the obvious opportunity issue. He was at the same places as the tries every time. The Kasperville Folk Festival, which isn't like him, and the ribbon cutting with Jayne, which is."

"What about the Constitutional Club shooting at Tori Brice?"

"He was speaker at Palmer Auditorium an hour earlier, not five minutes from the Constitutional Club."

"And he was done in time for the shooting?"

"Just barely."

"Where did you get this?"

"He gave it to me, may have known I'd find out anyway and was trying to throw me off. He wanted to hire me."

"I can't believe this. What's the motive?"

"That's where we loop back to your woman-hater profile."

"Max hates women?"

"He might. His wife confirmed that there are photos of her naked with another man on the Internet. Max's daughter is wrapping up her rebel-without-a-cause phase in a very colorful and public way. He might be a little down on women. Then Hal finds Max's name on the client list of a woman who has top CEOs and political people scrubbing floors with toothbrushes to even out their secret feelings about women or something. I'm not the profiler you aspire to be, but someone who tries that kind of service might be wrestling with woman problems."

"It's all so incredible. It does fall together and hold up, just a bit. Is there anything solid to back this up?"

"I'm not saying that absolutely, positively this is the way it is," I said. "It's just the way it leans at this second. You know about investigations."

"Max Bolens," she said, shaking her head.

The sun was slipping into the rolling green tree-covered hills as we pulled into Huff's lane. Some of the critters in the Huff camp were beginning to stir. It was too early for the armadillo, but I saw the roadrunner goose-stepping its way across the front of the house at a good clip.

Before we got out of the car, I said to Cassie, "You know how before you go into the morgue. . . ."

"Yeah. You rub some Vicks up into your nose so you can't smell the corpse."

"You think that might . . . ?"

She didn't let me finish. "He's your buddy. You have the close conversations with him this time. I'll take my chances with whatever animals are loose in there."

Huff swung the door open and waved us in. The lights were on and he'd made a rough stab at cleaning the living room, enough so that there were places to sit. Cassie headed for a chair with a sheet over it and no animals visible.

I said, "Can we take a look at that disk I left with you, Huff? You *can* look inside it, can't you?"

He pursed his lips at me. "Trav, Trav, Trav. Ye of little faith. Of course, I can." He led the way to a back room where computer terminals lined the wall. By the time I had tripped over a tangle of wires that sprawled across the floor, he had the disk in and was scanning its contents.

"What're you after?"

"A client list for this woman in Austin. I'll know it when I see it. Hal showed it to me back at the newspaper office."

"Then why do you want to see it now?"

"There. That's it," I said. "Now, scroll down."

"Who are these guys? Fat cats? I know a name or two—some are top dogs in high-tech industry there, software as well as semiconductor."

"Stop right there," I said. "It should be there."

"What?"

"Max Bolens' name. But it's not."

"But it was on the one Hal showed you? That can't be, Trav. These are exact copies."

In my excitement I had leaned too close and got a full load of Huff's personality—a whiff of his toxic breath that I'm pretty sure melted my nostril hairs. I didn't faint, but wished I had.

"They sure enough *were* exact copies once," I said when I could speak again. "That's one thing I wanted to come out and check on."

"What's the other?"

"You haven't gotten any contact from the feds, have you? Felt them checking over your communications or anything? I'm sure you could sense something like that."

"I can, and haven't," he said. He moved closer since I had taken a step or two back. "You think something you're working on might have drawn their attention to me?"

"That, or someone I'm working with."

"You worried about her?" He nodded toward the living room.

"I'm worried about you. I don't want anything I do to compromise you."

"Want me to find out what I can on her? I know it isn't like the old days. Firewalls are thicker than ever at the Bu and ATF. You can't begin to believe the reverse spike you could get from even nosing around the CIA. But there are easy ways to scope a person. That's gonna be one of the biggest concerns of the coming decade—the amount of info available on a person. Lawyers for big corporations like oil companies already know and use it. States don't help. They get revenue from selling Bureau of Motor Vehicle information. Most states generate ten million dollars a year or more off that kinda thing, so they aren't going to say no to that. I can also get you phone records, credit and financial data, and any amount of personal profile information, even more if she's ever surfed the Internet."

"I hope I never get so far in PI work I need to go that route, even about something like this."

"Then you don't want me to check her out?"

Huff was strung tight as a wire where it came to people, and had a way of knowing things without my ever knowing how. I said, "I did that by coming here. If she was fed, you'd have noticed some kind of contact or surveillance. You haven't."

"Just as well," Huff muttered. "Never could get to picturing you in bed with a fed."

CHAPTER SIXTEEN

Cassie stayed silent all the way back out to the car, even when something furry and difficult to identify rocketed past her legs. She gave a little jump as it went by, but didn't comment.

I could feel her tensing up over in the passenger seat. Two miles down the road, headlights on and cutting through the growing darkness, she said, "You know, Huff would make a lousy poker player."

I let that hang in the air for half a mile. I finally said, "Too bad you were never in such a frosty mood when I was driving the car that wasn't air-conditioned."

"You know damn well what's bugging me," she said. "When Huff came out of that room, doing whatever it was you two were doing back there. . . ."

"I think you can rule out French kissing."

". . . he acted differently. She cast a sideways glance at me. You know. You had to see him. You miss very little." When I didn't respond, she said, "Trav, you know him. He's one of the last honest men in America. Until now, I thought you were another."

"Not saying anything's not lying."

"It is too. It's lying by omission. You know that." Her voice went up half an octave.

"Gosh," I said. "Our first squabble." I didn't feel as light-spirited as I sounded.

"Don't try to sweet-talk your way out of it. What was said

back there?"

"Oh, nothing. Let it go."

"Where do you get off by being twisted tight? I'm the one who should be pissed off here."

"It's what wasn't said," I answered. "Huff offered to check on your background, to see if you were a government snoop. I declined the offer."

She ran silent and deep for only a second or two. I didn't hear any steam coming out her ears, but I could sense the explosion building. She spoke in a rush. "Oh, it's okay to sleep with me. But you're still hung up on the idea that I might be on the other side. Is that usually the only women who'll have anything to do with you?" Her voice got louder.

"As a matter of fact it is." I should have said nothing. I knew better—that giving any answer at all to this topic was to head in the direction where madness lies.

"Don't even start to say it." She clammed up and sat with her arms folded across her chest, huffing and staring out her window for a few miles. I let her stew. Every mile or so I'd look her way, get what I expected to see: a clenched jaw, her staring away from me. Instead, she seemed calmer than I expected.

"You know," she said at last, "I have to confess something."

"What?"

"I ran a background check on you."

"You what?" I felt a warm flush run up the back of my own neck.

"It was S.O.P., Trav. You were out there. We ran the same on Jimmy Bravuro, all your other buddies too."

"And?"

"You know, there's not too much on you to find out."

"Oh?"

"You've been a lot of places, and only one or two people talked. I thought I'd never get those Pima contacts to quit talking about how you managed to get a kidney dialysis machine for a little girl there."

"Regular saint, aren't I."

"Kid around, but it impressed me, more than you'll know."

"I'm not out to impress anyone."

"You were a foundling, weren't you?"

"A what?" There was a hitch in my voice. I knew what she meant.

"Someone left you at the reservation. You really don't know all that much about your own background, do you?" Her voice was soft, careful. Just a few ticks ago I had thought she was going to explode on me, now I wished she would talk about anything but this.

She gave me a minute or so to respond. When I didn't, she said, "Why Woodgrow?"

"What?"

"Your official records show just Travis Doe, but the tribe elders had it changed to Woodgrow. Why?"

"Just trying to be funny, I guess."

"What's funny about that?"

"They were Miami Indians, run out of Ohio and Indiana years ago. Little Turtle signed the Treaty of Greenville after General 'Mad' Anthony Wayne defeated the combined tribes at the Battle of Fallen Timbers. The Wyandot, Delaware, Shawnee, Ottawa, Chippewa, Potawami, Wea, Kickapoo, Eel River, Piankashaw, and Kaskaskia tribes were all involved too. By the terms of the treaty they were guaranteed the right to hunt the bulk of the western portion of their lands 'as long as the woods grow and the waters run.' Of course, history pretty much sums up how *that* went."

"I'm sorry."

"That was a long time ago, late eighteenth century. No reason to be sorry. At least they can joke about it with a name like

Woodgrow."

"I mean about nosing around in your background, when you respected mine. You're a very private man about that sort of thing."

"Let it go," I said. I glanced in the rearview mirror, more than anything to see if my face looked as warm as it felt.

She stayed silent for a few more miles before she finally stirred again. "We came all the way out here," she said, "and what do we have to show for it? You gave Huff his night-vision scope back. But other than that?"

I sighed. "We know it wasn't Max now," I said. Saying it made me sadder than I could believe.

"What?" She sat up in her seat, turned to stare at me.

"What I told you on the way out here, about Max; that was my straw dog. I didn't really believe that, though it would be nice if that's the way it was. All the time I had a nagging hunch in a different direction."

"What do you mean? You can't know who it is. I've been going right along and know everything you do."

"Let's talk about journalists for a minute, the ones who try to cause news instead of just report it, and I mean going all the way back to the William Randolph Hearst school of media, back when some say he blew up the *Maine* to get America into the Spanish-American War, a war that cost two hundred eighty thousand American lives."

"That's conspiracy theory crap," Cassie snorted. "Where're you going with it?"

"Whether the incident happened, or not, we're still talking about a kind of thing called 'yellow journalism'—sensationalism. You watch TV and read the papers enough and you might think that the lunatic fringe these days *is* the media."

"What the hell are you going on about now?" Cassie pushed herself away from me until the back of her head was pressed against the passenger window.

"You've seen TV announcers who shove the mike in someone's face and ask the person being interviewed if it wasn't time he announced his retirement, or made a public apology for something that happened years ago."

"Trav, you're scaring me, and not making a whole lot of sense."

There must have been a burr of passion in my voice. I could feel myself heating up. My words grew crisper. "This has been an unusually confusing and tangled mess for me. What I was having trouble getting a hook on was the common element."

"Hating women?"

"No. The common element was *him*. He was on hand to investigate each of the attempts. All the news that happened was not just coincidental to Max being present. He was there too."

"Who?" Cassie shouted. "You're going to have to be clearer than that. And what was that detail you were talking about that changed everything? You don't really have a clue about any of this, do you? That's what's so hard to admit."

"Forget it," I said. "It's something that's been gnawing at me from the first, a hunch I fought against. You'd better let me lance this boil myself."

"No. You've gone this far. What is it that makes you think you have any kind of a solution that makes sense of what you admit is a confusing mess?"

I sighed, glanced at her. "When you and I were at the newspaper office with Hal," I said, "I think Hal typed in Max's name, adding it to the client list."

"Hal? Your good friend Hal? Oh, come on, Trav. Get out of here. This is a huge stretch for me. All it does is change Max's being on the list. What about the other stuff?"

"Like Max being a woman hater? We don't know that. I'll be first to admit that I didn't buy all the way into that woman-hater profile stuff."

"Didn't buy into it?" Cassie's voice crackled with indignity.

I said, "Any chances of that kind of psychological profile paying off were diffused by Hal providing what he thought would be useless steers. If I hadn't stumbled onto Carol Myller and brought back a disk I wouldn't have caught onto the one detail that's changed all my thinking, confirmed my worst earlier suspicions."

"That it was Hal making the attempts? That he didn't mean to kill anyone, only get a whopping story, and maybe at the same time point any blame at Max. This is lame, Trav, and beneath you."

I went as silent as the cigar-store Indian Hal had accused me of being. The quiet filled the car for another mile before Cassie spoke.

"Trav, you're not making any sense. Why would Hal want to set up Max Bolens for attempted murder?"

"You remember when we were looking over the Max Bolens files, and the ones about his daughter being tangled up with paramilitary types?"

"Yeah."

"You remember seeing any née part about Audrey Bolens?"

"Where're you going with this?"

"I mean, in all the other newspaper files we looked at, or any others I've ever seen, there's always as much genealogy as they can cram in. There was nothing on Audrey."

"You think her maiden name was . . . ?"

"Jansen," I said. "It won't be too hard to confirm it once we're back to town."

"But Hal's motive? I mean, we are talking about a murder case."

"The murder itself was an accident, far more so than the murder Alvin committed. And remember, framing Max, and getting payback there, is just an added bonus, if this is the way things went. Being on the front seat of a story that could get Hal some recognition is far greater. I've known Hal for a while. He's always been a straight shooter with me. But he's had his head down for twenty-five years doing a job he's obsessed by. Would he do something like this—now—if he had a chance to get a breakthrough story that would put his career back on the map? Hell, yes. As for fingering Max, even if it's only to smear him, that would be like icing on the cake for someone who's slipped over the edge enough to orchestrate the attempts on women. Who's to say that's not long enough to crack, or that he's not someone who likes his revenge served cold. When I ask myself if he could be patient enough and manipulative enough to do things right, I have to say yes."

She looked at me as if I might bite. You start talking about one of your best friends being a killer, being a manipulator of Machiavellian proportions, and people are going to look at you strange. It's going to happen. Expect it.

"There's one other little bit," I said. "One that's hard to shake off. As soon as I waved an even juicier story within range of Hal's nose for news, all the attempts on women stopped, as did any mention of Max Bolens. If Hal wasn't the one behind the attempts, that is one of the damnedest coincidences I ever ran across."

She tried to force her voice to a calmer level, but didn't quite hit it. "But he's your friend. Shouldn't you at least *ask* him before flying to such an elaborate conclusion?"

"I intend to. We're going there as soon as we get to town. His hunger for a big break should be obvious to you. As for having it in for Max, think about this, Cassie. You're the psychologist. Hal's sister Audrey is shamed publicly. His niece goes off the edge. Some of his own failed entrepreneurial spin may have been caused by his sister. At the least it would be hard to see her live in style while he scrambles. What do you think?"

"Put like that it's within a long grab of plausible. *If* I was prone to grab. I wonder more about you having this stewing in your head all this time."

"I've met the two ladies in question," I said. "If Hal has any of their genes in his blood, he could be screwier than he acts."

I glanced at Cassie, thought she looked less convinced than I was.

She said, "Is it your theory that Hal's maybe crying out for help, like people who nearly commit suicide? Was this all a scheme to get caught and exposed? Or, do you think he's just an incompetent killer. Do you really think he's dippy or desperate enough to orchestrate attempted murders for heightened news stories, with exposing Max as the villain up his sleeve as a revenge?"

"I don't know what to think. The hardest part, if all this holds up, is that he's been using me for a dupe from the get-go. All I have is that everything points toward him, including my instincts. Hal's little trick of putting Max's name on the ZIP disk is the hard bit that makes it more that just a solid hunch." My insides felt torn up enough without trying to explain it.

Cassie said, "I hate to put it this way, but Hal does fit our profile much better than Max, if all you've said is true."

"In what way?"

"I mean Max is aggressive—there's no mistaking that. Hal is passive-aggressive. Whoever is making the attacks on the women is more likely someone like that, someone who had things build up, then snapped and went amuck. Even if all he did was frame Max. On top of that, Max has fame, of a sort. The pattern we've got suggests someone who's obscure, and not happy about it."

I nodded, frowning ahead at the road.

"Oh, Trav. I'm sorry if you're right. Hal. Of all people. If it's true, I'm so sorry."

"Don't think I like talking about Hal like this," I said. "I hope to hell I'm wrong. But Hal is a soul in torment or conflict if I ever saw one. He wants the fame and glory he never got, and he may hate women, just like you said—at least he would his sister. He might hate Max more, if he's been rubbing salt in Hal's wound, and that kind of thing fits with the Max I know."

"Okay," she said. "But you're still going to confront him and give him a chance to explain, aren't you?"

"Of course."

"Trav?"

"Yeah?"

"I'm sorry about being a little ticked off earlier. You must be pretty rattled. Hal's one of your few friends, isn't he?"

"He is that," I said.

"You know," she said, "you're sure an enigma. Friendship isn't just something you have. It's *all* you have."

Hal's small brick place was on Shoal Creek, in another of those pocket communities within Austin where you might expect to pay two hundred fifty thousand dollars for eighty thousand dollars' worth of house. One reason was the proximity to Tarrytown, where professors from the university liked to live in cozy stone houses with architecture occasionally reminiscent of Europe. Tarrytown's where James Michener lived, and one actor of significant fame had been arrested for being naked and playing the bongos in his living room at three A.M., something the locals said would have been okay down there in bohemian South Austin, but didn't sail up here among the less laid-back people. Shoal Creek didn't quite have Tarrytown's tone, and an average person could afford to live here if the house had been bought some time back, as Hal's had.

I'd been there a time or two when in one of his rare moments away from the office, Hal had me over for barbecue. Even though it was dark by the time I turned onto Hal's street, I could tell something was up. Within a block of the place I couldn't go any farther for all the fire trucks.

I got out of the car and, without realizing it, took off running. Cassie called out behind me. I pushed my way through the neighbors and passersby who had come out for a look. Hal's place was on fire, and had been for a while. I could see that as I got close. The roof was gone. Only some of the brick facade along the front of the house still stood. That's not what drew my eye. It was the circle of men setting up that all-too-familiar yellow tape around a spot on the lawn.

"No," I shouted, pushing and shoving my way through the crowd and past a uniformed cop keeping people back from the scene. "Nooo!" I ran toward the group on the lawn, got to them as the cop chasing me grabbed my shoulder and spun me around. I'd had enough time for a quick glimpse of a black charred spot in the grass that the detectives were being careful not to step in.

"Who do you think you are?" The cop had an unrelenting grip on my arm as I tried to turn back and look. He pulled me steadily away.

"Bring him over here," a voice commanded. Borster's. He stood near the yellow tape.

I still puffed when Borster turned from one of the MEs to look at me. Findlay stood there too, watching somebody poke at the charred spot with a stick.

"No," Borster said before I had a chance to speak, "I'm not the only damned homicide detective in the city, though it must seem that way at times. It just happens you're drawn to put your footprints all over cases I've been assigned to handle."

His saying that inspired me to look around. The grass was matted from all the activity. Where I could see anything like an impression, it could have been boot prints. It was hard to say with everyone mucking up the area.

"Is that . . . ?" I said, head bobbing toward the spot. "Is that Hal?"

"We think so," Borster said. He looked where I was looking, but kept me in the corner of his eye as he did. "One of the neighbors saw him early in the bonfire and thought he IDed him. But that could have been part rationalization. It's Hal's house. Who else would it have been? Pal of yours, wasn't he. Too bad you weren't here with some marshmallows on a stick to celebrate his final moments."

I leaped for Borster, and if the uniformed cop hadn't been standing so close with a grip on my arm I'd have had an assault against a policeman on my slate. As it was, the cop holding me yanked me a few steps away from Borster.

Cassie had been flashing badge and screaming her way to us. She came up and got close to Borster's face, yelled up at him, "What do you think you're doing?"

He turned his back to her, stepped away to say something to someone inside the taped circle. Findlay stepped over to keep Cassie from following Borster. When Borster rejoined us, he looked down at Cassie. "I thought we'd covered this thing about jurisdictions earlier. Do I need to refresh you on that?"

She shook her head and said nothing. Findlay and Borster both gave her a mixture of leer and sneer. I couldn't tell whether it was because she was a woman or because she was from a small town's sheriff's department. Not that it mattered. Either stung.

I shouted over the noise going on all around us, "Did anyone get a make on who did this? Was it those militia guys?"

Borster's weathered face twisted into what could be a grin, for him. "Boot marks on the lawn and driveway, broken bat over by where the door was broken down, public beating and burning of a victim? Now, what could make you think such a thing?"

"I'm going to get them, and when I find them. . . ." I recognized the voice screaming, identified it as my own. I shut up and glared.

"Oh, I wouldn't say you have anything to worry about there. Do you, Findlay?"

Findlay put in his oar: "No. You don't have to go after them. These guys—whoever did this—they'll just as likely find you."

I twisted to turn and walk away, heard Borster say, "Let him go."

The claw gripping my sleeve let go. I pushed back through the onlookers. Once through the crowd I broke into a sprint heading for the car. In the distance behind me, I heard, "Trav. Stop. Oh, Travis."

I climbed into the car and spun into a U-turn before Cassie could catch up. The anger and stirred up bile I felt I directed as much at myself as anyone, but that's not who I planned to take it out on. I pushed down on the gas and squealed down the street.

It had gotten late enough that there was little traffic from Hal's place all the way out to the warehouse with the "Mokey's Movers" sign. I noticed and didn't notice that the darkened gravel parking lot was empty as I raced into it and slid into a gravel-throwing skid of a stop. I leaped out of the car, thinking for the first time that I should have brought along Cassie's gun. I opened the trunk, hoping for one of those old-fashioned serious-chunk-of-metal tire irons. Nothing useful there. I looked around and saw a creosote-darkened four-by-four piece of wood over a yard long. I scooped it up and ran for the warehouse's side door, where I'd seen all the in-and-out foot traffic.

I grabbed the door knob. The door was locked. I stepped back and began to hammer at the door with the club. I may have been frothing and a little out of control. I pounded away for a good minute before two pairs of thick hands grabbed me firmly and spun me around.

CHAPTER SEVENTEEN

I sat silent, though still breathing hard, in the front seat this time. The two guys in flak jackets who'd grabbed me were in the backseat. The one formerly in the passenger seat followed us in my rental Toyota. Once again the conversation was as stimulating and provocative as before. Not one of them spoke.

We went down the ramp, slipped into the same parking place. Too bad the FBI doesn't have frequent-visitor points. I got out and joined the group in the elevator. We all went into a foyer. In another minute they ushered me inside Gareth Fields' office. His suspenders were red, and his tie was something in a yellow pattern by Tommy Hilfiger. He looked just as pleased to see me as I was to see him.

"You work long hours," I said. Now that I'd had a chance to cool off a bit I began to realize how foolish I might have looked, and been, in going to that warehouse. My getting kicked around, or killed, wouldn't have helped Hal's memory in the least—might have only added mine to it.

"I thought we had an understanding," he said.

"About what?" I asked.

"This operation I'm heading."

"Were you operating it when some of those paramilitary assholes set fire to Hal Jansen on his own front lawn earlier tonight?"

Gareth's head snapped to one of the men who stood beside me. The guy shot out of the room.

"I meant about staying out of our way, not hindering us in any way, and especially not hammering on the door of that warehouse. Are you on drugs?"

"An aspirin every now and again, but. . . ."

"Shut up. Just shut the mother-humping piss-up-a-rope." His cursing had not improved. He half rose from his chair. Sprinkles of saliva spattered the desktop. What he'd said didn't make total sense, but I caught the mood.

"As you may have observed, the men with whom you were tempting your fate are no longer where you found them before. We think your blundering around there earlier may be partially responsible for that. Their setting up in Southeast Austin, in the heart of the Hispanic and black gang communities, was a defiance move, a confirmation that they were of a strength. They were also there until some sort of deal—which has now gone down. Your actions may well be instrumental in our missing out on some of the details of what that deal was. The men have moved from that site. We're aware of only some, but not all, of the secondary and tertiary locations from which they operate."

"Where . . . ?"

"We are not sharing that information with you now. We don't intend to do so in the future. In fact, we want you to stay away from these men period, no matter where they are. Am I getting through to you this time? We want you off the scene. Out of sight. If you so much as come within a city block of these men I'll do everything in my power to see that you are locked up, out of the PI business, and, if possible, sharing a cell with someone who thinks you have especially pretty eyes and a cute walk. Do you hear me?"

It was once again the wee hours when they let me climb into my rental and cast about in the city for a place to flop. We'd checked out of the La Quinta, so it was hard to tell where Cassie had gone. Her mood might be a little tender, too, since I'd left her behind at Hal's house.

I called a few of the motels I thought she might have switched to, but had no luck. Then I sat in the Kerbey Lane Cafe, a restaurant open twenty-four hours, and alternately drank coffee and made phone calls. I could smell pancakes, maple syrup, bacon and eggs. I stayed away from food to keep awake. By four-thirty in the morning, even the crowd that had flowed in when the bars closed had thinned. I made half a dozen more calls, then tossed in the towel.

All things considered, the best shot I had of finding her, I reasoned, was to go back to my place, which I did. I didn't see her car parked anywhere near the office, though I circled the block a couple of times.

Still, when I pushed the door open at going on five A.M., I called out, "Honey, I'm home." I hit the light switch.

They stood and sat quietly in a circle, waiting. Two of them moved behind me and nudged me farther inside and away from the door. I counted. Eight of them, including Alvin and Donnie. It was a small office, and they filled it.

Much of the tape that had been around Alvin's face earlier had been removed. Thick purple welts ran along both sides of his face. His eyes were the same narrow squints I remembered. What pleased me less was the grin he wore.

"What goes around, comes around," Donnie said. He carried a baseball bat, which looked dirty and scarred from previous use.

The rest of his pals stood and stared, waiting. For the young, tattooed, and beer-drinking lot they were, they showed real patience.

Donnie and a couple of the others facing me began to stalk closer.

"Not here," Alvin said. Glitters of sweat came from between

the folds of skin beneath his eyebrows.

The others grabbed me and towed me toward the door. When the lights were turned off, someone hit me a solid punch in the kidney. Outside, they dragged me to the backseat of a sedan. One of them sat on each side of me. Donnie and Alvin rode in the front seat. The other four crammed into another car that followed us.

Barely a few hours ago I had hoped to find another of the places where these guys hung. Now I had my wish. And it looked like Findlay had been right. I didn't need to chase these guys—they had found me.

There was a fair amount of shouting, kidding, and beer drinking going on during our ride out into a stretch of backwoods. Alvin didn't join in, and I wasn't invited. They seemed to especially enjoy the native side of my heritage. One of the guys in the backseat kept sneaking punches at me, little rabbit jabs to my ear, my face, my ribs. Alvin snapped back at him, like we were kids fighting in the backseat on the way to Disneyland.

Quite a few miles out of town, after weaving through a few back roads into a part of the county where I had never visited, the two cars pulled back a lane, then parked. We all got out. The two fellows holding me made a game out of banging me into trees as we hiked another half mile back to a small gravel pit.

High above, clouds obscured most of the stars. The clouds parted to show a full moon. In that light the gang gathered around me. Alvin and Donnie faced me, Donnie with his bat. Alvin was still on crutches with his cast.

They had been careful back in Austin not to carry guns. They did not have any now—or need any. There were enough of them to accomplish whatever had brought us out here.

I figured this for some of my final moments. There would be a fight—they wanted that. But the outcome was inevitable. They'd brought me to the spot where I could expect to do some eternal resting. By daylight, perhaps the spot was not so foreboding, could even be pretty. I got no comfort from that. The guys holding me by the upper arms eased up and stepped back. I thought of making a bolt for it. They looked like they expected and wanted that.

"Okay, Shitting Bull," Alvin said. "You haven't talked yet. You feel like sharing anything now?"

I thought of a lot of things I could say. My mouth felt too dry to say them. I stared back, wondering who would make the first move. In that quiet of waiting, I heard gravel crunching beneath steps.

Heads swung back up toward the path. A small figure approached. As it got closer, I could see it was a petite woman, maybe five feet tall tops. I could make out longish straight hair tied back, and a lean, even bony face. She looked tanned as a saddle, and wore boots that came almost to the knees of her jeans. Her checked shirt had pearl buttons and was partially covered by a black vest.

One of the guys who'd been holding me said, "Hey, are you . . . ?"

Another said, "You're. . . ."

"Yeah. Joz Brosche," she said. "I know who I am. Who're all you chrome domes?"

"I've heard about you," Donnie said. The others spread out in their circle. She walked into the center and stood a couple of feet away from me. We were surrounded.

Donnie's free hand caressed the bat he held in his fist. "You may've heard of me too," he said. "I *like* pain."

"Good," she said. Quicker than I could follow, her left hand went behind her and up under the vest. It came out with a short pistol. I heard the sound of the shot before I even realized what she held in her hand. "This is your lucky day," she said.

My eyes traveled to Donnie, caught his wide-eyed stare. His

knees buckled an inch, then the red started to spread at the V of his faded jeans. She'd shot him right in the crotch. I had her figured as someone who would shoot a man in the knees. As if not to disappoint me, she fired twice more, hitting Donnie in each knee. His shocked face shifted to a mix of absolute fear and pain, as each leg jerked, sending him to the ground, screaming.

The others took only a half step forward, saw that she held a gun in each hand now. I hadn't seen her get out the second gun at all. She looked around at the faces of the men.

"Oh, what the hell," she said. She snapped off another shot. I saw plaster fly and red begin to show at the knee in Alvin's cast. He screamed as he spun, the cast snapping back. He toppled to his side.

That was it for the others. They turned and scattered in as many directions as there were of them except back toward their vehicles since that would have meant going past Joz. They left Donnie and Alvin behind, screaming and bleeding.

Joz turned to me. She slid one gun back up under her vest and carried the other in a hand that hung loose at her side. She looked at me. "What'ya say we blow this popsicle stand?"

I nodded slowly, licked my lips, which felt very dry.

She led the way back down the lane. I walked at her side.

"You know . . . ," she said. Her flinty eyes swept the woods around us, checking behind every tree. The woods seemed to be free of any of the ones who'd grabbed me. "People should be careful what they wish for."

"I've heard that," I said.

CHAPTER EIGHTEEN

Her vehicle, a beat-up hunter-green early-'seventies Land Cruiser, was pulled up behind the two cars my militia pals had driven. Before getting in, she drew her guns again so quickly I missed it. She shot out two tires on each of the cars. Without comment, she climbed in and started her engine. I got into the passenger seat.

"You follow us out this far?" I asked.

She nodded. That was all the conversation I got out of her for a few miles. I watched her drive. She was a tiny woman, but very flinty. I wondered if I hadn't seen her in action if I would look at her and think scorpion, rattlesnake, as I was doing now. I'd seen a few flickers of fear in the eyes of some of the guys when she first walked up to us, small as she was. She must be something of a legend out in some parts of West Texas. I had to wonder how or why she was roaming free. She seemed the type who might have stepped over the line once or twice.

I looked around inside the vehicle. The floorboards had rusted away enough below me that I could catch glimpses of the road, lit as it was by the headlights. On the door beside me, a row of bullet holes had been patched and painted over. "Nice car," I said.

"Held together by bondo and duct tape." Her voice came out terse and brisk, each word cut off like the cracking of a bull whip.

"Thanks for stepping in back there. I think they meant to do me harm."

Her head swept to me. One eyebrow raised. She gave a curt nod, went back to driving.

"Cassie ask you to watch me?"

She nodded.

A mile later, she said, "I had doubts, but Huff vouched for you."

"You know Huff?"

"I don't shack up with him, or anythin', if that's what you mean. I just keep an eye on his place. I've seen you come and go a time or two."

"Me?" I said. "Why does Huff's place need watching?"

"It doesn't . . . always. He's had a brush or two in the past, harmless as he is. We kinda look out for him. Me and a few friends."

"They as tough as you?"

"Oh, my. They blow me away. I'm the pussycat of that group, all right. They make me look like the princess and the fuckin' pea."

"Hard to believe," I said. She didn't respond to that.

Truth was, I wasn't as happy about being rescued as I should have been. I tried to reason with myself about whether it was because it had been done by a woman. Bottom line, though, is that people really prefer to get themselves out of their own scrapes. Accepting help doesn't come easily, or gracefully. It was something I would have to work on.

Joz stayed quiet for most of the way back to town. As we approached the outskirts of the city, though, her head snapped to me. She said, "So, okay, tell me. Where's the money?"

"Money?"

"You know, green stuff—tens, twenties, fifties. You use it to buy stuff."

"What are you talking about?"

"You know what the French say, *'cherchez la femme'*—means show me the female. They figure that behind every crime there's a woman. But then, they eat frogs and snails, so what can ya expect. I figure that in every case there's a little honey—translate that to read money. So where is it?"

I hesitated, then said, "What the hell." Joz turned her Land Cruiser onto Mo-Pac, named after the Missouri-Pacific railroad line that runs down through the median strip. She headed south. The sky to the east was getting lighter as dawn approached. Camp Mabry passed by to our right. "There *was* some mention of a possible million bucks or so," I said.

Her eager eyes swung my way. For the first time, I saw what she probably thought was a smile. It was the kind of thing you might see in a dark alley and be very afraid.

I told her all about Bent Lenny, what Johnny Gringo had seen when in the house, what was there now, about the photos Hal took, and the negs Huff might get in the mail any day. It was no skin off my back. The house was still staked out. The money meant nothing to me, and she *had* just saved my life. When I was done, I said, "So what do you think happened to Bent Lenny?"

"Two words," she said. "Jimmy Hoffa."

"That's what I thought. I doubt if the money that was shifted away ended up at the warehouse. That was a temporary place. I don't know the other haunts of this gun-toting homeboy set."

"I know a few," she said. I had the momentary uncomfortable feeling that I was setting the boys up for some grief. Bad as those fellows in the backwoods militia were, she seemed a lot to wish onto anyone. I wore a few recent scratches and lumps, which made harboring any sympathy for them a stretch.

Joz dropped me off at my office without having to ask where it was. The farther I went into this case, the more it seemed my life was an open book, and to people whom I would not always pursue as part of my crowd.

My office door was closed, but unlocked. I went inside. Early as it was, Cassie sat behind my desk in a folding green-and-white lawn chair. A matching chair on the other side of the battle-scarred desk seemed to call to me. I went over and plopped into it.

"You're hurt," she said. She started to rise. She looked fresh as tomorrow. She must have caught some rest somewhere. She had taken her gun out of its holster and it lay on the desk beside the wrapped bottle.

"Stay put," I said. "I want to apologize for running off on you."

"Did Joz . . . ?"

"Yeah. We've met. She just pulled my bacon from *that* fire. And I think you can put Donnie down on the serious injured reserve list for a while."

"I hope you don't feel emasculated by Joz. Some men do."

"Oh, I've still got more *cojones* than Donnie has. Let it go at that."

"I had your well-being in mind. Or your being at all."

"Okay. Okay. Enough said."

"I brought you a gift," she said. The twinkle was back in her eyes.

"I don't need. . . ."

She held up a small grocery sack. I reached for it, opened it. Inside were two small glass jars of dried beef.

"Since your heirloom crystal was ruined in the earlier fracas, I thought you needed replacements. I knew you'd feel uncomfortable with anything too much flashier than what you had before."

"Thanks," I said, and meant it. "For the boffo office furniture as well."

She stood and bent across the desk, offering her lips. At that second someone pounded on the door and without hesitation swung it open.

Cassie plopped back into her chair, a frown darting across her face.

Borster and Findlay lumbered through the door. Borster's lip curled at my temporary office furnishings, not that it was going to cost me sleep.

"Don't they have any crime back where you're from?" Borster asked Cassie.

"Nothing to compare with what you big-city fellers have," she said with as much twang as she could put in it.

Borster and Findlay traded looks. I thought, here it comes. When they looked back, an awkward half smile struggled across Borster's craggy face. "You got a couple of glasses, Trav?" he asked.

Inside I reeled. As cool as I could, I said, "Cassie, could you get out the good crystal, please?"

She grinned. "Sure."

She took out the two containers of dried beef, popped off the tops with an opener, and put the beef in a pile on the flattened brown-paper sack. She handed me the glasses, which still wore the labels.

I gave one each to Borster and Findlay, then reached to the bag holding the tequila. I poured them each a jolt.

Borster raised his glass. "To your health," he said.

"Yeah." Findlay glanced to Borster, then to me. "To your health."

They raised their glasses and took a sip. My eyes locked with Cassie's for a second.

"Look," Borster said when he'd lowered his glass, "it's time we let bygones be bygones."

"Wow," Cassie said. "You guys must really be in a hole."

Borster looked like he had just swallowed broken glass, then he switched back to his version of a smile. It wavered uncertain on his face, unused to being there, no doubt.

"We're working the death of your friend, Hal Jansen," Borster said.

"You're sure it's Hal?"

"Partial dental plate pretty well locks that in," Findlay said.

I felt as if he'd punched me in the stomach.

"You were seen at the newspaper office a couple of times," Findlay said. He caught a look from Borster and clammed.

"We need your . . . help," Borster said. His voice crackled like a small brush fire. That was hard to get out.

I looked at Cassie again. I could see that the whole thing made her about as comfortable as it did me, which was not at all.

Borster pulled out a notebook from inside his suit jacket and said, "He kept a regular series of reporter's notebooks. The last few pages of his current one were torn out. On one of the earlier pages we found something we can't quite make sense of. It says: *'When you open an oyster, whether you just get the meat or if you get a pearl depends on where you put the point of the knife.'* Any idea what the hell that's about?"

I shook my head. It didn't seem like anything to me, other than an excuse to come talk to me. I glanced at Cassie.

She said, "That could be Hal's epitaph for all that. The man struggled not to be a loser, and at this point he was attracted to a quick fix, one driven by greed."

"I thought it probably did have something to do with money," Borster said. "Hal was hurting financially. We've had a good look through his finances and know just how bad. He had to be pretty desperate by this point."

"It's no suicide note," Cassie said, "the man was stomped to death."

Findlay made a low gurgling sound.

"You mind," I said, "telling me who is giving you the hot foot. Is it Bolens? Fields? Randall?"

They traded looks, but shared nothing. Borster, though, was near the end of his leash. I could sense that. He finished off his drink, put the glass down on the desk. "If you do learn anything. . . ."

"You saw me at the Constitutional," I said, "so you know I'm working on who shot at Tori Brice. If that ties to who sent a truck toward Jayne Randall, and who thought they'd strangled Trish Mirandez at the Kasperville Folk Festival, then I'm working on all that, too. Cassie here is looking into the same connection possibility. Hal helped me with information. But it's hard to believe it led to his death. Maybe I could have been a better friend, listened more. I don't know."

"Like I said," Borster said, "if you get anything . . . you know. . . ." He gave Findlay's arm a tug. Findlay bolted what was in his glass and set it down. The two of them spun and went for the door. Findlay went out, Borster hesitated, then turned back to me and said, "Gareth Fields did say he'd like you to drop by his office ASAP. That's not just a casual request. I'd do it."

"Borster," I said as he started to leave. "How common is it for a field agent for the Bu to work with a handful of ATF men? I haven't met the Bu's agent in charge since I've been in this. You think he even knows what Fields is up to?"

"How would I know?"

"You think Fields might be bucking for some publicity on this? Score a reputation?"

"Could be," he said. "That could just well be." He tried for the smile again, to take off some of the edge, but he'd spent all the near smiles he'd saved up. So he slipped out the door and closed it.

Cassie gave it a few minutes, then said, "He doesn't seem like such a hardnose to me."

I let out a puff of air with a snap.

"What?"

"You weren't around," I said, "when he missed out on a reward that would've retired him and Findlay, and in style too. They blame me for that, though I had little to do with it."

"All that's interesting," she said, "but do you get the feeling that someone is setting the metronome up a few clicks?"

An hour or two later, Cassie and I went outside. The sun had struggled up through the jagged skyline of buildings, lighting streets that needed a good sweeping. My eyes felt like rings of fire, like Borster's eyes had looked.

I ignored the dark limo sitting behind the rental Toyota. I opened the car door, gave a sigh when the limo's back door opened and Max Bolens got out, still in an evening suit.

"What do you want?" I said. Cassie got into the passenger seat. She had slipped into her uniform so she could wear her gun.

"You know," Max said to me.

"What makes you think my answer has changed?" I asked.

"Won't you reconsider? It took a lot for me to come here and ask you like this," Max said. He twisted his hands, realized it and stilled them, moved them to his sides.

"There're lots of detectives in the phone book. Why me?"

"You have a number of friends on the force here. I talked with them. They say you're the guy to go with."

"Like Borster?"

"I *did* talk with him. You may not realize it, but he has respect for you."

"He has a funny way of showing it."

"You cost him a great deal of money." Max held up a hand

when I started to say something. "I know. It wasn't money he already had. But I understand he considers it was practically in hand when you intruded."

I felt sure Borster's version had left out a few details. I knew his recent visit had been as much fun for him as taking out his own appendix with a pocketknife.

"Fact is," Max said, "Borster said that you may go out of your way *not* to say something, but you'd be as equally ethically bound to share something once you were hired."

"You think I should put him back on my Christmas card list?"

"What I want to know is whether I can hire you or not."

"Not," I said. "But don't take it personally. It's just that I always avoid being employed by anyone who might be the culprit."

"You still suspect *me?*"

"I told you that you've been on the list from the first," I said.

I got into the car, winked at Cassie, and rolled the window down. He stood like a pillar of salt staring at me. "And you're not all the way off yet," I added.

"You think it could be *me?*"

"I'd like to," I said. "I really would. It would sure make things simpler."

I pulled away from the curb, noted in the mirror that Bolens stood rooted to the spot. I feared I was in for disappointment in thinking he was our culprit. But it wouldn't hurt him to feel human for a moment or two.

CHAPTER NINETEEN

I had to work from memory to follow the path I'd been taken when kidnapped by Alvin, Donnie, and crew. What I hadn't memorized going out, I recalled from the ride in with Joz. As I left the city limits, Cassie said, "What about Fields and the FBI?"

"To hell with them," I said.

"Thanks," she said as if she meant it, glad to have me over suspecting her of being their agent.

Back at the office she had suggested that we go and revisit where I'd been taken; she had done her insisting in a convincing manner. She still had a job to do: find Alvin. It tied enough to my own agendas to keep me interested, and I hadn't minded being convinced considering the way she'd gone about it.

"I can't believe she just left them out there, wounded that bad," she said.

I could have said that I had left them too.

She shook her head. "That damned Joz."

"These guys must have a doctor somewhere who patches them up without reporting bullet wounds and all that," I said. "Alvin's been fixed up a few times and you haven't found any hospital records."

"She shot out their tires too. You remember that?"

"You really think they'll still be there?" I could picture us finding two mounds of gravel in the pit containing their bodies.

"We'll see," she said, and went silent for the next few miles.

197

We left the county and got onto smaller and smaller roads. I caught each of the landmarks, got tense as we got closer. I also sneaked a look at Cassie from time to time until she caught me doing it.

"What's up with you?" she said.

I shrugged it off, but inside I wrestled with the awareness that for most of my life I had gotten by with an inner piece of me missing. When I was around Cassie, or thinking about her, it felt in place. Don't think that didn't scare me.

She had to be younger than me by almost ten years, which made me feel older than the Dead Sea scrolls. Not by anything she did. I brought *that* to it. She was so smooth, so soft, so vibrant and so alive. What niggled more, beyond the physical side, was that everything I had seen so far, her feistiness included, had only made her more attractive to me. She made me feel complete. I thought of the way I lived, my shambles of a home, my having no car. On the other hand, thinking of me coming home to a cozy brick house with a car in the garage somehow made me feel no better—in fact, it made me feel worse. For all of those reasons I argued against saying or doing anything more than I had. It was an old argument, but one I had always won—or lost, depending on your view.

The gate stood open on the lane that led back to the gravel pit. I nodded to Cassie as I turned in. She loosened the strap that went over the hammer of her revolver.

"The two cars are gone," I said.

"I'm surprised they drove cars. If you look over the vehicles these guys tend to drive, it's usually pickups with the occasional motorcycle. There's not too much of the family car with this crowd."

"Stolen, maybe," I said.

She nodded. We got out of the car, started walking slowly back the road that had seemed so long to me before. It felt shorter now. A light wind rustled the tops of mesquite and cedar brush. For a second I thought I heard the sudden rattle of a snake, but it was the clicking of a large grasshopper's wings as it flew across our path. We came to the clearing where the abandoned gravel pit spread out. We saw no one there. I felt the tension ease away. I led Cassie over to where I remembered standing and thinking that those were my last moments.

The bright sunlight showed wide smears of blood across the gravel in a couple of places, already baked brown and brittle in the heat. A confused buzzard circled high above us, due for a disappointment.

"That damned Joz," Cassie said again.

We hiked back to the car. "Where to now?" Cassie asked.

"We're not all that far from Huff's place, if you don't mind."

"You brought the Vicks, of course."

"Sorry," I said. "A well-prepared cop like you ought to have a gas mask on you someplace."

"I traded mine in for a bullshit detector," she said.

We drove all the way to the end of Huff's lane. It seemed quiet and still. We got out of the car and went up to the door and knocked, but there was no answer. Cassie reached for the doorknob.

"Don't open that," I cautioned. "If he's not here, the best that could happen is that you'd let half a dozen animals loose."

"And the worst?"

"It could be booby-trapped."

Warm as it was, the thick stands of trees that crowded Huff's place made it cool in the shade that spread across his porch. The breeze gave a rustling tug to the high limbs every now and then. I sat on the edge of the porch, Cassie beside me. After a few minutes I lay back, closed my eyes.

I woke to the sound of Huff's old Chevy truck rumbling

slowly down the drive toward us. Cassie's head lay on my stomach. Her eyes fluttered open. A possum and several small young possums had curled up in a pile pressed against us. They got up and stretched as we did. A doe and two small fawns stood eating at the low brush a dozen feet from us. They looked up at the approaching truck, but didn't take off into the woods.

The truck rattled to a stop and Huff got out. A large black smear covered the right side of his face.

"What happened to you?" I said. At the sound of my voice, the deer stiffened, twitched their tails, then bounded away into the thick of the woods. The possum and small ones moved toward Huff.

"What?" he said.

When he got closer, I said, "Your face has some sort of black soot on it."

"Oh," he said. He reached up and smeared it into a wider patch. "I better go around to the back to open up."

In a few moments he fumbled open the front door and came out to join us on the porch. He had taken a washcloth to his face, had made a clean circle of the center area. A small half moon of black still showed high on his forehead near the hairline.

"Well, you weren't playing in the chimney," I said. "How did you get so dirty?"

"And they call it smokeless black powder," he said. "Humpf. I was messing around with that and some Composition B. It burns as hot as C-four. But it's not quite as stable. Looks like I'll have to go with C-four, then."

"Go with C-four?" I said.

"Oh, nothing." He shrugged it off. "A little something I was fooling around with. I had to go a ways from the house so I wouldn't upset the critters. The black powder was from something else that didn't go right. What brings you out here?"

"I wanted to check something I forgot to look for before," I said. "On that ZIP disk I left here. Can you see if Hal Jansen's name is on the client list?"

"Sure thing. Come on inside for a sec, but watch your step. While I was gone, some of the fellas inside made a mess of the place."

"Maybe I'll wait out here on the porch," Cassie said. She watched the baby possums push at the side of their mother.

"Oh, come on," I said.

Huff ducked inside, and we followed, staying closer than I liked. He wove through the living area to one of the back rooms lit by computer screens. I stayed at one shoulder while he sat in front of one of the screens and shoved a disk into a slot. Cassie watched over the other shoulder. After a few minutes of tapping he said, "It sure is," he said. "There's a note next to his name too. It says: 'No More.' What do you make of that?"

I shook my head.

"Sounds like Hal got blacklisted by Myller," Cassie said.

"But for what?" I said. "This computer stuff doesn't give me as much to go on as people do."

"They're okay," Huff said. "Computers are good quiet company most of the time."

"I don't know. It does seem that there was a whole lot more to Hal than I knew about."

"People are mysterious," Huff agreed.

I didn't want to raise the touchy issue that most people don't usually "fool around" with C-4 like Hal was doing either.

"I've got one wife who's supposed to be naked on the Internet and busy with some other man," I said.

"Who?"

I hesitated. "Oh, what the hell. Max Bolens' wife Audrey."

"Let ya know more in just a sec," Huff said.

He clicked at the keys as his hands raced across the keyboard.

He hunched over like the Phantom of the Opera over an organ. "I'll just look and see what we get."

He went to an Internet search engine and typed in, "Austin amateur." He had to narrow that down after getting way too many responses.

"Gotta let a search engine do its thing," he said, figuring me, accurately, for not being as computer literate as I should be. He scrolled down through a list with names like "The Bearded Clam Wrestles the Pulsing Prong."

"Cute," I said.

Cassie let out a soft puff of air beside me.

"Lot of clumsy creativity going on out there," Huff said. "I don't mind that as much as the bait-and-switch, the spamming, other crap going on. Then too, it's easy to get the impression that the whole world out there is having more fun than you."

"You seem to know your way around pretty well."

"Here we go," he said. "We've got action, and amateurs, or so they say."

He started clicking open tiny pictures into bigger ones. "Thumbnails," he said. "Hey, those aren't amateurs. That's Peter North and Christy Canyon."

"Who?"

"Porn stars. They're from quite a while back too. The seventies or eighties."

"You know the *names* of porn stars?"

"The thing about masturbation," he said, "is that you don't have to talk to your hand after sex."

Insightful, but it pretty well ruled out my ever shaking hands with Huff again.

The small snort from Cassie was louder this time.

"Stop right there," I said.

"That her?"

It was Audrey all right. She was twisted into what I thought would be an impossible nude knot with a man who was *not* Max Bolens. The corner of the face of the man with her looked a lot like Don Briscoe.

"How do you suppose the picture was taken?" I asked. "And why?"

Huff looked at me as if I had just crawled sideways out of a crib. "Oh, Trav, there're lotsa reasons. Some people've made their fortunes on the Web, exposed their work and made career-boosting connections. But for every one of them, there are hundreds who just end up giving stuff away free." He glanced at Cassie before he went on. "For other people it's revenge. There are whole sites dedicated to people who want to get back at their ex-girlfriends or spouses by putting nude pictures of them on the Web. I understand them more than husbands who put their nude wives on the Web. A lot of people seem to live jaded lives. Sometimes the husband takes the pictures, other times it's a camera set up on a tripod. If you use a digital camera you don't even have to get the pictures developed. They come out on a disk, ready to share and you don't even have to compress or digitize anymore. Just about anyone can get involved these days. You don't have to Photoshop the pictures, or anything."

Huff caught my puzzled look and frowned.

"You're telling me more than I need to know," I said, and bent close to look at the background, trying to see if the room was in a motel or private home.

"Huff, we heard about some paparazzi-type shots Hal took. Any chance we could see some of those?" Cassie asked.

"You're too late. All of them have been yanked from the Web. A lot of the big and even medium stars have lawyers and paralegals who scour the Web looking for photos that don't help the star's image. They put the legal squeeze on the Webmasters, and how. The whole intellectual property issue's still fuzzy, but when a lawyer gets involved you can kiss some of the sharing spirit good-bye.”

“I thought you said Hal’s shots were pretty tame stuff, Trav,” Cassie said.

“They were,” Hal answered for me. “You know, the usual stuff—a woman wears an evening dress that turns transparent under a camera’s flash. On another, the strap of a gown slips. Then there are the shots of stars when they’re not looking their best—bad hair day, or just out of the Betty Ford Clinic. That sort of thing. Mostly females. Men seem to mind less, or make less interesting stories, unless you count that DWI photo of Nick Nolte he’d sure give a lot to have back.”

“They’re all gone from the Web now?” I asked.

“Haven’t seen one in quite a while.” Hal rubbed a finger under his nose.

“Some of the women got pretty testy with Hal, huh?”

“You can say that. It was a real mess. I’m surprised you didn’t hear more about it. The stuff made a huge stink. Jansen could’ve been sued for plenty, if he had anything worth suing.”

Cassie’s questions had headed the same direction my rattled brain had taken me. In the mindset I’d been in before Hal’s death, I could easily see him swiping the pictures from Audrey, maybe ones she’d taken herself with a preset camera, and putting them on the Web, out of spite at her better life. Maybe he took the pictures himself. There might even have been failed blackmail involved.

“I doubt if any of that matters to him now,” I said out loud. Thinking about Hal that way only made me feel more lousy. At bottom, I was feeling the kind of guilt anyone would when he hadn’t been around to help a friend.

“Oh, hey,” Huff said, with enough of his breath behind it to rock my head back. “I just got some negatives in the mail from you. What was that all about?”

Cassie stood up straight and looked alert.

"No secrets," I told her. "Hal dumped some negs on me from shots he took that night I had the jogging class at the warehouse—some kind of meet between Bent Lenny and the militia." To Huff I said, "Did you make prints from those?"

"Of course."

"Well, let's have a look at them."

Huff turned on a room light and brought the pictures out. He'd blown them up to eight by ten. The photos had an odd tint to them, and were fuzzy from being taken through a night-scope. There was Bent Lenny, the terrain of the top of Mt. Bonnell behind him. Donnie and Alvin were among the militia present. A couple of them carried suitcases.

"So, that's the last anyone ever saw of Lenny Coggins, huh?" Cassie said.

"Seems that way," I agreed.

"You wanna take these with you?" Huff asked.

"I don't," I said. "Do you, Cassie?"

"Nope. You better hang onto them, Huff. I'm still trying just to get a hook on Alvin. That's all I'm worried about."

"And you don't know where he is?" Huff asked.

"No," Cassie said. "But when he's well enough, I figure he'll come around looking for Trav here. He's drawn to him for some reason."

"Lots of people like Travis," Huff said.

We pulled into Austin as the sun was growing red on the skyline horizon.

"Where are we going?" Cassie asked.

"I thought the psychologist side of you might like to address some of the same questions that are bugging me."

"Such as?"

"Why would the executive of a major company set himself up for being naked and get verbal abuse while scrubbing a kitchen floor with a toothbrush? Why would that sort of thing be something Hal might try? And what caused him to be blacklisted from future sessions at such a delightful pastime?"

"You're right. That does hold my interest."

Carol Myller swung the door open, swept over me with a glance and fixed on Cassie, in particular on Cassie's uniform.

"Perhaps I wasn't clear." She waved us in, then closed the door and turned to us, her eyes still fixed on Cassie's uniform. "What I do is not illegal in the least."

"Aren't you going to ask us to sit?" I said.

"What wonderful views," Cassie said, looking out of each of the wall-length sets of picture windows. "Don't you have curtains or blinds?"

"They roll down from those overhead light bars when I need them."

"How *Architectural Digest.*"

"Oh, sit down," Carol said. She waved us to the couch. "I can assume you didn't call to discuss my interior design."

"Cassie is a psychologist with her department. She under-stands men fairly well."

"I'll bet she does."

"But she had some questions about how your business works. So do I."

Carol leaned back in her chair and crossed her legs. She reached for a cigarette from a silver box, then lit it with a silver lighter. The phone began to ring in the other room, but Carol ignored it. She pursed her lips and frowned, but said nothing.

Carol was a handsome woman, not past her days of turning heads. Cassie's youth and freshness, when seen side by side, seemed different, but not superior. They looked at each other, as two attractive women will.

"There's some desire for submission and dominance in everyone," Carol said. "Not necessarily the S-and-M model that springs to mind, being bound with ropes or chains and being beaten."

"Are you sure about that?" Cassie sat forward on the edge of her seat on what I knew to be a darned comfortable couch.

"Let me tell you how it started," Carol said. Cassie bent farther forward. "It's like I told Philo Vance here. I was in New York. I'd been the loving trophy wife and got cashiered out to be replaced by something that wore lowrider jeans and giggled. I was never good at the housework thing, and didn't want to spend any money. So I thought, 'What the hell.' I ran an ad that read something like: 'MALE SERVANT WANTED by former Mata Hari to clean my small Chelsea apartment once a week. No sex. No pay. Slavery is its own reward.' The next thing I know, I'm getting dozens of responses from men who want to clean my place for nothing. You'll notice that my place here is always clean enough to eat off any surface, and I never lift a finger."

"Why rent the men out?" Cassie still leaned forward in her chair.

"I had some qualms at first when I thought about hiring out some of my slaves," Carol said. "I had so many, and I needed the money. Besides, they were just men."

Cassie started a chuckle she suppressed when she glanced at me.

"I think the guys who respond to my ads are in some ways mentally healthier than the ones who don't, because they deal with their needs directly."

"Men *need* this?" I said. I'd heard a version from Carol before, but I had yet to fully grasp the concept.

"We all need something. A lot of men, executives to sports figures, office workers to religious figures, lead lives that make them kind of stiff authority figures, and it's a role they can't step out of at work or they'd lose all control of those around them, at the office and with their families."

She saw some question in my eyes and said, "Okay. I've got this one guy, who I'll call Pericles. He's a young major corporate executive here in town, but he's one of our best and most regular customers."

"He pays?" Cassie asked.

"No. But the woman who gets her house cleaned by him does." Carol tapped ash from her cigarette into a very clean crystal bowl. "Anyway, he shows up for a job I set up. He's wearing khakis and a dark polo shirt. He's brought along his black leather collar with metal eyelets. The woman, call her Lilia, says, 'There's some awful cruddy gunk under the refrigerator. Think you can do something about that?' 'Of course he can,' I say."

Cassie's eyes flicked to me, then back to Carol.

"So he's down on his hands and knees. . . ."

"Naked?" Cassie asked.

"Not yet. But he's scrubbing away. He says he needs steel-wool pads to do the job and offers to go buy them. I tell him he's got to wear his collar down in the elevator and to the store and back. He bows his head, but he goes. When he's back he strips down and cleans the whole kitchen. The woman's kind of uncomfortable, but I tell her not to squirm—the guy's loving this. He knows he's lucky. Normally he'd have to pay plenty to be treated like this. I put a foot on his back while, naked now, he works on the floor tiles, and I'm wearing spike heels. When it's time for him to leave, he dresses and bows to us both. I make him wear the collar to his car. I never get too close. They usually like it when the woman keeps her distance. It heightens the tension—he's never sure if we're going to be angry or pleased, and that's titillating."

"But not everyone takes to this," Cassie said. "I mean the men. Don't some try it and burn out?"

"Oh, lots. But for most of them it's just what they need."

"What happens to the ones who don't work out?"

"They aren't asked back. Some fail for various reasons. They thought it was something else, they aren't in touch with their inner selves, or they're just thrashing around hoping to land on something that scratches an itch they don't understand."

"I had a friend, Hal Jansen, a reporter, who tried it," I butted in. "I think he was one of the burnouts. Can you tell me what happened?"

"You know I don't break confidences. I won't even confirm if he was a client or not." Her eyes flicked over to the desk where she kept the disks. Maybe she knew she was missing a backup disk by now, but she was too cool to show it.

"He's dead," I said. "I'm trying to see what kind of itch he tried to scratch."

She sighed. "Well, it wasn't this. He was dead wrong for it. As wrong as you can get."

"Too dominant?" Cassie said.

"Too out of. . . ." Carol stopped herself. "I'm not qualified to talk about him like that. He was obsessive, not that that's always bad, but he was driven to fix something, and I wasn't all that sure he knew what. I do know he felt wronged, but what I offer didn't turn out to be any kind of answer or cure for him."

"Thanks," Cassie said. "You've been very helpful."

"Well," Carol said to Cassie, "maybe you can send Spike here back sometime for a workout. I'll bet he'd be something to look at in a tutu and nothing else while he scrubbed windows."

"I can think of some people who would pay to see that," Cassie said.

"You mind if we visit Audrey Bolens?" I said. "I'd kind of like to have you along when I visit her too." It was getting darker out.

Cassie gave me the one-eyebrow-raised look.

I drove to the Bolens' mansion and pulled up in front as if expected. Once again, Audrey opened the door. She wore a red evening dress, one designed to dignify while still making her look sixteen. She looked past me to Cassie, who stood behind me in uniform.

"What's he done this time, officer?" Audrey asked.

"Do you have a couple of minutes to answer some questions?" I asked.

"Oh, come in." She led the way back to the same room by the pool. Cassie looked around at the house. It was an eyeful on a first-time visit.

"As I recall, you enjoy brandy," she said to me. "Does the officer wish a beverage?"

"This is Deputy Sheriff Winnick," I said. "Cassie Winnick."

"Oh. It's like that," she said, playing at being the hurt female because I had used Cassie's first name.

"A glass of water would be fine," Cassie said. She was enjoying herself more than I'd expected.

Audrey brought the drinks over to the sofa. She'd made something for herself in a tall thin highball glass. The brandy snifter she handed to me was nearly full. She plopped into the chair.

"No coffee this time?" she said. Before I could answer, she said, "I know you're not much of a sipper, so I gave you the adult portion."

She crossed her legs, managed to share enough of them to show her stocking tops. She was one of those women who like to imply a history with a man in front of another woman. Cassie rolled well with it, though. I think she discounted a lot of Audrey, which seemed the appropriate way to take her.

"What brings you out here at this hour? Dinner's not for another hour. I'd enjoy some entertainment."

"It's about your brother," I said.

The highball glass stopped halfway to her lips. She lowered it slowly.

"You . . . you know?"

"Hal," I said. "Hal Jansen." Of course, I knew. It hadn't taken any major detecting to land on that.

She raised the glass again and drained it. "I believe I'm dry," she said. I hadn't taken so much as a sip yet. She rose. "Would either of you like another?" She walked over to the wet bar.

"Aren't you going to the memorial service?" I asked.

"I suppose," she said. She came back and settled into her chair. Her glass looked much darker this time. "There's so much going on, what with Donna still in trial and all."

"Is that why Max is around?" I wondered.

"You must have realized that Congress is in session. Yes, he's here doing all he can for Donna. It's election year for him too. All this couldn't come at a worse time."

"I thought I knew Hal pretty well. I'm getting the feeling I didn't know him as well as I thought."

She took a deep drink from her glass. I felt competitive and tried to match her with a drink from my snifter. "Hal was coming apart," she said, "I think. We didn't see that much of each other. He was a workaholic and a recluse for the most part. But sometimes he would spin loose with some pretty bizarre stuff."

I thought of Carol Myller.

"You might as well know," Audrey said, "that I think he was the one who got hold of some pictures I had and put me on the Web in the first place."

He must have been as fond of her as she was of him for him to do that. I asked, "He was taking some pretty expensive trips during the past years. Do you know how he was able to do that?"

"He was spending as if he was me, as if he had that kind of

money to spend. He didn't."

It struck me as a cruel thing to say. I asked, "Where did he get the money?"

"He tried a lot of things. You must know that for a while there he tried his hand as one of the paparazzi, hung around anyone famous, you know. In a town this full of rising stars, it wasn't hard. He found the men common—cowboys with talent, but men of the earth. I sense you're the kind of man who's comfortable with men like that, and your own lot in life. Hal wasn't."

"And the women?" Cassie asked.

"Oh, they shunned Hal. They were the ones who drove him off when he sold a few of his pictures to national tabloids. You know, petty, mundane pictures, the kind of thing the masses, the hoi polloi, the public wants. The women turned on him. Hal didn't take any of it well. He became a grubby little man, bitter. I imagine he's better off dead."

I swallowed, said in a scratchy voice, "He didn't get any more money after that?"

"Not from me," she said, raising her glass until the ice cubes clattered against her teeth. "Not from me."

CHAPTER TWENTY

It was getting on; dark had settled in on Austin. I drove Cassie over to Threadgill's where she could have a chicken-fried steak. I had the chicken gizzards, because, well, there just aren't that many places you can even get them, and I felt low and mean enough to want to make myself gnaw on something tough. I had whirls and wisps of smoke so far, but nothing in this case worth calling a step forward.

"Where do you want to stay?" I said when we got back into the car. "Should I scout out a new motel?"

"Your place is fine," she said between yawns. She lay her head against my shoulder. That's all the argument I needed.

Back at the casa, we took turns in my tiny bathroom. Then we made it to the cot. This time we made love; and that's what I mean. It was different than anything before, which had been so much raw, though exciting, sex. This was tender, fulfilling. She hovered over me, playful and childish for a moment; then she was very adult. There were times we both got animal, and then were nuzzling and comfortable. But there was something behind it all, beneath the embraces that got more intense. It was a feeling I hesitated to define, but if I had to say, I'd say it was a feeling of farewell, some of that bittersweet sadness. Naked, and dripping with sweat, we separated on the cot. I slipped to the floor where I had spread the spare blanket. I lay on it, thinking, wondering what had crawled inside Cassie to make her so suddenly and mortally sad, in a way that was

213

beyond words. Well, maybe I did know, but I said nothing about it. I listened to Cassie as she began to make small snoring sounds, which I heard for only a second or two before I joined her.

I woke, stiff in the morning—and I mean in the back from laying on the floor. The sound of the shower had awakened me.

I pushed myself up slowly from the floor and spent a few minutes pulling at the edges of the tape wrapped around my chest. I couldn't tell if the tape was what was making me so stiff. I suspected that came from sleeping on the floor. The tape was definitely what made me itch and feel hot beneath the wrapping.

Someone banged at the front office door and stirred me from my deliberations, made me grab for my shirt and pants.

I had myself together, shirt tucked in and shoes on by the time I got to the door. The banging continued. There was no peephole in the oak door, something I'd have to discuss with my landlord. I lifted the mail slot flap. Jimmy Bravuro's eyes looked in at mine.

I rose, in several slow stages, and undid the lock. Jimmy, Dutch, and some other fellow the size of the state of Kansas came pushing into my office.

"Dark in here," Jimmy said, and flipped on the light. "You ought to think about putting in some glass in your picture window."

"So far," I said, "it's buffered me from early morning shocks, such as yourselves."

Jimmy perched on the corner of the desk. Dutch eased into one of the new lawn chairs, cautious at first, then with a thumbs-up to me. The big fellow stood by the desk, not knowing where he should go. He was a slab of a fellow, six-foot-six or so and at least three hundred pounds. His hair hung down to the middle of his back in a waterfall wave that had been care-

fully washed and conditioned. It glistened in the office light—
quite a mane.

"Oh, this is Lionel Rainey," Jimmy said.

Lionel held out a cautious hand, and I was expecting one of
those bone crushers. Instead I got a firm and brief shake, though
my hand was lost for a moment.

"Lionel's an agent in the music biz," Dutch explained.

"Not our agent," Jimmy threw in. "He represents a number
of other artists you'd know."

"The point is . . . ," Dutch said.

Jimmy cut in, ". . . that he represents the organized cluster of
musicians paying for the investigation."

My head had been going back and forth between them. Lionel stood with hands hanging down at his sides. He looked at
me, but had nothing to add.

"And you're out of money," I said.

"You see," Jimmy said to Dutch. "Cut right to it."

Lionel spoke for the first time. "I'm really sorry. But we . . .
just never . . . hadn't thought out the costs." His big face, wincing in apology, showed more sensitivity than you'd expect to see
in a man his size. No one would call him weak. He looked like
he could crush Brazil nuts with his teeth.

Cassie chose that moment to come out from the back room
in jeans, cowboy boots, and a white blouse. Her hair hung
straight and wet down her back. "Hi, guys," she said.

Jimmy and Dutch both jumped to their feet like they had
springs up their asses. I introduced Cassie to Lionel. Dutch
stood wiping his hands on the sides of his jeans before shaking
her hand.

"Go ahead. Sit back down," she said. She sat on the other
corner of the desk.

I waved for Lionel to take the chair behind the desk. He said,
"Oh, that's okay," and lowered himself slowly to the front edge

of the desk while I went around. We made a nice little cluster around the scarred wood. I hoped the bricks holding up one corner of the desk could take the combined weight, now that Lionel had sat. The desk seemed to hold up just fine.

"How close are you?" Jimmy asked. "Any chance of wrapping up soon?"

"You fellows haven't paid Travis *anything* yet, have you?" Cassie put in.

Lionel spoke up. "We intend to. It's just that our resources have . . . a limit, one which we may have already exceeded."

"Didn't you two check with Lionel before you asked Trav to investigate?" Cassie asked.

Jimmy looked embarrassed. Dutch stared at Cassie with a look that was hard to define. She did look very wholesome and tasty, sitting there on the desk. I was quietly proud, in spite of all my efforts otherwise.

"It doesn't matter," I said. "You all know I'm going to stick with this until I unravel it—whether it's some random kook or a calculated plan against women, musical or merely prominent. I've had a setback or two, but I'm in for the trip."

All three of the men let out a little air, and the tension that went with it. Cassie looked at me in a way that gave me a glimmer of what she found attractive in such a weathered bit of furniture as me.

"That's a comfort," Jimmy said at last.

"You'll have," Lionel said, ". . . that is, we'll find some way of thanking you."

"Free tickets to a Trish Mirandez concert?" Cassie said. "Maybe a pre-release CD?"

"A CD would be something," Dutch said. He looked around at the otherwise bare room. "Is he going to spin it on his finger?"

"We'll think of something," Lionel said. "Something appropriate."

"What about this other business?" Jimmy asked. "These thugs who trashed your car and office?"

"Still looking into that," I said. I could imagine that the militia thought of me as unfinished business as well.

When my morning visitors had filed out, Cassie asked, "What's on your dance card?"

"First a shave and shower. Then I should visit Gareth Fields before he visits me. Are you going to do anything about tracking Alvin?"

"You're still the best bait in town. I may just wait here, see if he shows."

Somehow, that didn't make me feel any better. I vowed to myself to make my visit with Fields a short one.

A secretary ushered me into the office this time, the day crew at the Bureau office being in. Gareth looked up from his desk. He'd missed his shave and his eyes looked like red holes burned in a blanket. He put a hand over the receiver he held and said, "Have a seat."

He wrapped up his conversation and put the phone down, then closed a couple of dark-tan numbered files on his desk, moved them to the left corner of his otherwise-clean cherry-wood desk. He stood, stretched, went to the window, looked out, then came back and sat.

His wore a rumpled shirt and had gone back to dark suspenders. A stain of sweat marked where his shoulder holster pressed against him. He ran the fingers of one hand through his reddish-blond hair. I noticed a few white hairs for the first time.

"You took your time getting here," he said.

I waited. It was his party.

"I asked you not to meddle in my investigation," he went on. He leaned back in his chair, looked up into a corner of the room. "But there have been some ripples in the pond. You may have even detected a different attitude on the part of the local police."

I nodded. Borster sure seemed to have a burr up his butt, one Gareth had put there.

"Some of them have . . . reasons for feeling compromised. They want to cooperate."

"Pressured into cooperating, eh? Not much has changed since J. Edgar, has it?" I said, knowing right away I should have kept my mouth shut. I watched color dance around on his pale face. At least I hadn't said anything about Bu guys wearing dresses or anything.

"Other parties—those in a position to . . . matter—have also begun to assert their interests," he said. "In a way that doesn't make my job any easier."

"It's easier to yank me around than them, huh."

His lips pressed together. Oh, he had buttons, and I was hitting them.

He took a deep breath. "You should know something about these men about whom we have a common interest. They're not outright skinheads or neo-Nazis. They're the combined dregs of several cast-off bunches, working together to protect what they perceive as their own way of life, and we think money is involved," he said. "But, they're disrupted. Something has changed their whole confidence. It's sent them to holes now where even we can't locate them."

"Is that a bad thing?"

"It is when my job is to keep track of them and bring them to justice."

"Don't you have anyone on the inside?"

"Two key informants we had are missing, presumed lost."

"Donnie and Alvin?"

"Not those two," he said. "Neither of them were ever in pocket, though they were part of what we were looking into.

The point is. . . ." He stopped, got up and walked over to his window again. Must have been something damned interesting out there. He stayed there for a moment or two.

He turned back to me. "Someone's killing these guys, able-fighting militia though they are. Do I have to tell you how difficult this makes my job?"

I shook my head.

He looked at me, expectant.

"And you want me to do *what* about it?" I said. "Did you call me in just to vent? This case hasn't been a bowl of peach cobbler for me, either." Oh, yeah. I don't talk much. When I do I can be a smart-ass.

He settled back into his chair, looked around the room, then at the files on his desk. In an abrupt move, his left arm shot across the desk and swept the files into the file cabinets that lined the walls. The files hit and fell, the sheets of paper and photographs in the folders opening into sprays of bent pages as they tumbled into loose piles on the floor.

"Go on," he said. "Get the bent dick hell out of here."

Call it a hunch, but I doubted I would be getting any holiday greetings from him.

The drive back to my office seemed a longer one than getting to the FBI office. I suspected that Special Agent Fields intended more lumps to come into my already lumpy life.

I turned the corner and was debating on parking the rental in front of or behind the office when I saw the open hole in the front wall of my office. Les Bettles stood looking at it, his fists on his hips.

I hopped out of the car and rushed over.

"A damn fine mess you have *this* time," Les shouted as soon as he spotted me trotting his way.

I brushed past him, didn't try to open the locked oak door,

just pulled myself over through the gap and stepped across the smashed plywood inside.

"Cassie," I yelled. The desk had been knocked onto its corner, and the chairs scattered every which way. I ran into the back. It was empty back there as well.

I came back into the sunlit office as Les unlocked the door and stepped in. "You're going to have to pay for all this, you know." He looked around the otherwise empty insides for more damage.

Les is a burly, roundish fellow whom I have never seen in his happier moments. I did admire the way he shared his threats—far more direct than the FBI. I said, "I may have to consider moving out anyway. This place isn't safe, and too many people know about it now. The wrong kind of people." I looked around for other signs of violence. The office bottle lay shattered.

"Come on, Trav. It's just some busted plywood. The glass guys are coming today anyway." His chances of renting out such a hole in the wall to anyone else weren't great.

I nodded. "You mind if I take some of this plywood?"

"Mind? Hell, no. Help yourself. I guess we're gonna have to tear it out anyway. Someone just saved us some bother."

I looked for all the pieces I could find that had heavy boot prints in them. Bits of stone from the bottoms of the shoes had been smashed into the wood from the violence of the entry. I bundled them in my arms and ran back to my car, opened the trunk, and put them inside.

Les stuck his head outside, watched as I fired up the car and pulled out with a small screech. He must have figured me for more than a little loony. But he still had a tenant.

That was all the time I had to worry about him. My mind was on Cassie, and on the ones who'd kicked the front of my office in and snatched her.

Chapter Twenty-One

I'm one of life's most impatient drivers in the first place. As I fishtailed my rental car through a sea of Volvos on my way to the University of Texas campus in the middle of town, I was at my worst. To make matters worse, I wasn't sure which building I needed. I did know the corner of the campus where most of the physical science and engineering buildings were. I parked the car off Twenty-Sixth Street, gathered an armload of smashed plywood, and headed over to the brick buildings of the campus.

A student pointed me toward the geology building. It was just across a fountain from me. I circled around the spraying jets of water, hiked to the building, and went inside. The directory told me where to find the Department of Geological Sciences. In seconds I burst through the door with my armload. I spoke too quickly and too loud to the department secretary, saw her head snap back an inch as I said, "I need to find someone who knows Texas geology."

"Well, there are a number. . . ."

"A specialist . . . on identification."

She looked over the tops of her glasses at the lumber I clutched, probably deciding whether or not to call campus security. Whatever urgent plea showed in my eyes led her to say, "You might try Professor Vance P. Marsh. He's down the hall."

She started to give me a room number, but I had taken off, moving in brisk strides in the direction her eyes had pointed. I read the name tags by the doors as I went, finally came to a sign with Professor Marsh's name and office hours posted. It stood open.

I gave the door a rap in passing and stepped inside. The guy behind the desk was younger than I expected, but had already cultivated a dark beard that shot out in several directions. He looked up at me through glasses that magnified his eyes to the size of golf balls. "Yes?" he said.

"If I furnish some rock samples, could you tell me what part of Texas they're from?"

"Why, of course." He lowered the copy of some technical journal he had been holding close to his face.

I took a deep breath. "Sorry. I'm a private detective. Someone's life may be hanging on this information."

"Oh, I hardly think geology's life and death. Though, in the case of some earthquakes we. . . ."

"Well, it *is*," I said, far more loudly than I'd intended. His head rocked back and his mouth closed.

"Please," I said. "The rocks I need checked are stuck in these pieces of wood."

His face lit up. "We all enjoy a challenge now and again. Let me see what you have there."

I handed him my plywood pieces. He pulled some clear glass dishes from his desk drawer and began to scrape and pick as he put all the pieces of stone into the dishes. While he did this, he picked up the phone, held it to his ear with his shoulder, and punched in a number. "Shirley," he said, "can you come to my office if you're not busy with something."

He hung up the phone and whistled. He looked up, saw me watching him and said, "A colleague. In structural petrology."

I said, "Oh."

A woman in a white lab coat came into the office. Her hair was short, straight and blonde. The glasses she wore weren't quite up to the strength of Professor Marsh's, but they made up

for it by having very large lenses. They kept her face from looking cute, gave her the intelligent air she seemed to prefer.

"Shirley Rasher," she said to me. I introduced myself.

She looked at the rocks in the dishes. "Where did you get
these?"

"Some may be from around here," I said. "It's the other pink
ones I'm interested in. I'm a private detective. Finding the
source of those other rocks may well save someone's life."

She gave me the same look Marsh had given me, but it faded
from humor to serious when she saw how I looked back at her.
"Let's see what you have. Some of these are definitely not from
here," she said. "They look to be from a granitic gneiss terrain.
You're lucky you came to me. I specialize in structural deposi-
tion."

We then entered the phase where she and Marsh chattered
back and forth in a dialect of which I understood only an occasional word. They waved me to a chair and took off down the
hallway with the samples.

I looked around at the books that crammed every inch of the
shelves, some on their sides on top of other books. Piles of
magazines stood in stacks around the floor. It looked like Huff's
place, except for the subject of the journals and books.

I tried to keep my mind off where Cassie might be, or what
might be happening to her. On the wall were maps of tectonic
plates, topographic highs and lows, and one of Texas that had
each mountain sticking out from the map. Some of this stuff
looked dry as six-week-old toast. Professor Marsh had been
what I'd expected when I came to campus. But Professor Rasher
had surprised me. That's the way it should be. If someone as
young and as attractive as Professor Rasher found stones exciting, I say power to her.

I could hear them talking together as they came back down

the hallway to the office. They seemed to be having a great time.

They burst into the office with the little glass dishes of rock. Professor Rasher's eyes twinkled at me. Professor Marsh looked goggle-eyed and shy, suppressing a giggle about something.

"We ran a couple of standard routines just to be sure," Rasher said, "but you don't have much of a mystery here. Between our electron microbe, gamma-ray spectroscopy, and whatnot, your little rocks didn't stand a chance. Of course, the tests just confirmed what we already knew."

Marsh chuckled as if she had told a slightly off-color story.

"You see these little pink fellows there?" Rasher poked a finger at some crumbs of rock.

"Town Mountain Granite," Marsh said.

"Precambrian exposure," Rasher added. "Putting aside a couple of relatively small spots in far West Texas, the main exposure covers a few square miles and is just to the west of the buried Ouachita Mountain Range."

"Can you tell me exactly where the rocks are from? Because I need to go there." I hated to butt in and interrupt their fun. But there was Cassie.

"Absolutely," Rasher said.

"No problem," Marsh said. "We can distinguish Fredricksburg granite from that which is mined near Marble Falls, and, to put a fine point on things, we can even tell apart igneous rock that comes from the same county."

"Well, *where* then?" My voice seemed very loud in the tiny office.

Both their hands went up to the same spot on the bas-relief map. The spot they pointed to was to the west of Austin and slightly north.

"In earth person terms," I said more softly.

"Enchanted Rock State Natural Area," they said in unison.

"The whole area?"

"No, if you want an exact match, you might look here." Marsh's finger moved north on the map. "You see, we can tell. The mica, for instance. . . ."

I had gone, already out the door and hearing their voices fade behind me.

I swung by my office. A crew was putting new glass in my front window. I stayed just long enough to dig out a Slim Jim that had survived all the recent chaos by hiding flat along the top of a door sill. I used it to open Cassie's parked car and get her gun out of the glove box. It was a .38, blue steel with a five-inch barrel.

I gassed up the rental car and wheeled into the nearest Academy sporting goods store long enough to buy two boxes of ammo. It had been a long, long time since I had allowed myself to pack a gun. As far as falling off the firearms wagon went, I figured that now would be the time to fall hard.

The car held the road well. I hummed along at about eighty-five mph out toward Llano where I would turn south toward Enchanted Rock.

The spot the two professors had identified, with some precision, was outside the park and up in some rough country, typical of some of the sites for militia retreats I'd heard mentioned.

For most of the miles, I tried not to think of Cassie. Instead, I let my mind drift back to the chatter between the rock professors as I was darting from the office. I gathered I was driving past an outcrop of Paleozoic sedimentary rock—mere baby rocks compared with Precambrian. The professors had touched on Balcones volcanic rock and a few other types before I'd escaped. I wished I'd paid more attention so that it could distract me more now.

When I'd played out that line of thought, I turned on the

radio, found a station that played the kind of music Jimmy and Dutch sang. My mind drifted in and out, but I swear I heard a song that went, "You got her drunk. You take her home."

Almost to the cutoff road to Enchanted Rock park, a truck had pulled to the side of the road with a sign saying the guy was selling homemade beef jerky. I stopped and went over and bought some of the jerky. I asked the pimple-faced boy sitting on the dropped-down tailgate of the truck if there was any kind of training camp nearby. I got a blank look back.

My insides were wound up like a vehicle in overdrive. Before I had to calm myself and try asking anything else, I saw a pickup truck go by painted in camouflage colors. Both guys in it had fuzzy bowling balls for heads.

I rushed to my car, threw the jerky in the backseat, fired up and followed, keeping back as far as I could. They led the way through fourteen more miles of twisting, turning, and climbing roads that hadn't seen maintenance in the last two or three presidential administrations. I felt glad that the car banging around under me wasn't my own.

In a thickly wooded stretch of the two-lane road, I came around a sharp corner and saw a long open straight reach of road ahead, but no truck.

A small two-rut gravel cut led off into the trees to my left. Small dust clouds swirled above the ruts.

I slowed, eased over until I came to a flat spot where I could edge my car off the road. The car plowed into and through the thicket of bushes. I drove until I eased behind a couple of trees and a stand of brush that concealed the car from the road. I put both boxes of ammo in my pockets, for balance, and tucked the gun into my belt. I followed the path my car had made back to the road, standing up bushes and broken brush to cover the tracks. Then I slipped across the road like Rambo in a suit and began a careful hike up along the twin ruts that led deeper into the dark of the thick woods.

CHAPTER TWENTY-TWO

The big trees around me were live oaks. The smaller mesquite trees and other brush filled in for a dense wall of shadows and green that surrounded me.

The vegetation began to thin about the same time I could make out sounds ahead. I'd been walking for two or three miles, had passed a broken wooden sign that confirmed that long ago this had been a camp called "The Last Cowboy Summer Camp."

I stepped into the woods off the trail to the right, pressed that way until I came to an exposed wall of the pink granite that made up the composition of much of the gravel I'd seen so far. Good thing it was here or I'd have never found this place. It began to look like my two rock hounds were right.

The area along the pink rock face was too open, like a road. I had to push into a sticker-filled patch of tight green growth to get closer to the source of noise. I took my time, eager as I was. No sense making any noise. I kid myself a lot about the Indian side of my heritage, but I always have been good at being quiet in the woods.

I got close enough to look out from behind the bole of a tree and a thick clump of sage. Below, an encampment spread out through the opening along a stream. Several weathered wooden tent-shaped buildings on short stilts stood in a row—probably where the boys once stayed. A main building, big enough to hold a mess hall, stood across from the row on the other side of the clearing.

Somewhere behind me, a mockingbird chattered away. I heard voices of the men moving between the buildings in the camp down the slope below me. The gravel walks between the buildings were pink, the same crushed stone that had given the place's location away to me. Hard to tell how many men were there. I could only see ten or twelve. From the cluster of trucks and motorcycles parked near the lane, there were quite a few more men than that here. Cassie had been right about their not using cars much.

An open stretch of once-mowed grass made creeping any closer risky. The sun beat down on me; sweat ran down my collar and in a cool trickle down my spine. I considered waiting until dark to get closer.

A rustle of trees behind me caused me to ease low in a squat in my thicket. The sound was light enough to be a squirrel, but had the wrong rhythm to it. Instead of something furry scampering from limb to limb, this sounded like someone trying to be quiet.

I pressed tighter to the ground, kept still as death.

Branches snapped back into place like leafy whips as the soft rustling came closer. Through the thickest part of green leaves surrounding me, I could look through and see dark khaki and a glimmer of white. When I caught a corner of the face, I pushed out and grabbed an arm.

Harmon Cuthers spun, stared at me. It was hard to tell if he had nearly fired his gun or dropped it. The shock in his face eased away to surprise. "You scared the Bejesus out of me, Travis. Why are you here? Oh, Cassie. Have they got her?"

I nodded, looked down to the encampment. I didn't think they could see us from there. I pulled Harmon farther back into the woods before I asked him, "Is this a full-fledged operation?"

The embarrassment in his face saved him having to answer. We weren't even in his county. I said, "Are you crazy? What were you going to do by yourself?"

"I could ask *you* that," he said.

It was a good question. I mulled it over while he looked over my shoulder and said, "No, Hazel. He's with us."

I heard the hammer being lowered on a gun behind me. I turned slowly. The fellow wore a uniform similar to the sheriff's. He stood an inch or two taller than my six feet. His face was the color of a Hershey bar.

"My new deputy, Hazel Martin," Cuthers said. "He's the head count replacement for Alvin. Cassie has the investigative slot. That is, if she's alive."

"We're going to get along better," I said, "if you stay as positive as possible about that." To Hazel I said, "It's good to have you along." I held out a hand.

He smiled, gave me a firm shake, said, "Pleased."

"I'll bet you're the kind of person wears red to a bullfight," I said to Harmon.

He smiled. "Hazel can take care of himself. You think militia who lean to the racist side like Indians any better than blacks?"

"What do you plan to do to them?" I asked.

"Do to them?" Harmon said. "I'm here to save as many of them as I can. Now that I know Cassie's down there I want her out as much as you do. Though, that's not what brought me here in the first place."

The first explosion went off before I got to ask him what the hell he was talking about.

The concussion knocked all three of us to the forest floor. I could only imagine what it was doing to the men back at the camp. My ears were still ringing when a second and third explosion went off.

I scrambled forward and pushed apart the leaves. Several of the vehicles were in flames and smoking. One of the smaller bunk cabins was gone. I put my fingers in my ears, watched as four more explosions took out all the motorcycles, several more of the trucks, and two more of the small cabins. Someone thought, as I had, that Cassie was being held in the large building. None of the explosions went off near it.

There were bodies scattered across the lawn and between the buildings. One man on fire ran and leaped into the stream that ran behind the cabins. Several men came running out of the large building and some of the smaller ones. They held assault weapons. A couple began to spray the woods around them in all directions. I ducked back down as a string of bullets sizzled around me, snipping off leaves.

I put my head back up and watched the men below frantically looking for anything to shoot at. Each time one began firing, he would tumble flat. Another would open fire in the direction he thought the sniper had fired from, and *he* would fall. After a number had been hit, the rest caught on and dove to the ground, taking what cover they could.

You know, you think about a militia camp, where they train and prepare for the day when the dreaded terrorist hordes or even their own government (they think) will come busting in and try to take their guns or something. For all that training, the first few moments of this firefight had these guys in utter confusion. I didn't see a single woman in all the running about below, though there were some normally competent militia men rushing around like so many confused girl scouts.

I heard the hollow thump of a howitzer, saw rockets zip in at the men from at least three directions. Some of the men were so shook they were firing straight up in the air at one or two flares on parachutes that floated across the parade ground.

Harmon and Hazel lifted their heads on either side of me and watched the chaos below.

"If those boys weren't riled up before, they'll sure enough have the green apple nasties now," Harmon said.

Somewhere in the woods on the other side of the encampment, a .50-caliber machine gun opened up. Its patterns of fire forced some of the militia, who were trying to dig foxholes with their hands, to jump up and start running back and forth, only to tumble to the ground from shots fired from another side.

I ducked low and started to crawl down the hill through the brush. If I stayed low and followed the vegetation I could get closer to the main building.

"Where're you going?" Harmon said.

"I didn't come to be a spectator," I called back to him. "Why don't you guys stay here until this lets up. If you want to do something, lay down some ground cover for me when I make a break for it." I turned and started forward, almost put a stick right into my eye. Better pay attention, I told myself. I heard bullets sizzle through the leaves above where I crawled. They sounded like angry metal bees.

When I had worked myself as close as I could get to the main building, half deafened by more explosions and the steady firing, I looked over at the ground I had to cover. Black smoke billowed and rolled with the slow breeze across the open area. One or two men lay still. All of the vehicles had been blown up by now, and most of the cabins were leveled. The corner of the main building was just beginning to burn. Shots came out of one or two of its windows. I saw some of the men on the ground crawling toward the trees. As soon as one made it, he'd stand up and run, though I did see a couple of them tumble back.

I shook some of the bullets from one box of ammo loose into my pocket, took a deep breath, and started a scrambling run toward the building. As I ran, I saw one or two dirt furrows fly up, but wondered why I wasn't drawing more fire, not that I craved it. I glanced to my right. From the center of the billowing black smoke I saw a small figure burst through, firing away with a pistol in each hand. Two thick men stood from where they lay, but before they'd swung their assault weapons to her, they fell to Joz's firing. Without breaking stride, she shoved one automatic back into her belt and scooped up an assault weapon. I watched two more brave, or foolish, defenders fall while completing my own not-too-bright of a run.

I ran at full tilt toward the side door of the main building when I saw movement in one of the windows on this side. I fired off three shots at it, saw someone fall backward through the opening.

I hit the wooden door at full speed. Its latch and hinges gave at the same time. It flew several feet into the room, along with the fellow who had been standing behind it. He lay where he fell. I stood in the open dining area. Someone in the kitchen fired at me. I squeezed off the last three shots in my gun and dropped to the floor. I knocked one of the thick dining tables onto its side, flipped the cylinder of the S & W open and popped out the empties and began shoving in more bullets.

Shots rang loud, echoing through the dining hall. A string of holes appeared in the table I hid behind, and they were progressing toward me. I dropped flat and rolled in the opposite direction of where the holes appeared, only inches below them. I rolled until I came out from behind the other end of the table, stopped, and from the prone position fired twice. I saw the man shooting fall back and clatter into hanging metal pans.

I got up, gun held forward in both hands. My head snapped to each corner and any place someone could hide. The room was quiet, the smell of cordite still thick in the air.

A large pair of closed doors led from the dining area to the rest of the building. I ran to them, gave a tug. Nothing. They were locked, barred from the other side. I spun and ran back to the outside door. I slipped outside and started to edge around the building.

Down at the edge of the green, I saw Harmon Cuthers standing and firing in the direction of three men trying to get around one of the smaller buildings to be on the other side of Joz Brosche. Hazel Martin ran, firing as he went, getting into a flanking spot. Joz crouched low, shoving new magazines into her pistols.

I popped around the corner, fired at an opened window. The weapon sticking from it fell forward onto the long wooden porch where a couple of tumbled rocking chairs served as meager cover for another fellow firing at Joz. I unloaded the rest of my rounds on him, saw him roll sideways off the porch, leaving behind his gun.

I pressed back against the building, reloaded, then darted around the corner and ran toward the front door. Shots were still coming from the building. I glanced back and saw Joz running toward me. She fired past me and took out one of the shooters. Then I saw her drop her guns, grab at her side, and drop to the ground.

Chapter Twenty-Three

I ran at full steam, hit the door with my shoulder and bounced back two feet. I grabbed for the knob and twisted. It was locked. I took a step back, aimed at the lock, and shot a hole through it.

This time when I kicked, the door swung open. Shots from inside punched two holes in the door as it moved. I dove and slid inside on a hardwood floor. I spun onto my back, aimed and shot at the guy who stepped away from the window to shoot at the door. One of the three shots I squeezed off lifted him off his feet and dropped him.

I scrambled forward on hands and knees, picked up the automatic weapon he'd held, a nine-millimeter built to look like an M16. I was pulling three extra magazines out of the fallen guy's shirt pocket when the door behind me opened. I squeezed the trigger and sent a three-round burst into the man coming out. He flew back into the room.

The room was shaped like a hotel registration area, with a couple of beat-up vinyl couches, designed to serve as a lounge area. Dust and cobwebs covered most of what I could see. I looked around but didn't spot anyone else lurking. I saw a door behind the registration desk. Before I went there, I eased to the window and looked out. The sound of the fighting out there had shifted.

I couldn't see Joz anywhere, though that didn't mean she wasn't still lying out there where she'd fallen. I could see what had changed the tone of the fighting. Hazel Martin scurried from place to place in the parade ground, leaping in and out of some of the small cover spots the militia had made. Most of those men still fighting, who hadn't run or fallen, shifted their entire fighting to trying to get him. You drop a black man in uniform into the angry bee's nest of a now-paranoid racist militia camp and you can expect a result like that. I only hoped Hazel could last until I got back out to help.

I turned back to the business at hand and went across the creaky wooden floor of the room to the door. I turned the knob, pushed the door in and went inside, ready to cover either side of the doorway on the inside. There were only two people in the room. One of them was Cassie. She lay on a mattress stretched along the wall, her wrists and ankles bound. Silver duct tape covered her mouth. Beside her, in a wheelchair, where he'd been able to shoot out the small window that faced out toward the back of the building from the office, sat Donnie. He held a gun, a mate of the one I now carried, aimed at Cassie's head.

"What's the matter with you?" he screamed. "She was our insurance. You want her dead, I'll blow her away. I mean it, man." His face flashed red all the way up through his scalp that showed beneath his buzz-cut hair. He had casts on both legs and he wore what looked like a hospital gown. His face and neck were covered with sweat. He had to be on some heavy pain medication. This had been his hospital room, perhaps, until Cassie had been brought to the camp.

"I swear, Donnie," I said, "is your voice getting higher?" I wanted him to swing the gun away from Cassie, to give me a second's chance.

"Put the fucking gun down," he screamed. The end of the barrel wavered with the shake of his hands, but stayed too close to her head the whole time. I could see his hand tightening on the stock and trigger. "I'll kill her. I really will. Don't even doubt me for a second."

I lowered the barrel of the M16 clone I held, caught movement at the window behind him.

"But what about Joz Brosche?" I said.

You talk about small kids and their boogeyman. Donnie's face jumped a shade of red and I could almost see more sweat pour out of it. "Don't bullshit me, man."

"Right here behind you, scumbag." Her voice sounded like tearing sheets.

Donnie whirled, dropping Cassie out of the way. He lifted the barrel of his gun as he did. Joz hung by her armpits on the window sill, both thin arms inside the room holding guns. Flames shot from each of the guns half a dozen times and the racket filled the small room.

Pieces of Donnie splattered across the room. I was out of the line of fire, but not of all the spray. Donnie flew out of the wheelchair and lifted to land with a thud to the floor, the wheelchair falling to its side across him.

I rushed to Joz. "Are you all right? I saw you get hit out there."

"Give me a hand inside."

I grabbed her wrists and lifted until I could shift and grab her waist. I pulled her inside the room. Her shirt was soaked with blood, front and back, from a spot at the side of her waist where a bullet had passed through. You see people in movies and cartoons get hit with bullets and they bounce back or move right along. That doesn't happen in real life. The shock of getting hit with a round is enough to send most people into shock. But Joz had pulled herself to the house after losing a fair amount of blood for a small woman. I eased her down onto the mattress, propped her up so her back was to the wall. Then I reached for the ropes binding Cassie.

She pulled off the tape from her mouth as soon as her hands were free. "Trav, Joz," she said.

I finished undoing her ankles. "We've got to move," I said. "Harmon and Hazel are out there taking fire. We need to help them." I handed Cassie one of the assault rifles and a couple of the clips. She rubbed her wrists and moved her jaw from side to side as she got back to normal.

"What about Joz?" Cassie said.

"I've got her."

Joz had been busy prying the bullet out of a 9mm round. She poured the powder onto the front entry wound of where she'd been hit, pulled out a lighter and held it to the powder. There was a small flash. She gritted her teeth, but didn't scream.

"Good lord," I said. I'd heard of people doing that in battle, but didn't think I'd ever see it.

Cassie yanked off the robe Donnie had been wearing, tore strips from what hadn't been soaked in blood. With that and the robe sash, she did a makeshift binding job on Joz's wound. It looked like the bullet that hit her had passed through the lean fleshy side of her waist and hadn't hit any organs. But she'd lost blood and had fought off the effects of shock. Her normally serious face looked a step closer toward a death mask. She put fresh clips in her guns while Cassie did the wrapping.

Cassie stepped back. I handed her the .38, then bent and scooped up Joz, who was a handful of dense weight in spite of looking small. I carried one of the automatics along with Joz. Cassie led the way. Joz had both guns ready.

The three of us burst out the front of the lodge. Flames covered a much larger portion of the building by now. We ran through the smoke out into the open ground, saw where half a dozen of the opposition had Hazel pinned down at the corner of one of the remaining cabins. The closest of them was still twenty yards away. They were all firing and moving closer.

Covering shots came down from the sheriff's direction, behind a tree at the base of the woods. Two of the militia had deployed in that direction and were working closer to where Harmon was holed up. The rest of the encampment area was quiet by comparison, except for occasional fires and the sound of moaning coming from one or two of the men who hadn't been able to crawl away.

Cassie and I ran toward the men shooting at Hazel. We were ten yards from them before any of them saw or heard us. When they did, I can only imagine they saw Joz, who could not look pretty to them. Two of them spun to return fire—the others jumped and ran, falling at once to the fire from both of Joz's guns and Cassie's automatic. Hazel stepped out from the building and sent a few shots into the air.

The two men who stalked Harmon dropped their hunt and cut in a run for the woods. Cassie sent one of them tumbling to the ground. The other fell back just as he got to the woods. I couldn't tell if Cassie got him or if I got him with the rounds I fired while shooting from the hip and running with Joz in my hands. I knew Joz's guns didn't reach that far.

It seemed suddenly very quiet all around us. Harmon waved at us to get out of the clearing, just in case. Hazel jogged our way. Cassie and I kept up our pace and swung toward the sheriff.

The four of us on foot, with me carrying Joz, worked our way through the skirt of the woods until we got to the two ruts of the lane that had brought us here.

We kept a close watch as we walked, but saw none of those paramilitary guys in the area. Soon it was just thick woods around the trail. The air smelled green and alive after all we'd been through, all the shooting, fire, and explosions we'd left behind.

"Thanks," I said to Hazel. "You sure took the heat off us at the right time."

He grinned at Cassie and me, gave a wink to Harmon. "I endeavor to give satisfaction," he said.

CHAPTER TWENTY-FOUR

Joz Brosche was all bone and muscle. I carried the heft of her, and she never let up on looking around us. But a person can't take a bullet through the side with no effect. She shuddered every once in a while on the walk back, though she never complained. She did squint in the sheriff's direction and say, "You know, Harmon, I couldn't help notice you missed your mark a few times back there."

Hazel said, "The sahib shot divinely. But Providence was merciful to the game."

"You didn't notch up your gun much either," Joz said to Hazel.

"I realize," Sheriff Cuthers said, "the concept's a stretch for you, Joz. But we're 'peace' officers. I think the accuracy of Hazel's shooting was just what was called for."

Joz grumped back, "That's somethin' you coulda had put on your stone if Cassie and Geronimo here hadn't been more on the bead. You know, Trav, for a guy who never carries a gun, you were a pleasant surprise. You musta been motivated."

I grumbled back some sort of answer.

Cassie walked closer and put a hand on my shoulder. "Thanks," she said, "for everything."

"Thank me when it's all over," I said.

"I will," she promised.

"You be careful I don't steal this one from you," Joz said, in her gravelly voice. "He's got some good in him . . . somewhere."

Her voice was forced, someone tired who didn't want to doze off.

"You think we'll see any of them this way?" I asked Harmon.

"Depends," he said.

"On what?"

He nodded to Joz, but said no more.

"Were there others there with you, Joz?" I asked. I was seeing Huff with the smear of black powder on his face, and hearing his comment about "fooling around" with C-4.

"Let's say there were," she said. "Don't you think, if there was, they'd have had the sense to skedaddle? Someone somewhere had to hear those explosions. It's only a matter of time before the area's lousy with the law. Beggin' your pardon."

"No offense taken," Harmon said. "Hazel and I would be in as much trouble as you if we're found here now in this mess. Cassie too, for that matter, although her presence wasn't as a volunteer."

Where we walked, there was only the sound of our steps on the pink gravel ruts and of limbs bending with their leaves rustling high in the thick growth of trees. Sound seemed to dampen in the woods. The area near the encampment wasn't too populous. I counted on that to give us time to get out.

"When we get to civilization, Harmon," I said, "it might be a good idea to call a tip in to Gareth Fields about this. I wouldn't make the direct call yourself. Maybe route it through your old pal Jayne Randall."

"What's that about?" Cassie asked.

I asked Joz, "You wouldn't happen to know anything about someone killing some of those militia guys, would you? I mean, before today."

She stared back at me in stony silence.

"It might be," Hazel said, "that whoever was doing such a thing probably knew it would make the group paranoid enough to cluster together in a gathering like we found today, with no women present. Whoever set this up, though, couldn't know that the militia would kidnap Cassie for insurance."

"Thanks again, everyone, for getting me out of there," Cassie said. She looked pale and tired, but her smile was genuine.

"They didn't do anything to you?" Hazel asked.

"They were afraid to. Something had them very shaky."

"With good reason, it seems," I said. "How did you come to be out here, Harmon?"

"I did some tracking of my own," he said, "and listening close 'round where I live. There may be frost on the mountain, but I still can pay attention to what's going on around me." The corner of his eye flicked to Joz, then back to the trail. We were nearly to the road. I began to watch for cars or any other movement.

A few more steps, and I could see road. I breathed a sigh that we had had no encounters.

"Just take me to my wheels," Joz said.

"Where're you parked?"

"Way the hell and gone to the other side."

"I'll drive you there," I said.

"I'll ride to Fredricksburg with Harmon, come back in to Austin and get my car later," Cassie said. The look she gave me had promises, questions, all manner of things in it. Her eyes glittered at me in round wetness. From the corner of one, a tear started down her cheek.

"We'd better all scramble," I said.

Harmon stood still for a moment, though. He looked back toward the encampment. "What I want to know," he said, "is did anyone see Alvin in all that mess?"

I drove back into Austin knowing I had an empty pantry at home and a nearly empty pocket. I'd spent some of the last money I had on ammo, the remainder of which I had given to Cassie when I returned her gun. I was thinking strong thoughts about that cot back in my office. But I didn't allow myself to go there just yet.

My mouth carried a bad taste about what I'd been through. On the way in I'd whirled through the news radio stations, but hadn't heard a word so far. It would likely be tomorrow's breaking story, though without my name anywhere in the tale, which was fine with me. I pushed the rental car through traffic and aimed it toward Max Bolens' sprawling place. The sun was going down; some people were flipping on their headlights.

The limo was parked in front of the house. As I wheeled up behind it, Max stepped out of the front door. He wore a burgundy long-sleeved shirt and gray slacks with cordovan loafers. A lot of tension seemed to have peeled away from his face. He smiled and waved.

I got out. "You really *do* have this place under a close watch, don't you?"

"That will end soon. Thanks to you," he said.

"I guess you've heard." I didn't have to ask his source of information. His pipeline came right from federal sources—he'd almost certainly been the one pressuring Gareth to put the vise grips on Borster.

"I sure have." He beamed and held out a hand. I ignored it.

I said, "I want to head off any wrong ideas. Some of what went on has a vigilante flavor. I don't want you to think I condone that."

"It got the job done."

"There were other circumstances." I didn't want to go into Cassie's abduction. "But understand me. When it comes down to it, my bottom line is that people can wear their hair any length they like, they can have any kind of heritage, they can speak out in any way they like, they can bear arms, and they can be rich sons-a-bitches—as long as they respect one another while doing so. It's the hate that bothers me, whether it comes from right, left, up or down."

"You're the last person I'd expect to hear endorsing the system."

"I hope I'm not doing that," I said. "But there's always been a crowd that thinks whoever doesn't agree to the letter with them ought to be lined up and shot. You, and whoever agrees with you, don't ever really want that to kick in. Because I'm here to tell you that there are far worse people than you out there, by far. You might find yourselves being the ones lined up."

I turned and started to get back into the car, as upset once again with myself as with him.

He called out to me, "You know, whatever happened, it means just one thing to me right now. Most of the prosecution's key witnesses are gone. My daughter's trial is likely to be dismissed and she can come home. That's all I've wanted. I'd really like to repay you somehow."

"You could keep the feds off my back," I said.

"I wasn't able to do that for myself," he said. He meant off Donna's back.

I got in the car and closed the door. Through the open window I said, "That's what I thought."

He leaned close, bent forward until his crossed arms rested on the bottom of my open window. "Look, I'll be the first to admit that I didn't marry well. But I stayed loyal to her all these years. I stuck by her, no matter what. I did the same for my daughter."

He took a breath, glanced at the house. "I made some money, that's true. And I was fortunate politically. But I don't have servants. I only ride in the limo because I'm asked to, since it's bulletproof. Do you see where I'm going with this?"

"Yes. Yes, I do. I begin to see the paradigm shift you've sold yourself, and to enough others to bring in the vote. Before I buy, I want the answer to one question."

"What?"

"You use people. Does that let you sleep well?"

"When? What do you mean?"

"Did you send Don Briscoe to my place to snoop around and see what I'd found so far?"

He gave me a glare that could cut glass, but said nothing.

"Before you answer," I said, "I need to tell you that whoever did send him there put him in the wrong place at a very bad time. Whoever sent him carries some blame for his death."

He stood and stared back, suppressed waves of shock rippled across his stoic face. He was giving me some real cigar-store-Indian silence.

I said, "Sometimes at night, the faces of friends I've lost haunt me. I only hope some of your friends, on whose heads you've stepped to be where you are, worry you as much."

"You know," he said at last, the words as pinched as if they were squeezed out of the tail end of a toothpaste tube. "I'm going to tell you something I wouldn't dare tell another soul." He glanced around, then leaned closer. "My biggest concern about my daughter's trial was that it might reveal just how close that acorn fell to the tree."

"Do you mean . . . ?" I'd had to think my way to what he meant, and couldn't believe it then, much less get myself to say it.

"That's right. Those buzz-cut bastards might just have been on the right track. I know I could never admit that in the open, but since you've been so graceless about my thanks I'll share it with you. I wouldn't care a good goddamn if every mick, kike, nigger, or especially Indian, was loaded onto a boat and run off

245

the flat end of the earth. Now, then. How do you feel about that?"

He smiled the oiliest smile I've ever seen and rose slowly and stood hovering by my window, waiting to see what I would do.

Anything I might have said boiled in poisonous pools on the softest tissues inside me. All I could see was a red haze. Anger pumped blood through me in small red fists. Everything in me wanted to climb out of the car, tear his arms off, and beat him with the bloody stumps. But, if I did that, I knew I would be no better than Alvin and his ilk. I forced myself, with a leaden arm, to reach and put the car in gear and ease away as he stepped back. It was a triumph for me, but a painful one. I saw him alone and small in front of the massive house as I drove down his lane, and getting smaller the farther I drove.

Hunger and being tired in more than a physical way gnawed at my insides as I pulled up to my place. The new window and blinds were in place, and Les had even done a little touch-up patching and painting. I could see a little scar here and there, dark as it had gotten. That just gave the place personality.

I went in and locked up behind me. I didn't even turn on the office lights. All the bouncing around and rolling hadn't done my ribs a world of good. When they'd bothered me before they'd just been warming up—now my ribs felt like they were on fire. I ached for some serious cot time. It took me a couple of minutes just to tug off my suit coat, which I found had been ripped into uselessness in a half dozen places. I threw it in the corner of the back room and sent the shoes and pants after it. With little more fanfare than that I collapsed onto the cot and lay there. Even without the cactus juice sleep remedy, I had no problem drifting off.

My eyes slapped open to the dark room. My heart was beating

like the late Gene Krupa showing off with his drums. It hammered and thumped inside my chest. My face and chest were covered with sweat.

I'd been back in the middle of the battle with the militia. I had been pinned down by fire where I lay flat on the parade ground lawn. Guys rushed in at me from all sides, firing their assault weapons. Then, from the billowing wall of smoke a figure burst through, firing pistols with each hand. The men attacking me fell with every shot, lifted up and were thrown back into the gray and black smoke. As the figure got closer, I could see the face. It was Cassie running my way and firing.

I took shallow rapid breaths as I came back to normal. My heart began to slow. I felt rather than saw anything at first. I knew there was another presence in the room.

My eyes swept the room until they came to the white cast. I panned up from that, saw the bulky, muscular body hovering at the head of my cot. I stopped when I came to Alvin's slightly battered face.

"Having a bad dream?" he said.

Chapter Twenty-Five

The more my eyes adjusted to the dark room, the less I liked what I saw.

Alvin's face didn't seem to be healing well, or right, and it showed a great deal of pain. The leg cast he wore looked new. That knee had probably been shattered from the shot Joz had put through it.

He stood on crutches and wore a camouflage shirt held in place by a black leather weapons belt. An automatic was shoved in near the buckle, and his right hand hung down by the crutch on that side. I didn't need to make extensive calculations to know how things would come out if I tried to roll off the cot and scoot for the door.

I lay in T-shirt and boxers, waiting. It took only a second to run through my options. I heard a sound that added to the tension. It was the sound of a long steel very sharp polished blade being slid slowly from its scabbard. Anyone who has ever heard this sound in a dark room will know why the hairs on my neck twitched erect.

"How smart do you think I am?" Alvin said.

"What?"

He repeated himself. I could hear him rubbing the blade against the side of the cast, honing it.

"Do you think I'm some sort of half-wit? Me and the other fellows as well?" he said before I could formulate an answer.

I could hear his labored breathing. If it came to a foot race, I knew I could take him. It didn't look like it was going to get that far.

"I mean," he said, "the way you look at me; you act like I'm some sort of lesser being. You being an Injun. Yet you think I'm like . . . white trash or something. You understand why that's hard to take?"

I didn't think I was going to win any debate with Alvin, so I decided to stay out of this one. The steady, unrelenting sound of that knife stropping on his cast, though, was making my insides try to crawl inside themselves.

"Oh, what the hell," he said. "None of that matters now. Any of us getting near Austin was a bad move. I see that now. I don't know if there's half a dozen guys left. We sure stepped in it. Did you see Donnie out there? How'd he take it? Did he fight to the end?"

I wrestled with several things I could say, finally said, "Yes."

"That damned Joz Brosche," he said. "If we could have, we should have done something about her long ago."

I lay in silence, listening to my heart rattle around in my chest.

"We tried, you know. Long time back," he said. "She's something." There was admiration in his voice. "None of this is clicking with you, is it? But then, you never knew Marle Brosche, Joz's husband. He was a big man, made me look like a cub. And he was a mercenary, a good one, one of the first true militia men in Texas and one of the best. Until he crossed Joz, and she snuffed him out like a short cigarette. He was a leader while he was around. But he made one mistake, and that was Joz."

I felt on the verge of telling him to get to whatever he'd come to do. This dragging it out with folklore stories wasn't doing me any good. That's when he hit me with the spin.

"They're sisters, you know."

"Who?" I squeaked.

"Joz and Cassie. You knew that, didn't you?" He waited a moment. "I didn't know it when I was on the force. I wish I had. Doesn't matter now. I always wondered how someone who looked like Cassie had stayed single. Can you imagine anyone wanting to be brother-in-law to Joz Brosche?"

I thought about the little kid who told the author, "Your book on penguins told me more than I wanted to know."

"It's all over now," Alvin said. "You may not think I'm smart enough to parse it all out, an' Lord knows I thought of running for the border or something. But I know when the hounds are at my door. That's why I'm here."

What little light there was in the room seemed to focus on the gun so handy in his belt, and the long silver blade he was waving around while he talked. He lowered the blade and gave it a couple more strokes on his cast, letting the sound of the sharp metal send an ice cube up my spine.

"I wasn't such a bad cop as you think," he said. "But if I'm caught I'll do some hard time. If I stay on the loose, I'll be hunted down by the law—or worse, by Joz. I'm caught in one of them horned dilemmas."

I could have told him that the Aryan population in prison might be the best support group for someone like him right now. But I had slipped to the other side of feeling chatty.

He held the knife over my chest and turned the long blade in the air so that the long silver blade swayed back and forth like a cobra about to strike. "I can't let anyone take me without a fight, without taking out as many of you sons-a-bitches as I can. You understand that?"

I was in no position to argue.

He swallowed so loudly, the sound filled the tiny room. "You don't know what it was like for the ones who she got to and took down before everyone headed out to the encampment. I mean, they were tortured first, for quite a while." He talked faster now, leaning on his crutches while careful to keep the knife hand free and handy. "One of our guys we found," he swallowed again, "she'd used a knife to cut patches of skin out of his cheeks. Then she sliced thin layers of skin away until all of his lips were gone, just his teeth and gums showing. I bet he talked, talked and sang, told her stuff he knew and didn't know. I know I would."

I lay there stiff as a corpse myself, each breath I took shallow and raw.

"Fascinating as all that is," I finally managed to say—my voice a thin shadow of its usual self—"why are you telling it to me?"

"I have to kill you, of course," he said. The blade stopped its waving back and forth and lifted into a swoop headed toward my throat.

I grabbed the sides of the cot and pushed with my legs against the wall to my right. Knowing I couldn't run past him, I crashed into him instead.

A sharp pain rippled through my ribs as my chest smashed into his cast, crutches, and his good leg. His own weight pitched forward with the knife thrust—all of his bulk was balanced on that good knee. I felt it bend backward, then buckle and pop as I rolled into him. His arm swept down and the knife chopped against the side of the cot.

Alvin, crutches, cot, and I all tumbled into a heap with Alvin on top of me. Alvin screamed. Unlike the late Donnie, he did not enjoy pain.

He was close to two hundred and fifty pounds or so, not counting the plaster cast. All of it pressed down on me. I squirmed to grab the wrist that held the knife. He must have dropped both knife and gun, to grab at his crutches as he fell, because his hands were free now. Fingers thick as sausages closed around my throat and squeezed. I reached to pull at the fingers, but I might as well have tried to pull apart the bands of a steel trap. His thumbs found my esophagus and began to press. Lights began to whirl in white flashes and then in color through what had seemed a dark room. His massive forearms jerked my head up, then slammed the back of my head down against the wooden floor, again and again. My eyes were open, but I could barely see the dim pale and swollen shape of Alvin's head above me as I got closer, then farther. I let go of his fingers, spread my hands, and the next time he raised me I brought my palms together as hard as I could about where I thought Alvin's ears should be.

His fingers snapped away from my neck and let my head fall one more time to the floor. Both his hands went to clasp his broken ear drums. I couldn't wait for him to recover and get angrier. I shoved the stiffened fingers of my right hand under the chin of his puffy head and felt the fingertips jam into his throat.

He made gasping sounds and rolled partially off me. I pushed him the rest of the way off and scrambled to my feet. Both his hands were scurrying across the floorboards searching for knife or gun. I stepped back and kicked him as hard as I could. My foot caught him under the chin. His head snapped back and his whole body lifted to slam back into the wall. He slowly sagged down along the wall and settled into a heap. I stood, pulling hard to get air down my painful throat. I stood on trembling legs, ready to kick again if I had to, but there was no need.

The sun was up and it was all the way to mid-afternoon, the office heating up into a real oven by the time Cassie, Harmon, and Hazel pulled up and unloaded from the sheriff's cruiser.

Alvin lay stretched along the wall, his hands and legs tied with strips of army blanket cut with his knife. He no longer bounced and fought against the restraints, though he had struggled while I had showered and shaved. I did what I could with my tattered suit, which was little. I felt both hungry and anxious to move things along. I imagined he was hungry too. Though I hadn't done anything to gag him, he didn't say a word, just lay there and glared. Neither of us had anything left to say.

The sheriff and his two deputies came inside. Harmon and Hazel put the cuffs on Alvin. He had a resigned look. As they led him to the backseat, he looked at Hazel's dark face and said to Harmon, "So it's come to this."

I followed along, watched them close the door once Alvin was in the backseat.

Hazel stood beside me, looked up and down me and said, "You should look into your *accouterment,* my man. You look absolutely frazzled." He walked around the car in quiet dignity and got into the front seat. Cassie was getting a small bag out of the trunk. I wasn't sure how I felt about that.

While she was busy, I pulled Harmon to one side and asked in a low voice, "You hear any more about Joz Brosche?"

He glanced over at Cassie, then his eyes locked with mine. His scratchy voice quivered. "Son, I like you. Let go of that one. Don't follow the thread. I been doing what I do for the better part of forty-three years, and even I don't know quite what to do about handling Joz Brosche. I know more'n I wish I did. Can't do nothin' about any of it."

"She hasn't committed any crimes? Anything like that?"

"Joz likes money. She usually gets near it. Often as not, it's when it belongs to someone who shouldn't of had it in the first place. In a way, she'd kinda like a friendly cancer that way. How do you feel about being a pal with a cancer?"

I didn't get a chance to respond. Cassie walked over and joined us. "What're you two up to? Tradin' lies?"

"I wish," Harmon said under his breath. He turned to Cassie. "Gotta go. You have a safe drive back, now, y'hear." He sauntered over and climbed into the cruiser.

She waved at Harmon and Hazel as they drove off. Alvin looked out the back window at us, but there was no expression on his face.

Cassie turned to me, looked at my face, saw whatever I can never find there. "You going to ask me in?"

"Sure," I said. "Sorry. I haven't eaten in who knows when. My attention span is a little suspect."

She looked up at me from lowered eyes, turning pages in me where I didn't even know there was a book.

Inside, she headed for the back room. "Let me get out of this uniform," she said.

I started to say something, but she headed me off, said, "Then we'll go get you some food. Don't worry. I'm not going to make you do anything you're not ready for."

I don't know where she got that. It bothered me more that she'd been so accurate.

She came out in her boots, jeans, white blouse. She wore a black vest this time. "It's good to have all this over with," she said.

"Will be," I said, "when the other shoe drops. But that's due too."

She gave me a raised eyebrow, but didn't prod. "We might try Hut's," she said. "Their dress code should allow for your new casual look."

I looked down at where my left pocket was held in place by a safety pin. "I can leave the jacket in the car while we dine," I said.

"Thanks."

As she walked by, I patted her back, felt the gun tucked in the small of her back.

"You're the one," she said, "who says it isn't all over yet."

We shuffled down to Hut's in the car, where I ate two burgers and a full order of onion rings. I would have been more embarrassed by that if Cassie had not pulled her own weight at the trough. She paid the tab, waved off my attempt to dig into an empty pocket.

Storm clouds were gathering as we went back out to the car. That, and the evening darkness setting in, cast a pall over the town. Here and there lights flickered on. In the distance I saw the first bolt of lightning, and in a second heard the thunder.

"I noticed you didn't have a bottle at your place," Cassie said. "You want to pick one up?"

"I'm giving that a break for a little while," I said. "The shelf life on bottles at my place hasn't been so hot lately."

She grinned, but wiped it off her face when I looked at her.

"You know, for a fellow who doesn't pack a gun, you handled yourself awfully well out there."

"It's not something I'm as proud of as I should be," I said.

"You don't have to tell me that. You know now that I'd been working on myself to be not quite so quick to go to the gun when all this came along."

"I did notice a little reluctance at first," I said. I thought of my first tangle with Alvin and his pals in the parking lot at the Kasperville Folk Festival.

"Where're you going? Isn't your place the other way?"

"Yeah," I said. I turned on the lights. It was getting dark and the lightning would flash and knock out the mercury-vapor streetlights now and again. Each light would struggle to slowly flicker back on in a sickly purple hue. Traffic had thinned. Folks knew a real gullywasher was coming. The ground gets so hard in summer that, when it does rain, the water doesn't soak in. Whole school buses have been swept away in the flash floods.

They were nothing you wanted to be around when they happened.

"You see the papers today?" I asked.

"That business out at the militia encampment was all over the place," she said. "They didn't have any answers, just said the guys must've fought among themselves. Something about some of the assault weapons being from that Fort Worth heist a few months back."

"The point is, anyone keeping an eye on those militia guys would feel that cannon is safely spiked for the moment."

"And?"

"We'll see," I said. I followed Mo-Pac north until I came to Bull Creek Road. I got on it and headed west.

The last of the streetlights combined with a flash of lightning and lit up the inside of the car just as I happened to be glancing over at Cassie. She sure looked good.

"What?" she said.

I shook my head.

I turned left and started up the climbing road that led to Mt. Bonnell. I don't know when I've seen the sky so black and threatening. It had a midnight-blue cast to it that surrounded each burst of lightning.

At the top of the hill was a row of parking spaces. One car sat at the far right end of the row, near the path that led up the back way. The front way led up the stairs over by the monument to Big Foot Wallace, who had holed up on Mt. Bonnell when on the lam.

"What are you after?" Cassie said.

"I'm not positive yet," I said. "It'd be a help if you stay by the car and watch that other car for me while I go up."

"Okay, Kemo Sabe," she said.

I got out, hesitated for a step, almost asked to borrow her gun. But I wanted her to hang onto it. I started up the trail.

The wind blew. Any second the downpour was going to start. From this high up, and without any lights around, I got a good look at the lightning. It was worth looking at. Each bolt once again looked like an upside-down electric white tree with wide branches, flashing down and cracking. They were coming closer together, too. Sometimes two or three at a time crashed down. The thunder was getting to be a steady drum roll.

Mt. Bonnell isn't really a mountain—it stands only 785 feet above sea level. Hiking up the stair side can be done in five minutes, but it'll have you huffing. The hill sticks out far above any surrounding hills and overlooks Lake Austin. On a clear day, it's something of a lover's lane for strollers. Tonight wasn't a good one for that, especially for anyone wearing a lightning rod through such a sustained and eerie display of bolts splashing and cracking in all directions around me.

There are eighty-seven steps, I believe. I counted each irregular one of them, lifting one tired foot after the other, trying not to think about the choice I had. I could just go back to Austin and put a nipple on a bottle of tequila, pretend I was just as in the dark as I'd been most of the way. I hesitated, with one foot halfway in the air to the next step. No, there was never any choice for me at all. I hated that in me, the stupid inflexible honesty in me that would never let me live with just turning back and going down the stairs. Was I incapable of choice on that? My next step fell, on a damp and uneven step. Guess not. I kept going.

I worked my way up the hill until it leveled off. The path led along a cliff. I followed it in soft steps, not that it mattered with all the thunder.

The saxophone I hear at times playing in my head was rifting in some frantic and off chord hysterical shrieks—like nothing I had ever heard before.

Up ahead a stone gazebo looked out over the river to one

side, and offered a view of Austin back in the other direction. A few feet from it a loose pile of flat stones had been lifted and piled to the side. A figure bent over behind one of the rocks. Dirt flew up in the air like a dog burying a bone.

I eased closer. A bolt of lightning cracked down within yards of where I stood. The figure stood and looked at where the bolt had hit, then the face swung to me. In the next flash of lightning I got a good look at the face.

"Hello, Hal," I shouted. "What brings you up here?"

Chapter Twenty-Six

What little hair Hal had stood out in a slant the way the wind blew. His face looked stark and pale in contrast to the strange sky that got darker each second. He looked at me with wide eyes and yelled, "The money's gone."

I stepped closer. The stones that had been pulled away opened into a hole. I bent closer, got a glimpse and caught a nasty whiff. That was enough for me. Looked as if, unlike Hoffa, Bent Lenny had bobbed back to the surface of life, at least what was left of him. I had seen just the corner of his face, what hadn't been eaten away. It was enough.

"What money?" I said. A bolt of lightning punctuated my question.

"You know what money." Hal slumped onto the pile of stones that had been pulled away. "Someone came and got it." In spite of any effort he made to control it, he was rubbing his dirty hands together. A shovel lay tossed to the side of the hole. Hal's khaki slacks and pale-blue shirt were covered with smears of loose soil.

"You're alive," I said. Thunder rumbled in a growl. The wind picked up.

"I think you've had to know that for a little while or you wouldn't be here," he said.

"Hal," I said. "Tell me. What made you contrive all this?"

"Aren't you even going to give me hell for letting you think I'd died?"

"Oh, I get a faked death about every other case these days, it seems." It hurt me to try to act nonchalant, yet to feel as stupid as I did. I had thought it, but not believed it until I saw him. "Who *was* the dead guy who burned on your lawn?"

"Just some migrant without a green card who I picked up near the Salvation Army building. Making it stick cost me my partial dental plate. What do *you* care?"

"That's what made it hard, what stood in my way, Hal. I couldn't see you killing anyone. The woman in the trailer, this migrant."

"*You've* killed people."

"That's. . . ."

"Different? Think hard on that, Trav. Do you sit on the right hand of God and I don't?"

I could expect to get nowhere arguing with him when he was like this. Cassie had explained something about passive-aggressive people to me. I think we were past passive with Hal. I tried to move closer. He moved back.

"You weren't . . . sorry?" he said.

"Of course I was, Hal. What the hell were you thinking?"

"You . . . you're the detective."

"I figured out Audrey's tie to you when she said, 'That's thirty.' Only someone who knew journalism would know that's the newspaper way of saying 'The End.' I can guess the way they treated you too. Her especially. And, yeah, I know enough to recognize envy and resentment when it's become something far more than sibling rivalry."

He seemed very tired and old to me, disappointed in life, maybe it in him. "You don't know what it's like, me slaving twenty-five years, and all Audrey has to do is open her thighs and she's rich."

"You steered me to Jimmy Bravuro's problem in the first place," I said. "That should have rung some bell for me. Then you had me bouncing around like some patsy. Was I supposed to frame Max for you? Was all that to hurt Max, or Audrey? And did you just lose interest in all that when the Bent Lenny opportunity came up?"

I took a sideways step closer. He matched it with a half step away. Our eyes stayed locked.

"You're the one who screwed up everything—who caused. . . ."

"Who caused what, Hal? Sure, I let you know about the Bent Lenny situation, probably shouldn't have. I didn't know then you'd drop your first harebrained scheme—trying to kill women and lay the blame on Max—only to slip to an even loonier one by trying to move in on Bent Lenny's loot. What the hell's eating at you?"

"You couldn't know," he said, his voice a whisper. He looked down. It had gotten too dark now to make out any features on his face.

"Try me, Hal. We were friends." The familiarity of my own words gave me a stab of ache low in my stomach.

His head snapped up at the tense. "If you'd been an even better friend, you'd have known what I was going through." His hands hung at his sides. His shoulders were bowed.

"I've found out a good bit," I said. "The travels. The cleaning in the nude with a toothbrush, or whatever that bondage trip was about."

"Just that once. The one time. What'd Myller tell you? Hey, Max's name was on that disk."

"You put it there, Hal. To replace your own name. You're the one who started me out on those people, the path that led me to Carol Myller. I was fooled at first, even thought all that might be some kind of cry for help. Then I realized I wasn't supposed to get as much out of the visits as I did. You never wanted me to talk to Myller and had to scramble to keep my nose pointed toward Max, the way you intended to steer me all along. You didn't respect me enough to think I could muddle my way through all this to you. Respect's a two-way street, Hal." Thunder muttered, then exploded.

"No," he shouted. "I . . . I . . . tried a lot of things to get myself back together. You know how people like Max can be— he's the one who set out to wreck me, because I put some pictures I found of Audrey on the Web. Then every woman I'd ever snapped in the least negative way jumped on and helped. You don't know how hard it was for me to live a humble life. It comes easy for you. I thought going to Myller would help me. It didn't. I'm just not a 'giver' like you, Trav. All that was left was to get away from all this, and now the money's gone. The money was going to make everything right."

"You saw the militia bury it out here, that night they did in Lenny. How much of it did you see?"

"All of it," he said. "You'd know if you were a good detective. The negs I gave you were numbered. The missing ones show the hit. I hid them someplace else."

"In an envelope taped beneath the middle drawer of your desk at the newspaper office?" I said.

"How did you . . . ?"

"I didn't, until now," I interrupted. "It just figures, given the cornball spin you've put on everything else." Lightning lit up his face. It wasn't pretty.

"Trav, I'm warning you." I saw him grab the shovel. The first raindrops began to fall, accelerated from a sprinkle to a pour in seconds.

He leaped across the hole, slipping as he did. I backed off a few steps. "Hal," I yelled. "Get hold of yourself. You're in enough trouble."

I don't know if he even heard me above the pour and continuing thunder and lightning. Oh, we were a scene of high drama, all right. Scrawny Hal swinging a shovel, almost knocking himself down every time he did. Me in my tattered wet suit squirting around, slipping and falling, scrambling back to my feet just ahead of the next swing.

He rushed toward me. I faked left and dodged right, but not before he caught me a clip on the shoulder. His swing had more punch than I had thought. I ran in the accelerating rain toward the stone gazebo, got behind one of the pillars.

Metal clanged on stone as the shovel bounced off the pillar beside me. I darted to the next pillar. A bolt of lightning hit a tree somewhere a few feet away from me down the slope. It made a cracking slit of a noise like the earth being torn in half. I must have turned my head that way. I looked back just in time to duck the shovel blow.

I jumped up onto the concrete ledge and scurried across it, leaning out and around each pillar. Below and behind me was a fall down the cliff face I didn't want to think about. My wet shoes slipped and I clutched the stone. The shovel face bounced off my left hand. I let go with it and nearly fell.

I swung with my good hand back in the other direction, jumped off the ledge onto the ground and ran under the swinging blade of the shovel. I could hear Hal sloshing along behind me as we scampered along the trail. I looked back to dodge his next swing and slid down into the hole with what was left of Lenny.

Mud covered me. I spun and lay on my back, looking up. Hal stood poised at the edge of the hole, the shovel drawn back behind him. He began his swing down toward me. There was no place for me to twist and get away.

The front of his shirt jerked. I saw the dark color appear and begin to ooze in the rain. His head lifted and looked past me. The shovel dropped. He twitched back a half step, then twirled slowly and began to fall. I heard two more shots between the thunder this time. He fell back before they hit him. But he was just as dead. The last look on his face was one of disbelief.

I lay where I had fallen, sucking in big gulps of air and rain.

Cassie came up to the hole, gun hanging in one hand. I leaped out of the hole in a surge that startled her. She took a step back. My arm shot out and I grabbed the gun from her—she let her fingers go loose. I turned the gun and pointed it up into the air, screaming. I fired two shots into the air, then handed the gun back to her, butt end first. Her face showed concern as she took it and slowly put it away at the small of her back. Then she took a cautious step forward and raised my lowered head. A thick strand of her wet blonde hair hung down against her face. I lifted a hand to move it away. She moved closer, pressed her lips to mine. The rain poured in sheets, hammering us.

When she pulled her head back, she looked hard into my face, said, "Trav. Hey, Trav. Yo, Travis."

"Yeah?" We both shouted to be heard over the rain. I stared over her shoulder at Hal's crumpled body.

"I'm sorry."

"About?" It was hard yelling above the rain. We moved our bowed heads closer until they touched. Then we could hear.

"I just shot your friend."

I was too tired to even force a shrug.

"I'm sorry too. But he was already dead. He let me adjust to that once. I can do it again."

"Harmon was right about me, wasn't he," she said. "It's too easy for me to pull the trigger. I'm no different than Joz."

"You were defending me. Do you think I'd have it different?"

We stood, slipped, then steadied ourselves enough to start down the hill. We got only a third of the way down before we saw a dark figure in rain gear slogging toward us, up the side of Mt. Bonnell in the unrelenting downpour. The head lifted. It was Borster. His glistening face twisted into a look I couldn't place at first, finally realized it was a genuine smile. I thought that it was having me in a spot that gave him joy.

"Let's go back up and wait," his scratchy voice growled at us. "Findlay's down at the car getting the right people on the way."

I felt as if I had no bones left in me, and Cassie slumped against me, probably feeling as bad or worse. But we went with Borster to the top.

He looked around, saw Hal, saw the big hole Hal had dug that was now a muddy soup with what was left of Bent Lenny still visible.

Borster nodded toward the stone gazebo. Once we were there and out of the direct rain, he gestured to the bench. Cassie and I plopped into place. I listened for the sound of a saxophone playing in my head, but heard nothing.

Before he could speak, I said, "I killed him, Borster. Have one of your guys run the gunshot residue analysis on my hand. You'll see."

"Don't let him pull that noble savage crap on you, Sergeant," Cassie shouted. "I was the one who shot him. I wish I hadn't, but. . . ."

Borster's eyes swept back and forth between us. He looked amused.

"You better give me the piece," Borster said to Cassie.

She sighed, took out the gun and handed it to him, butt first.

"This isn't your department gun, is it?"

"No."

"Traceable?"

She hesitated. "No." It wouldn't do to hide anything Borster could clear up later.

"Good," he said.

He turned from us and walked out into the rain again, went over to Hal. I could barely make them out in the rain, thought I saw him putting the gun in Hal's hand, lifting the arm. Squeezing Hal's hand, Borster fired a shot into the air. The blast and flash of light startled me. He could not have surprised me more if he had fired at us.

Borster let the arm flop back into the mud with the gun in it. He came back to us, stared down at us, water dripping from his short hair, running down along the scar on his face. He didn't say anything. I sat wondering just what the hell he could possibly be up to. The look frozen on his face could be a smile, or something else now. I didn't want to know. He stood beside us and stared at where Hal lay. Rain poured off Borster, but it meant nothing to him.

"So that's why you fired my gun in the air," Cassie said. "I thought you were beside yourself in grief."

"I was all of that," I admitted, feeling my insides trying to eat themselves. Then we both sat in quiet and waited. The look she gave me now had softened from a glare to a puzzled frown.

The guys from the ME office were just zipping up the bag on Hal. I sat shivering under the gazebo. Bursts of rain still swept in under the rock covering and splashed at us. I'd given my suit jacket, damp and muddy as it was, to Cassie, to slip around her shoulders. She had the vest, but her white blouse had soaked through by now and I'd seen Findlay and some of the others staring.

"There wasn't nothing you could do, Deputy Winnick," Findlay was saying to Cassie when Borster came over to us. Findlay was also treating us far too nice. That made me uncomfortable. "A guy sets his hat for suicide it's hard to talk him down."

A suicide? A man shoots himself in the chest? It wasn't the usual suicide shot. If I was the detective here I would have split up Cassie and myself to see if our stories matched. Or I would have tested my hands and Cassie's with the old five-percent nitric acid solution to see if either of us fired the gun. I felt drunk, or dizzy, unable to figure out what was making Borster and Findlay act so unlike themselves. I felt Cassie tense up as Borster came over and ducked into the gazebo with us again.

Findlay said to him, "Looks like we've wrapped up Bent Lenny's disappearance and that business at Hal Jansen's place all in one night. Not too shabby."

My left hand still throbbed from Hal's shovel blow, but one of the men on the ME crew had examined it and said nothing looked broken. I couldn't tell if it was my ribs aching in my chest, or if it was my heart that hurt like twisted ends of bone.

Borster said to me, "I put a hook on that bit that Hal scribbled in his reporter's notebook. I can guess what drove him to suicide." He looked at Cassie. "The pearl meant money, just like I thought." He swung his glance to me, maybe to see how I was taking it. "The photo spread he did about Bent Lenny and money laundering was there at the newspaper office and I looked at it. He thought Lenny Coggins was some kind of Pulitzer story. He had it figured for a story with money in it. Maybe he wanted the money for himself. Maybe the story doesn't hang together without hard evidence of the cash. He dug a hole big enough, but there's only Lenny in there. You and Deputy Winnick got onto him, but not in time to stop him from popping himself in frustration. Too bad. The little fella might've been nuts, but he took some good pictures in his day." Borster's head swung back and forth between Cassie and me. The intensity of his stare went up a notch.

I blinked through a spray of rain and looked deep into Borster's eyes. It was thin, very thin. But it was *his* story. He was selling it. I just couldn't figure out why.

Findlay moved away. He came back a few minutes later in an ebullient mood. I did not wish to experience Findlay as ebullient. But there was no getting around it.

"That crime scene is nothing but soup," he said to Borster. Behind his words, there was a note of hysterical laughter on the verge of being released.

I didn't know what these fellows had been sipping, but I hoped I could get a bottle of it somewhere. I did wonder whether Borster had seen enough of the hole before the rain turned it into a small pond to know that objects the size of suitcases had been removed.

"Yeah," Borster said. "Looks like old Hal was as fooled as the feds about Bent Lenny having a fortune stashed away some-place."

"But . . . ," Cassie said. I nudged her in the ribs. I had started to figure out Borster, and though it wasn't pretty, I let him ride with his yarn.

"Set fire to his own place," Borster said. He shook his head. "I sure bought into those militia being right for that one. But then, I wasn't the only one pulled along after *that* herring." He looked down the trail where Gareth Fields was struggling up through the mud. The agent seemed to ignore the dark, the cold, and the wet. His face looked flushed, though that could have been from the climb.

"You," Fields shouted when he saw me. "I thought I was done with you."

"They're still digging Lenny Coggins out of that hole over there." Borster nodded toward a cluster of men. "That's the only part of this that is federal now as far as I can see. The suicide we just bagged will be handled by our department." I could see that he got a lot of joy out of talking to Fields that way.

That's when the curtain pulled all the way away and I figured it out—knowing Fields as I did, and his personality, his out-of-control ambition. He had put the vise grips to Borster and Findlay earlier, perhaps egged on by Max Bolens. That's what had made Borster and Findlay act so squirrelly in their last visit to my office. It came down to this: kicking sand in Fields' face, after whatever he'd pulled on them, weighed a whole lot more with them this time than whatever had happened to Bent Lenny's loot.

But, no, that wouldn't be enough, as much as Fields had rubbed Borster the wrong way. It was the money—Borster knew or had suspicions about it. After all, he'd followed me out here to Mt. Bonnell. Maybe he thought I'd collared the cash earlier. I suddenly felt sure I'd be hearing again from him later myself.

"Yeah," Borster said to me. He rubbed his hands together and I couldn't help thinking of Hal doing that. "Everything's in a tidy bundle." Another trickle of rain ran down along the scar on his face. He leaned closer, gave me a small slap on my wet back. "And we get it without even having to give you a salary or benefits. I gotta love that." He turned to walk over to where Fields was waving his arms. His head spun back and he did something I never thought I'd see, that I'd never wanted to see. He winked at me.

CHAPTER TWENTY-SEVEN

The guy from the phone company had just wrapped up hooking up the phone again when it rang. I went to the desk and picked up the receiver.

"How much of it do you want?" The voice was barbed wire scraping across glass.

"None," I said.

"I thought you'd be like that." She hung up.

"Who was that?" Cassie asked.

When I didn't answer, she said, "It was Joz, wasn't it?"

I took a deep breath, winced and nodded. My ribs still felt tender.

"You know," she said, "I had to sort out why you'd tell Joz about Bent Lenny's money, but not me. It wasn't just because she saved your life. Then it came to me. You think money corrupts. Don't you? You thought you were protecting me from its influence."

"It wasn't Bent Lenny's money," I said. "It came from those guys who, like Fields said, were neither true paramilitaries nor skinheads, just militia thugs cutting a deal. The cash probably came from a number of deals, like the sale of assault weapons, the kind we found at the encampment. Lenny was supposed to launder the money. But he was being watched. Fields was using ATF men. Time got short when these guys killed Lenny. They had to leave the money behind. Now there aren't enough of them left from that group to come after it."

Cassie sat in one of the lawn chairs. She tilted back and looked at me from beneath lowered lids. "Did you know it was Hal all along? That he was behind the attempts on the women?"

"No."

"Oh, you had a sense of it. My being around distracted you."

"A lot of things distracted me."

"You've always worked best alone."

"How do you know that?"

"Don't argue with me. You know as well as I do."

"What are you saying?"

"I'm going back to Kasperville," she said. "You know that, don't you."

I nodded, while sorting through a tornado whirl of broken glass in my stomach, the kind I get when I try to make sense of what the contact between two people means. Was our time together trivial, doomed from the get-go, or was it more complex than any mystery I'd ever unraveled? It sure did look like the fellow with blue eyes and an Indian face was, once again, not going to get the girl. I wondered for part of a second if I would have rushed to her rescue in a mad panic if I'd known that then. Well, of course I would have. I'm loathe to encourage self-pity, so I kicked myself in the mental pants and tried to stand up straight.

"Did you hear me?" she said.

"Yes, ma'am," I said, wincing at the twinge in my chest. "I nodded my head. Sorry you couldn't hear it rattle from there."

"Oh, don't be that way. You know that beneath all this, I'm probably more wildcat than you need around. It's the same thing that worries Harmon. He thinks I've still got a few rough edges that would be smoothed out by being around him."

"If there are any rough edges," I said, "I didn't find them."

"You know what I mean. I *enjoyed* seeing you shoot at those militia, or whatever they were, more than I should have for

271

someone who's going to be a fair lawperson. And worse, and I'm sorry to admit this, I got a kick out of doing Hal after all he'd done to string you along. I know he was your friend. But he had become one psychotic package. I think your friendship's the very thing that blurred that for you. Yeah, doing Hal felt good. That's where I'm different from Harmon—and Hazel, for that matter. And as far as rough edges go, you have a few yourself. It would only be so long before I'd be looking around for curtains, or yelling at you about the cactus juice."

"Or shooting someone."

"Or shooting someone," she agreed.

"You know," I said, "I don't really care if your uncle is Genghis Khan. I hope you'll come back and visit."

"Oh," she said. "I didn't tell you about Uncle Genghis?"

"That ought to do it," the phone man said. He'd been giving us sideways glances while he put all his things back in his tool-box. Now he sidled for the door and shot outside.

Weird shadows were cast across the room by the new wrought-iron bars Les Bettles had put across the window, whether for protection or what I couldn't tell. They gave the front of the office a New Orleans look from the outside. I was still getting used to the prison-like shadows the iron bars cast.

The door hadn't quite closed before it was yanked open again. Jimmy Bravuro stood framed in the doorway. "I like what you've done to the place," he said. He carried a suit bag on a hanger. I felt a little cramped and crowded. This tail end part of a case is always a crawl across broken glass for me. But I worked out a smile.

"I hope I got the size right," he said to Cassie. She looked away when I glanced at her.

He held out the bag to me. "Have a look," he said.

I took the bag and opened it. Inside was a new dark suit, in the same size and style I usually wore, although this was far better material.

"Try it on," Jimmy said.

I slipped on the jacket. He said, "Check the pockets."

I pulled a slip of paper out of the inside breast pocket. It was a check, and for an amount that made me take a step back.

"The musicians weren't the only ones who wanted to say thanks," Jimmy said. "Several people were affected when you found Bent Lenny had no heirs. The music rights reverted back to the performers, including Johnny Gringo."

"Is Max Bolens behind any of this?" I asked.

"And Jayne Randall, and half a dozen others," Jimmy said. "You can't sort out Max's money this way. It's laundered in with the rest. He really does want you to have it."

Cassie looked over my shoulder. I felt her checking out the fabric of the suit as she did. At least that's what I think she was doing. "Wow, twenty-five thou," she said, then added, "But you deserve it. Think of all the risks you took, not to mention damages."

"And aggravation from us," Jimmy said.

I handed the check back to him. "Well, unlaunder it," I said. "I'll think about taking a fair check then, but only from you people who hired me."

"See," Cassie said to Jimmy. "The last honest man in America."

"Gonna be a poor one too," Jimmy said.

"At least look in the other pockets," Cassie said.

I slipped a hand into the other inside pocket, came out with pieces of cardboard. "Tickets," I said. "A pair each for Trish Mirandez at the Backyard, Jimmy Bravuro at La Zona Rosa, Tori Brice at the Constitutional Club, Dutch Hitchcock at Gruene Hall, and Johnny Gringo at Luckenbach."

Cassie said, "I guess I could swing back to Austin for a few visits to help you with those."

"You could," I said.

"And something that's not in the jacket," Jimmy said, "is a desk Jayne Randall is having sent over here. She says it's the kind that suits senators and private detectives. Who knows? Maybe you'll get a whole new class of customer in here."

As if on cue, the door swung open again and Dutch Hitchock came in. "Well, if this isn't enough to make a cat laugh," he said, looking around at our little gathering. To me he added, "Nice threads."

"If he had another brain," Jimmy said, "it would be lonely."

"Oh, go fry ice," Dutch said.

"Guys. Guys," I said.

"You wouldn't think it to look at him," Dutch said, nodding to Jimmy, "but he used to have a girlfriend so ugly he took her everywhere with him just so he wouldn't have to kiss her good-bye."

"An intellect rivaled only by garden tools," Jimmy said. "You just know he's a few feathers short of a whole duck."

"Stop it," I yelled. "Stop."

"Okay," they grumped in unison.

"Oh, by the way," Dutch said. "I brought you something. It's a gift, from Joz Brosche."

My eyes connected with Cassie's. "What?" I said.

Dutch reached in his pocket and pulled out a set of keys. He tossed them onto the desk. "We all know you don't have a car anymore, and the rest of us can't afford to furnish a rental forever. So she sprung to get you new wheels."

I hesitated.

"Take them," Cassie said.

I reached and picked up the keys. My eyes snapped wide. I moved to the door and swung it open. There, parked out in front of my office was a new silver Volvo. My mouth hung open.

I could hear the three of them laughing back inside, slapping each other on the back and having a good time.

"The least you could have done," I said, "was put some dents all over it so that I would feel at home."

The phone rang. It startled me. Having it ripped from the wall for a spell had been a pleasant break. Jimmy, Dutch and Cassie had moved closer to the doorway. I went between them over to the desk and picked it up.

"Travis?" It was Borster's growl of a voice.

"Yeah."

"I'm thinking about money," he said. "A lot of money."

I was going to answer as soon as I thought of something to say. I didn't get the chance.

"You start showing some flash, loose spending," he said, "I'll get ideas."

"Look, I. . . ." I was thinking of the new suit and new car.

"I'll be by to talk sometime," he said. "When you least expect it, expect it."

I hung up, because there was no longer anyone on the other end.

I wondered for a second what would happen if I just gave him Joz's name—who'd win that little confrontation. I played it out from either end and couldn't find any loser except myself.

"Who was that?" Cassie asked.

"No one," I said. *A muted cornet murmured far back in my head, bubbling low and rifting up slow through swirls of smoke.* At least, I thought, it wasn't playing taps.

ABOUT THE AUTHOR

Russ Hall lives by a lake in Texas Hill Country, northwest of Austin.

For over twenty-five years he was an editor with major publishing firms, ranging from Harper & Row to Simon & Schuster to Pearson.

He has had more than a dozen books published, including a series featuring Esbeth Walters and a previous collection of short stories featuring the Blue-Eyed Indian.

He has also published numerous short stories and won the Nancy Pickard Mystery Fiction Award.